ONCE AROUND

BARBARA BRETTON

BERKLEY BOOKS, NEW YORK

ONCE AROUND

A Berkley Book / published by arrangement with
the author

PRINTING HISTORY
Berkley edition / August 1998

The Penguin Putnam Inc. World Wide Web site address is
http://www.penguinputnam.com

ISBN: 0-425-16412-8

BERKLEY®
Berkley Books are published by The Berkley Publishing Group,
a member of Penguin Putnam Inc.,
200 Madison Avenue, New York, New York 10016.
BERKLEY and the "B" design
are trademarks belonging to Berkley Publishing Corporation.

PRINTED IN THE UNITED STATES OF AMERICA

10 9 8 7 6 5 4 3 2 1

For TCB, with love.
Your stories gave me the key.

I owe an enormous debt of gratitude to my editor, Judith Stern Palais, whose patience and understanding, wisdom and kindness, mean more to me than I can possibly convey. Judy, you're the best.

I owe another debt of gratitude to my agent, Steven J. Axelrod, who has received more than his share of my "There's good news and bad news" phone calls over the past year with admirable equanimity and amazing optimism.

And I couldn't forget the Klatschers whose own stories and encouragement spurred me on. I love you all, but there are a few I must single out.

Tim Bowden, a brilliant writer whose vision and dedication keep the choir singing.

Reloj, even if he and Rita opted for Spain instead of Times Square. Julie and Gene and Joyce B for friendship and encouragement. The Second Trimester gang for their help. Joyce Y, David, Lee, John, Beth, Tonny, Jim S, Al, Tony H, Valerie and David, Bob/Robin—for various and equally important reasons.

And, always and forever, my husband, who must sometimes wonder why he ever married a writer.

ONCE
AROUND

ONE

❧

Princeton, New Jersey

When Molly Chamberlain's husband Robert called to say he wanted to come home, she thought her prayers had been answered. Robert had been living in Manhattan for two months now, ever since the day he'd told her it was over between them. But Molly knew better. All he'd needed was some time to come to his senses, and apparently that moment had finally arrived.

Molly sat down on the edge of their brand-new sofa in their brand-new living room and held the phone as close to her ear as she could. She didn't want to miss a single word when he told her how much he loved her, how much he wanted to make things right again. It didn't matter that she couldn't remember the last time he'd told her he loved her. All that mattered was that he was coming home to stay.

"I want to get the rest of my things," Robert said,

and for a second she thought she was upstairs in their bed, having one of those nightmares where he told her he'd never loved her at all.

"I'm sorry," she said, cupping her hand over her ear and closing her eyes. "There's a lot of noise in here. What did you say?" Okay, so there really wasn't all that much noise inside the house, but somebody in the neighborhood was mowing his lawn. Those riding mowers could drown out a jumbo jet. "Robert? Would you repeat what you said?"

"I found a place, Molly. I want to come by and get the rest of my stuff." He'd nailed a great apartment within walking distance of the office and he was ready to set up housekeeping with the woman of his dreams.

Robert said he would come over the next afternoon, and Molly said that was fine because she'd be at the obstetrician's office, making sure the baby in her belly—*his* baby—was healthy and developing on schedule.

"Great," he said. He didn't sound embarrassed. He didn't even sound as if he cared. "I'll be out of there before you come home." Then he said something about not wanting to disturb her, which they both knew was a lot of baloney, because if he really hadn't wanted to disturb her he wouldn't have left in the first place. He would have stayed in their house where he belonged. She wouldn't even have asked him to stay forever. Just until the baby was twenty-one or married or ready for retirement.

But, of course, she didn't say that to him. Why bother? She'd said everything there was to say the night he told her he was leaving her for a judge's daughter with a law degree of her own and a nice fat trust fund that would keep them in Saabs and Land Rovers in perpetuity.

Sometimes in the middle of the night when she sat alone in the family room watching Mary Richards muster up the courage to ask Mr. Grant for a raise, she could hear her own voice coming at her from out of nowhere. *Don't go, Robert, please . . . I'll do anything . . . don't leave me . . . tell me what you want, Robert, and I'll never ask you for anything else.* That was the biggest humiliation of all, the way she'd turned into someone she didn't recognize the second he told her he was leaving.

She'd begged him to stay, begged him like some pathetic fool who couldn't live on her own without a man to protect her. It scared her to realize that she would do it all over again if she thought there was even half a chance that he would come back to her and they could pretend they were happy.

Molly had no problem with pretending to be happy. Pretending was a good thing. It was better than chain-smoking marriages the way her parents had been doing for the last twenty years.

But Robert didn't want to pretend he was happy. He said he'd found the real thing with Diandra, that what he and Molly had shared was nothing compared to it. Nothing, he said. Those years they dated in college. The first time they made love in the park behind the lake. The night she told him she was pregnant with their first baby.

"So what are you saying?" she'd asked him, hearing the edge of hysteria in her own voice. "That nothing before Diane mattered?"

"Diandra," he'd corrected her and said no more.

When you came down to it, what more was there to say?

Their almost ten years of marriage had been nothing to Robert but filler, something he did to pass time while he waited for his real life to begin.

That was two months ago. Her only communication with him since then had been through his lawyers, and their conversation a few hours ago, when he asked about coming over to pick up the rest of his stuff. She'd thought it was strange he'd bypassed his attorneys, but she chalked it up to Robert's natural arrogance—one of the many things she'd been foolish enough to love about him.

She couldn't sleep that night. She knew not sleeping was the worst possible thing for the baby, but every time she closed her eyes she saw visions of happier days, and they came close to breaking her heart. Finally she got up, slipped a robe over her T-shirt, then wandered downstairs to the kitchen. When she and Robert first moved into the house, they'd joked about needing a map to find each other. Ten rooms, two stories, full basement. They'd fill it with children, she'd said. Why hadn't she realized that Robert said nothing at all?

She wandered from room to room, sipping a glass of milk and trying to outdistance her thoughts. She tried to place Robert in the kitchen, the dining room, the huge family room with the stone fireplace and wall of windows, but couldn't. If he hadn't left his books and records and clothes behind, she'd have wondered if he'd ever lived there at all.

The house had been his choice. The neighborhood came highly recommended by one of his colleagues, and it carried with it a certain cachet. Cachet was important in Robert's world. More important than she'd ever realized. You wanted the right firm, the right house, the right car, the right wife.

She'd never had any doubt she was the right wife, not even when their sex life started sliding downhill around the second year of their marriage and neither one of them seemed to notice or care. Sex had never been the defining force in their relationship. Robert wasn't at all like her friends' husbands who demanded sex morning, noon, and night. They made love weekly—sometimes not even that often. And it was all right with Molly. Her parents had had one of those fiery, sexually passionate marriages and see where it had gotten them. To divorce court, that's where.

So she'd never worried about their lack of passion. Their friendship had turned into love, and love had somehow developed into a partnership. That's what a good marriage was, wasn't it? A partnership of the best possible kind, where two people worked toward a common good, a common goal. Maybe they didn't light up the skies in bed, but so what? What they had together was better than momentary passion.

Too bad she was the only one who'd actually believed that.

"Your blood pressure's elevated," Dr. Rosenberg said as he took the cuff off her arm in the examination room the next afternoon. "I'm not crazy about your rapid pulse either."

She forced a smile. "And I'm not so crazy about your tie."

"I can change my tie," the doctor said. "It's going to take a little work to bring down that pressure."

"Give me time, Doc," she said, noticing the goose

bumps running up and down her arms. "All I need is a good night's sleep and I'll be fine."

"I was sorry to hear about you and your husband," he said, scribbling a few notes on her chart.

"So was I." For once she didn't reach for the easy joke. "He's at the house right now, picking up his golf clubs and law books."

"You're not serious about that, are you?"

"Why wouldn't I be?" she countered. "He called yesterday and asked if he could drop by. He said he'd be long gone by the time I got home."

"Did you speak to your attorney about this?"

A sense of unease danced across the back of her neck. "Robert called me out of the blue and—" She stopped and regrouped. "It was after business hours. I meant to call a lawyer this morning, but . . ."

The doctor capped his pen and slipped it back into the pocket of his white lab coat. "Robert's not on your side anymore, Molly, and the sooner you realize that, the better off you'll be."

"You sound like my neighbor Gail," she said, trying to lighten the atmosphere.

"If your neighbor Gail is telling you to protect your interests, then I'm in agreement."

"I promise," she said. "As soon as I get home, I'll call my attorney." What she didn't say was that she had to find one first.

"Get dressed," he said. "We'll talk in my office."

But I don't want to talk in your office, she thought as she ducked behind the screen. She was so tired of hearing all the divorce horror stories. Being pregnant and alone was bad enough. If she had to worry about Robert doing something terrible behind her back, she'd go crazy. Besides, he'd already left her for a younger woman. What more could he possibly do to her after that?

She pulled on her perfectly tailored black maternity pants, the cream-colored silk blouse, the beautiful sapphire blue jacket. They felt more like a suit of armor than clothing, which was exactly the effect she'd been looking for. "Put your best foot forward," her mother used to say, back when Molly was a little girl with a mouthful of braces and bad skin, "no matter how bad you're feeling about yourself."

She wondered what she was going to do when her belly outgrew her current wardrobe. Her part-time income as a first reader for a New York publishing company was barely enough to pay the utility bills on her house. Unless Robert paid his fair share of the mortgage and upkeep and obstetrician bills, she and the baby would end up living in her Jeep Cherokee.

She used to believe she knew exactly where her future would take her: the two-story suburban home, the family car, the baby, the golden retriever, the husband who came home the same time every night and left the same time the next morning; stability, security, someone to grow old beside.

She had the house and the car and pretty soon she'd have the baby. Beyond that it was anybody's guess.

Dr. Rosenberg didn't spend much time instructing Molly in the fine art of divorce negotiation. He had other more important issues to discuss with her.

"I'm concerned about your pressure, Molly. We have to bring this down to a more acceptable level."

"It's stress," she said, placing her hands over her

belly, as if to shield the baby from bad news.

"I think it's more than stress, but I won't know for sure until we run some more tests."

"Tests?" She met his eyes across the desk. "I can't afford tests, Doctor."

"That's not something I like to hear."

"Then we're even, because it's not exactly something I like to say. I don't have insurance." Check and mate. Now she'd see how concerned he really was about her pressure.

"I've known you a long time, Molly. I'm not going to let this stand in the way of your health."

Tears filled her eyes. "Damn," she murmured, blinking quickly. "I wish you wouldn't be nice to me. Yelling at me I can handle, but this"—she waved her hand in the air—"does me in every time."

He let her cry for a few moments, until she managed to pull herself back together.

"I won't tell anybody about this if you won't," she said, forcing her usual cheerful grin. The one Robert used to love so much. Unless he'd lied about that, too.

"Maybe *you* should be telling somebody about this," the doctor countered. "Your parents. Your divorce attorney."

"My parents don't know Robert is gone," she said. "Let's keep it that way."

Dr. Rosenberg sighed loudly and leaned back in his plush leather chair. "Pregnancy isn't the time to decide to go it alone, Molly."

"I didn't decide to go it alone. Robert decided it for me."

"Point well taken, but you don't have to be alone. You have a family. Let them help you. This isn't just about you, Molly. There's the baby to consider.''

She sat there and nodded, pretending that every word he said made sense. He meant well. She had no doubt about that. Dr. Rosenberg was a good man, and he wanted the best for her. It was something they had in common.

Molly stopped at the supermarket for milk, eggs, and bread. Three items, she told herself as she pushed the cart up the cereal aisle. She wasn't going to be swayed by the seductive displays of ruby red raspberries or the leafy green Boston lettuce or the plump containers of creamy chocolate ice cream that cost more than a phone call to Tokyo.

Robert used to look at her as if she were crazy when she came home from Super-Fresh with radicchio and ice-cold plums and without the milk she'd meant to buy in the first place. Other women didn't make those mistakes. They drew up lists, organized their coupons, and set forth to do battle. No random radicchio for her stalwart neighbors. They bought what they needed and turned a blind eye to the rest. Maybe that was the problem in her marriage, she thought as she pushed the cart up one aisle and down the other. She was too scatterbrained, too disorganized.

Too impulsive.

What was it her Grandma Jean always used to say to her? ''You've got to quit listening with your heart, Molly, and start listening to your head.'' Her heart was always getting her into trouble, rescuing stray cats, nursing injured birds, hanging onto a husband who no longer loved her. Her neighbor Gail wouldn't have made that mistake. Gail had a sharp eye for reality. Gail would

have recognized the signs right from the start and set
out to save her marriage.

Molly hadn't a clue until it was too late.

She paused in front of a display featuring imported
Belgian chocolates. The packages were beautifully
wrapped in navy blue foil with silver stars. Two of them
leaped into her shopping cart.

Milk, eggs, and bread, she told herself again, staring
down at the chocolates. That was what she needed and
that was all she'd buy. Except for the chocolates.

Robert used to tell her they couldn't afford Belgian
chocolates, not until he got himself settled in with a
good law firm. Well, he was all settled in at Dannenberg
and Silverstein now, wasn't he? She should be able to
buy any damn thing she wanted. By the time she reached
the checkout counter, she had added two containers of
Häagen-Dazs, imported feta cheese, balsamic vinegar,
and double-thick lamb chops. She didn't have enough
cash to pay for her purchases, so she fished her wallet
out of her enormous tote bag and pulled out the handy-
dandy plastic rectangle that made all things possible.

"Swipe it again," the checkout clerk said. "It didn't
go through."

Molly dragged the magnetic strip through the reader
once again. "I probably had it upside down," she said
by way of apology to the five people on line behind her.
"I'm always doing that." She was always apologizing.
Once she'd apologized to a step stool for bumping into
it. She got as much of a response from the step stool as
she had gotten from Robert near the end.

The woman closest to her, the one with the full shopping cart and two small children tumbling together on
the sticky tile floor, sighed loudly. Molly turned away.

It could have been worse. She could have been on the eight-item-only express line with her two dozen items. That would really have given the woman something to sigh about.

The clerk motioned for Molly to swipe the card a third time, which she did. She hoped the sighing woman didn't notice that her hand had started to shake. She wouldn't want anyone to get the wrong idea.

"I use that card so often it probably has whiplash," she announced to no one in particular. "I'm surprised steam isn't rising from it."

An older man in a gray fedora laughed. Encouraged, Molly met his eyes and smiled. *See?* her smile said. *There's nothing to worry about. This kind of thing happens all the time.*

The clerk reached for the telephone receiver adjacent to her register and said a few words into the mouthpiece.

Molly's smile faltered for an instant. "What now?" she asked, keeping her tone light. "Am I over my Häagen-Dazs limit?" When in doubt, make a joke. Make fun of yourself before anyone else has the chance.

"The manager will be here in a sec," the clerk said, avoiding her eyes. "Just wait."

Her mind went blank. She could almost hear the air whooshing between her ears. She told herself to take a deep breath, but her lungs refused to cooperate. Things like this didn't happen to her. They happened to other people every day of the week, but not to her.

The manager, a harried-looking man with an overgrown mustache and tired eyes, approached. His khaki trousers rode low over an enormous belly that strained against his white cotton shirt.

"Your card was rejected," he said without preamble. "We've been asked to confiscate it."

Her backbone stiffened in response. This used to happen to her mother every time her father's outgo outstripped his income. It was always an error, the kind that a call to the bank rectified one, two, three. "There must be some mistake. I just used it yesterday, and there was no problem."

"There's no mistake," he said. "We'll be keeping your card."

"No!" The word shot from her mouth like a bullet. "You can't do that."

"We have no choice," he said, sounding bored, as if he'd done this a thousand times before. "Now, if you'd like to pay cash for your groceries, we can all get back to work."

Pay cash? If she could pay cash, why would she have whipped out her plastic?

"I can give you a check."

"We'll need two forms of ID." He paused. "A driver's license and something other than a credit card."

"I don't have anything other than a credit card."

"Then you'll need cash."

Her eyes burned, and she felt the telltale twitch in her chin. Oh, God, she was on the verge of crying. And not just crying, but sobbing like a baby. She had to get out of there fast.

"I'm afraid paying by cash is impossible," she said in as calm and cool a voice as she could manage. She placed her hands on her nearly flat belly and let her gaze sweep over the manager and the clerk and the nosy people on line behind her. "I didn't think I'd need cash when I went to see my obstetrician today." It was a cheap shot, and she knew it, but it was the best she could come up with on short notice. They wouldn't embarrass a pregnant woman, would they?

Head high, she turned and walked slowly past the pimply-faced clerk at Express Line 1, paused a half second until the electronic door swung open, then strode through the parking lot to her car. She couldn't let her control falter for an instant, or they'd see right through her.

Her hand shook so hard that it took three tries to fit the key into the ignition. "Damn," she whispered, keeping her head down. The key had worked a half hour ago. There was no reason it shouldn't work now. She almost cried with relief when the engine started up.

Her mind was a tangle of questions. Had she paid last month's credit card bill? Come to think of it, she wasn't sure she'd paid the mortgage or the phone bill or the other utilities. Hadn't Robert said not to worry, that he'd take care of everything? For all she knew, she'd get home and she'd have no phone or electricity. What on earth was the matter with her? She wasn't a stupid woman. How could she have let this happen?

She backed out of her parking space and headed for home. Robert had said he would take care of everything, and she'd believed him. Same as she'd believed him when he said he'd love her forever and always, until death did them part. A horn honked behind her, and she realized she'd been stopped at a green light. "Get with it," she muttered, moving forward again. "Pay attention."

The last few weeks had been an endless loop of Robert's voice telling her he'd never really loved her at all. She heard him saying those words when she went to sleep at night, and he was still saying them to her when she woke up in the morning. But no matter how badly he wanted out, he wouldn't turn his back on his own child. No decent man would.

And Robert was a decent man. No matter what else he was, she knew that for a fact. "It's a mistake," she said out loud as she tried to concentrate on the road. Computers were only as good as the people operating them. A payment must have been overlooked or posted to the wrong account. She was getting herself upset over something that would probably turn out to be nothing more than a minor blip on a computer screen.

Still, the episode in the supermarket had managed to shake her up, and maybe that was a good thing. She'd been in a state of suspended animation since Robert walked out on her. The baby was the only reason she got up in the morning and washed and dressed and ate well. Sleep was a tough one, though. Sleep eluded her for days at a time, until she was punchy with fatigue. She felt as if she'd been living inside a glass bubble, and the slightest movement would shatter the only barrier between her heart and unbearable pain.

Maybe this was exactly what she needed, a small reminder that it was time she started to pay attention to her own life, before she found herself in real trouble. She'd get out her checkbook as soon as she got home and take stock of her situation, no matter how much the thought scared her.

Traffic was light on Route 206. She sailed through Princeton proper and made her way to the pricey cul-de-sac she and Robert had called home. Their house sat on top of the rise called Lilac Hill, a nice blend of stone and shingles and high expectations. Her neighbor Gail called Lilac Hill a corporate ghetto, populated with doctors, lawyers, and scores of executives from Johnson & Johnson and AT&T. Molly hadn't paid too much attention to Gail's assessment of the neighborhood. All she'd cared about was her home and the family she and Robert would raise there.

They'd planned to build a life together in that house. That house was where the hard work and long hours would finally pay off. She'd found out she was pregnant the day before closing and she'd sailed through the afternoon on a cloud of wonder and excitement. Every single thing they'd dreamed about, every miracle they'd dared hope for was coming true. Could life be more perfect than this? She told Robert over supper in their old apartment, and you would have thought she was announcing the arrival of the Four Horsemen of the Apocalypse. His face closed in on itself, and he didn't talk to her until they went to bed.

"Are you sure?" he'd asked under cover of darkness as the air conditioner clanked in the background. "Could there be a mistake?"

"There's no mistake," she'd whispered. She'd told herself that he was worried, that's all. Not unhappy or disappointed or angry. "I'm positively pregnant."

He'd thrown back the covers and left the room, and she didn't see him again until the next afternoon when they met at the real estate office to close on the house. She should have known then. She should have seen the signs, made changes, loved him more before it was too late.

Maybe that was one of her problems. She'd spent her early childhood with her head buried in the sand. She pretended she couldn't hear her parents arguing late into

the night. She told herself that all families lived in deep
silence. The only thing that mattered was that they
stayed together.

The sun was beginning to set as she pulled into the
driveway, but it was still light enough for her to see
everything that was wrong with the place. Dandelions
speckled the front lawn like an old man's whiskers. The
azaleas and rhododendrons were overgrown and leggy.
The property looked neglected and in need of tender
loving care. If Robert hadn't walked out on her, she
would have called the landscaper and had him send out
a crew to mow and weed and trim, but those days were
gone. Right now she couldn't even afford to pay for her
groceries.

Next time she'd drive up into Hillsborough and shop
at Edward's, where nobody knew her. She could even
use coupons without having her neighbors laugh at her
or speculate about her fiscal health. Maybe this embarrassment wasn't such a bad thing after all. Not if she
learned something from it.

Her neighbor Gail had left a stack of self-help books
on her doorstep the day after the news of Robert's defection became public. Most of them were a waste of
paper, but the one message they all had in common was
learn from your mistakes. Molly wished someone would
write a book about how to avoid making those mistakes
in the first place. Now, that would be a book worth buy-
ing.

Gail was standing in her front doorway. Molly lifted
her hand to wave, but Gail apparently didn't see her.
She slipped back inside and shut the door after her. At
least one thing had gone right today. Root canal rated
higher than a friendly chat with Gail.

She pressed the remote control and waited for the garage door to roll up. When it didn't, she pressed it again. Still nothing. Robert used to see to it that their electronic devices always had fresh batteries in them. Another thing she'd have to get used to doing on her own. She shut off the engine and climbed out of the car. Okay, no big deal. She'd go in through the front, then open the garage from the inside.

The front door was unlocked. That hit her as strange. Robert was as fanatical about locks and alarms as she was. She couldn't imagine him forgetting to lock up when he left. She pushed open the door and stepped into the foyer. The faintest hint of sweat and aftershave lingered in the cool air. Lagerfeld, she thought. Robert's scent. The sweat, though, puzzled her. Robert didn't sweat. Not even at the gym. And never in bed.

She was about to chalk that up to imagination when she moved into the living room and what was left of her world came crashing down on her.

TWO

∽⊙∾

Rafe Garrick had just climbed out of his pickup when he heard the sound. He stood by the open door, pinned to the spot by the woman's cry. It was deep and anguished, so filled with pain that his gut twisted in response. The last time he'd heard a sound like that was years ago on a Montana mountaintop. A wolf had been hopelessly caught in a trap, and Rafe, just fifteen at the time, had had to put the animal out of its misery with a weak blast from his 16-gauge shotgun. Sometimes, late at night when the hours lay heavy against his mind, he could still hear the wolf keening in terror and pain, still hear the blast and the deadly silence after.

This sound was dark with anguish. Unrestrained. Definitely at odds with the prim beauty of the surroundings. Did people feel pain in Princeton? Up until that moment, he would have said no. How could you feel anything when you were cushioned by three hundred years of money and tradition and privilege? Last week he'd done some repair work for a jeweler on Nassau Street and he'd found it hard to keep his mind on what he was doing. For five hours he watched as a stream of Princeton elite marched through the door in search of tiny diamond studs for a granddaughter or a perfectly matched set of pearls for a new bride. He was supposed to be fixing the shelving in the supply closet—not exactly the toughest job he'd ever had—but it took all of his concentration to bring hammer to nail.

They all looked alike. Why didn't anyone ever mention that? The men were all tall and lean, and they all carried tennis racquets. The women were all rich-girl blondes. Even if they were brunette. They spoke like television news anchors, as if they'd been born somewhere in the middle of the Atlantic Ocean and didn't know which way to swim. The jeweler didn't have any trouble telling them apart, but Rafe would've been hard put to match names to faces without I.D. Of course, they wouldn't have been able to identify him either. He was invisible. Just some faceless, nameless guy with a hammer and a tool belt who was doing all of those things that keep a rich man's life running smoothly.

Bitter? Yeah, sometimes he was. Sometimes it swooped down on him like a hawk in a field of mice. That was how he'd lost a wife, wasn't it? Some rich man swooped down and snatched her up, took his daughter, too, and nobody said a word. Not even him. He stood there and watched them go, and maybe, just maybe, deep in the black hole he called a heart, he was glad to see the last of them. Glad to forget what a fucked-up failure he was. *This is for the best,* Karen said. *He can give Sarah things you can't even dream about.* Sarah was only a year old. He hadn't made an impression on her. He wasn't sure if Karen made sense or if he'd just wanted a way out. It didn't much matter. Either way he'd ended up alone.

He'd been waiting five weeks for Robert Chamberlain to pick a start date for the work on his basement. Twice he'd called Chamberlain's office, but so far the SOB hadn't bothered to call him back. So he'd decided to show up at the guy's front door and see if he could get an answer out of him that way.

He tilted his head slightly to the right and listened. The woman's cry had been absorbed by the quiet neighborhood, as if it had never happened. He wasn't sure which of the three huge houses the cry had come from, but his gut told him it was the Chamberlain house. Something about the place didn't look right to him. The yard was overgrown. One of the shutters hung slightly at an angle. The front door was ajar. Small things, but here in Stepford small things signified. He took off across the rise of lawn and a minute later found himself in the middle of a foyer the size of a hotel lobby. The skylight centered in the cathedral ceiling could have been a window to heaven.

But heaven didn't sound like tears. He followed the low weeping past the winding staircase to a sun-filled room with cream-colored walls and more pain than a heart could bear.

She was bent over at the waist, her arms wrapped tightly around her middle. A cascade of vibrant, sun-streaked auburn hair almost brushed the floor. He couldn't see her face but he knew she was beautiful. The graceful curve of her back, the long elegant arms—they told the tale.

He approached her the way he'd approached the wolf all those years ago. She was in agony, that much was clear. He wanted to reach out and gather her into his arms and hold her while she cried, but he knew he didn't have the right to touch her. She didn't seem to have any idea he was standing there, not ten feet away from her.

He cleared his throat. "Mrs. Chamberlain." She gasped in surprise. "Don't be scared. I—"

She straightened up, pushing her heavy curls back from her face with both hands, then took a step away from him. He was right. She was so beautiful she made his teeth ache. "Who are you?" Her voice was low and clear. "How do you know who I am?"

He hated the look of fear in her big blue eyes. Even more than he hated the tears. "Rafe Garrick," he said.

He noted the subtle shift in her posture, the way her right arm slid across her belly. A protective gesture, he thought, then noted the barely rounded swell beneath her blue jacket.

"Should I know your name?" she asked.

"Your husband didn't tell you about me?"

"My husband isn't here anymore." The fear in her eyes gave way to something even more disturbing. He saw anger, fierce and hot. "He didn't tell you?" She threw his words back at him, and he wondered what kind of mess he'd stepped into.

"Look," he said, "I thought you knew about this. I'm here to finish the basement."

Her laughter held an edge of hysteria. "I don't think so," she said, both arms wrapped around her midsection now. "I don't know what Robert told you, but I can't afford a finished basement." Another burst of wild laughter. "In case you haven't noticed, I can't even afford furniture."

He glanced around the room. The rug bore the outline

of couches and chairs and tables, but there wasn't a stick of furniture anywhere. "You were robbed?"

"You could say that." She seemed to sway on her feet then caught herself. "I'm sorry you made the drive over for nothing, but the basement's going to stay the way it is."

"I've already been paid."

The anger in her eyes battled with a burst of curiosity. "Robert paid you?"

"Half. We could negotiate the difference."

"Or you could give me a refund."

"Nonrefundable deposit," he said. He'd used most of it to pay his back mortgage and buy supplies.

"Then I'd say we have a problem."

Her face was pale, and he didn't like the slight hesitation between words when she spoke. What he did like was the way her hair tumbled over her shoulders and down her back in ribbons of red and gold. He fought back the urge to reach out and glide his hand down the fiery length of her hair. He'd never been this close to anyone like her before. He could smell the faintest traces of perfume and shampoo. He wondered if she smelled that way all over, then forced the darkly erotic images from his mind. This was a pregnant woman. Another man's wife.

"If you want furniture, I'll build you some furniture." Anything, he thought, if it meant he could stand there and watch her breathe.

"I can't think about this right now," she said, her voice softer than it had been a minute ago. "I—"

He watched in horror as her legs crumpled beneath her and she started to slide toward the floor. He caught her long before she reached the ground, just gathered her up in his arms and felt the warmth of her body against his, and he knew that in that one singular moment something in him had changed and wouldn't change back no matter how hard he wished it would.

"I'm fine," Molly managed as the stranger swooped her up into his arms. "There's no need for this." What was his name? He'd told her, but she hadn't been listening. She wished she could remember what it was, especially since he had her cradled against his chest, so close that she could hear his heart beating beneath her right ear. Oh, God, it felt good to be held again. The last time she'd been this close to a man was the night she and Robert conceived the baby. She hadn't realized how much she'd missed it until right this minute. "You can put me down now."

"And watch you drop like a rock? Just hang on, and I'll find you a chair."

He had a husky, very male voice and right now he sounded unbearably kind. She wasn't in the mood for kindness. She wished he would just go away and leave her to her misery the way her husband had.

He carried her into the foyer. "He didn't take your stairs," he said, then placed her carefully on the second step. "I'll get you some water."

"I wish you wouldn't do this."

"Save the thanks for later," he said, softening the words with a quick smile. "Just point me toward the kitchen."

She didn't have the energy to argue with him. She pointed him toward the kitchen, then leaned back against the carpeted steps. She couldn't see much of the living room from there, but then there wasn't much left to see.

He'd stripped pictures and paintings from the walls, taken embroidered pillows, the crystal jar of potpourri, and the chunky candles from the mantel.

All that was left was the pale cream-colored carpet and the stack of magazines that had rested on one of the now missing end tables. She was surprised he hadn't tried to pry the house from its foundation and cart it away in a giant U-Haul.

The top of her head felt ready to explode. Her ears throbbed with the sound of her blood pulsing through her body. She could feel her heart beating loudly in her throat, her chest, her temples. The baby shifted position then kicked sharply, and she placed her hand against her belly and willed herself to calm down. "You're all that's important," she said out loud. "You're the only thing that matters."

The helpful stranger—if only she could remember his name—walked back into the hallway then handed her a glass of orange juice. "You still have a fridge."

"That's good to know." She took a long sip of juice, closing her eyes as the cool liquid slid down her throat. "Listen, this is very kind of you, but I'm sure you have better things to do with your time."

"No," he said, crouching down in front of her. "I don't."

His face was inches away from hers. His eyes were a shade of blue that bordered on navy. She'd never seen eyes like that before. His lashes were thick and straight and inky black. A woman would kill for lashes like that. He wore his dark hair long. It brushed the collar of his denim work shirt. He had a small crescent-shaped scar on his left cheek, a wide and sensual mouth, and a strong jaw. She'd never seen anyone like him. He certainly didn't look like the kind of man you'd see walking the streets of Princeton. There was something vaguely uncivilized about him, as if he didn't know the rules and wouldn't play by them if he did. "You don't have a wife holding supper for you someplace?"

"She's holding supper for her second husband somewhere west of the Grand Canyon."

"Sorry to hear that," she said.

"I stopped being sorry about two years ago," he said. "Only took me eight years to reach that point."

Eight years? He might as well have rolled an eighteen-wheeler over her. The thought of feeling this pain for eight more years was overwhelming. Labor couldn't possibly hurt more than Robert's betrayal did.

She took a long sip of juice. The man in front of her looked appealingly uncomfortable. Very protective and very male. *Your wife must have been a fool,* she thought. Robert had never been this solicitous of her. Not even back when they were newly married and still happy. It had always been about Robert's comfort and Robert's needs and Robert's expectations. Not that she had complained. She knew the score when she signed onto the team. The most important thing was that the team stayed together.

"I'm sorry I can't help you about the basement," she said, standing up. "I'm also sorry you can't return the money."

"So am I."

"I almost believe you mean that."

"I do mean it."

"Well, there's nothing we can do about it now, I suppose."

"Your lawn's overgrown," he pointed out. "Your

shutters need fixing. I could work off the money that way.''

"I don't know," she said. "I'm in the middle of a divorce. I don't know what's going to happen next." Her laugh held more than a touch of fear. "Want to hear something funny? I don't know how I'm going to pay next month's mortgage." She didn't know why she'd said that. It wasn't something she liked to admit even to herself.

He didn't look shocked or judgmental. Maybe in his world not being able to pay the rent was as commonplace as a summer cold. "Do you work?"

"Part-time."

His eyes followed the movement of her hands as they instinctively cradled her belly. "You're pregnant."

She nodded. "Fourth month. The doctor doesn't think I should commute to Manhattan on a daily basis, so I've been freelancing." She waited for him to ask what exactly she was freelancing, but he didn't. Why should he? They didn't even know each other. "I'm looking for some local work." She forced a smile. She was good at smiling. People didn't look too closely when you smiled at them. "Need an editor?"

He blew right past her question. "How many rooms have you got here?"

She blinked in surprise. That wasn't the response she'd been expecting. "Five bedrooms, three baths, full basement. What does that have to do with anything?"

"You could rent out a few rooms to help pay your mortgage."

"To boarders?"

"Yep." He hooked his thumbs through the belt loops

of his jeans. "Good way to make some money without
doing much of anything."

"I couldn't live with strangers."

"Just an idea," he said easily, watching her with a
combination of curiosity and something uncomfortably
close to pity. She hated that look in his eyes. It made
her want to turn away in embarrassment.

"Not a very good idea," she said.

"So forget about it."

"I will."

"What do you want to do about me?"

"I can't do anything right now," she said. "You're
throwing questions at me, and all I can think about is
whether or not I still have a bed to sleep in."

"Then you'd better find out."

"Listen," she said, "I know what you're doing and
I appreciate it but I'm fine. I'm not going to pass out on
the floor or dissolve in tears the second you leave."

"You're not going to call the cops?"

"Why would I call the cops?" she countered, puzzled. "You didn't do anything wrong." So what if he
couldn't return the money. That was Robert's loss, not
hers.

"Somebody around here did something wrong," he
said. "You were robbed."

She felt heat rise up from her chest. "Don't worry.
I'm not in any danger."

"How do you know?"

"Believe me, I know."

"Why don't I check the house for you?"

Her temper flared up. "Why don't you—"

"Molly, oh, my God, I can't believe what—" Gail
from across the street burst into the foyer and stopped

dead. Oh, God, not Gail of the three perfect children and the adoring husband who showered her with Land Rovers and trips to Paradise Island. Gail thought Molly was just like her, a matron-in-waiting, a mother-to-be who'd do all of her being right there in her big, beautiful house where she was queen of all she surveyed. A woman who believed she'd been born to be served.

"Who are you?" Gail demanded, staring at the man whose name Molly wished she could remember.

He turned his slightly amused gaze on Gail. "Rafe Garrick. Who are you?"

Molly watched, amazed, as Gail's cheeks reddened. "Who *is* he?" Gail asked Molly. The righteous tone in her voice got under Molly's skin.

"Rafe Garrick," Molly said. Good thing she'd been paying attention this time. "He just told you."

"I mean, what is he? To you, that is."

"Did you want something, Gail? I'm not in the mood for social chitchat right now."

"I'm not surprised, after what Bob did. I never thought I'd live long enough to see a husband do this to his pregnant wife."

Rafe Garrick met Molly's eyes. "Your husband did this to you?"

She was too angry to be embarrassed. "You didn't think a stranger would be so sneaky, did you?"

Gail's beady little eyes didn't miss a trick. Molly knew the woman was filing away every word, every detail, so she could pass the gossip on to all of the neighbors. "We couldn't believe what was happening," Gail confided to Rafe, as if Molly weren't even there. "Bob was the nicest guy . . . just the nicest. He helped me with the flat tire I got down on Route 1. When Edie and I saw him pull up in that big U-Haul—well, it just about broke my heart."

"You saw him do it?" Molly asked. "You actually saw him stealing the furniture?"

Gail shifted her weight and glanced away for a second before answering. "I don't know that I'd call it stealing."

"He took the furniture out of my house," Molly snapped. "If that's not stealing, I don't know what is."

"I'm just telling you what he said."

"You spoke to him?"

Gail looked as if she wished she were anywhere but in Molly's foyer. "Just for a second. I had to make sure you weren't being robbed, didn't I? I mean, not being robbed by a stranger."

"You should have called the police for me," Molly said, struggling to keep her tone as even as possible. Gail Lockwood had disliked her from the first moment Molly and Robert moved in. "Maybe then I'd have some furniture."

"Oh, I don't think he took everything," Gail said in a cheery voice that rang as false as her helmet of blond hair. "I'm sure he left you more than enough."

Something in Molly snapped, and she grabbed the woman by the forearm and marched her to the entrance of the empty living room. "Still think he left me more than enough?"

Gail's cheeks were stained an ugly liver red, and the corner of her left eye twitched rhythmically. Twitch . . . twitch-twitch . . . twitch . . . twitch-twitch. Molly smiled in grim satisfaction. At least she wasn't the only one feeling embarrassed and uncomfortable now.

"It's just one room," Gail managed, pulling away

from Molly's grasp. She rubbed her arm with elaborate, melodramatic gestures. "You have the rest of the house."

But Molly knew better. She'd noticed the dirty footprints on the center staircase, seen the nasty scrapes where furniture butted up against the bannister and railings. She'd been cleaned out.

This was the stuff neighborhood legend was made of. Thirty years from now they'd still be talking about Molly and Robert and the way he'd moved out after only a handful of months and taken everything with him but the house itself. She'd be an old woman, pushing her shopping cart through Super-Fresh, and the young ones would point at her and whisper, "That's the one who was dumped."

She dragged Gail across the foyer to the dining room. The *empty* dining room. "What would you call it, Gail? How about minimalist—how does that sound?"

Gail stared at the empty room. "The bastard really did clean you out."

"You knew that before you came over," Molly said with deadly calm. "You and the rest of your pals watched as he stripped this house of every piece of furniture, didn't you?"

"You make it sound terrible," Gail said, looking toward Rafe Garrick for help. "What was I supposed to do—throw myself in front of the moving van and stop him?"

"Mrs. Chamberlain's right. You could've called the cops," Garrick said. If Gail was looking for an ally, she was out of luck.

"I don't think they would have appreciated it," Gail said with an edge to her cultivated voice. "We don't

call the police for every little thing in this neighborhood.''

Molly stepped forward. "Okay," she said, "that's
enough for one day. I'd like you to leave now, Gail.''

Gail's patrician jaw dropped open in surprise.
"You're throwing me out?''

"No," said Molly patiently, "I'm asking you to
leave. If you don't, then I'll throw you out.''

"You have a hell of a nerve," Gail said. "You
haven't been the friendliest neighbor on the block. I only
came over here to help you.''

"If you wanted to help me, you would've tried to stop
Robert.''

Gail looked over at Rafe Garrick, as if trying to determine where he figured in the scheme of things. Rafe
looked back at Gail with a closed expression on his face.
Molly was reasonably sure she was having an out-of-
body experience. The whole day felt as though it belonged to somebody else.

"Fine," said Gail, squaring her shoulders. "I have
supper to make for my husband and children.'' She
started for the front door, took a few steps, then stopped.
"I hate to be the one to say this, but we're not at all
happy with the way you've been keeping up your property since your husband left you. It's your business if
you can't pay for your groceries. Just don't take the rest
of us down with you. Maybe you don't care about things
like property values, but we do.''

"I hate her," Molly said as she stood in the doorway
and watched Gail saunter across the street.

"That's like hating a copperhead," Rafe said. "She
is what she is. Don't waste your time on it.''

Robert would have lectured her on controlling her

temper, the dangers of stress and negative thinking. He would have had her apologizing for everything, from her red hair to her bad disposition.

"I can't believe she knows about the supermarket. It's been less than an hour since it happened."

"What happened at the supermarket?"

"Let's just say it was a good opening act for what happened here."

"I'd better shove off," he said. "You've probably got things to do."

"I'm sorry about the job," she said. "I'm sorry Robert treated you so unfairly."

"So am I," he said. "I could've used the money."

She looked at him. "Me, too."

She wasn't sure if it was her words or the way she said them, but he met her eyes and started to laugh, and, to her great surprise, she found herself laughing right along with him.

"We've got us a problem," he said as the sound of their laughter faded. "You need the money back. I don't have it to give you."

He'd give it to her if he could. She could see that in his eyes. "So keep it," she said with a toss of her head. "This is between you and Robert. You don't owe me anything." In fact, she kind of liked the fact that Robert was out a healthy sum.

"You could use some lawn work."

"Right now I don't care if the weeds strangle this entire neighborhood."

"Call me when you do," he said, "and I'll take care of it for you."

It was the right thing to say. Polite. Generous. Insin-

cere. Why would he want to mow her lawn? She nodded. "I'll do that."

He hesitated for a moment on the top step. He looked
as if he wanted to say something. She couldn't imagine
what. They were two strangers who'd just happened to
share the worst day of her life. She could feel her defenses sliding back into place.

"See you around," he said at last.

"Yes," she said. "See you."

Polite talk. She'd never see him again. Not in a million years.

She closed and locked the door behind him, then set
out to assess the damage.

The downstairs was as empty as an abandoned warehouse. All she had to do was follow the trail of footprints—big muddy boot marks and the slightly smaller,
more precise markings of expensive Italian loafers—to
see what they'd been up to. Maybe she should thank
Robert for making her life easier. She should be able to
zip through her housecleaning in a fraction of the time
now.

She followed the footprints upstairs. Robert and his
crew had been remarkably thorough. She had to admire
their attention to detail. The bedroom had been picked
clean. That set her back for a moment. She could understand taking the armoire and the triple dresser and
the nightstands, but the bed? Mattress, box spring, heavy
oak frame—every single piece of it.

What kind of man would bring his marital bed with
him to his next relationship? She tried not to think too
hard about that question. She'd loved him once. Maybe
she'd even still loved him this morning when she woke
up, when she still believed he had her best interests at

heart. When she still believed he at least cared about their unborn child.

The den had been stripped of her books, the computer, monitor, printer, office supplies of all description. He'd even taken the bulletin board that hung over the desk and the *Far Side* wall calendar, her favorite one, with the barhopping elephants and angry housecats on the prowl.

He left the guest room untouched. She supposed that shouldn't surprise her. The guest room was their old life made visible. They'd emptied their entire apartment into the guest room when they moved. The cheap assemble-it-yourself Ikea knockoffs, the double bed from Dial-A-Mattress. Paperback books and photo albums from their wedding and those silly little stuffed animals he'd won at the Fireman's Fair three Augusts ago. No, Robert didn't want any of those things. He probably never had. He left them behind for Molly.

She moved down the hallway to the last bedroom, the one near the octagonal window. Not much he could do to that room. The only thing in there was a lamp with a split shade and no bulb.

The lamp was gone. She couldn't believe her eyes. He'd actually taken that miserable garage-sale reject and left the fractured shade on the floor near the window. The idea of fussy, style-conscious Robert living with that monstrosity struck her as so absurdly fitting that she started to laugh for the second time since she'd stepped into the nightmare. He deserved that lamp. He deserved every rotten thing that befell him and his blue-blooded lover. What kind of rotten son of a bitch would steal the mattress from under his pregnant wife?

Of course, she knew the answer: The one she'd married, that's who. The one she'd pledged to love and honor and stand with shoulder-to-shoulder through every dark moment life threw their way. She'd never figured Robert would turn out to be her darkest moment.

She picked up the shade then put it down on the windowsill. One of Gail's children was Rollerblading in front of her house. Even the woman's children were perfect. Their clothes never wrinkled. They never fell off their bikes and skinned their knees. They probably liked homework.

But Molly had to admit that her sharp-tongued neighbor was right. She hadn't given property values a second thought. What had seemed like an old man's innocent stubble a few hours ago now looked like an indictment of her worth as neighbor and homeowner. Each dandelion probably reduced her property value by five hundred dollars. Maybe even a thousand. If she had to sell the house at some point, every thousand mattered.

She pushed the thought from her mind. She'd lost her husband, her credit cards, her furniture, and a good piece of her pride. If she lost the roof over her head, she might as well give up the ghost. A part of her wanted to call Robert on the phone and beg him to come back home. Another part of her wanted to grab the handgun they'd kept locked in the bedroom closet and shoot him dead. And then there was the part that wanted to run home to her parents and let Mommy and Daddy make everything right again.

What a joke that was. Her parents had been divorced for ten years now. Besides, they would push her back to Robert even if he didn't want her. They'd remind her that she probably couldn't do any better, that it was a big cold world out there, and girls without great gifts of beauty and talent should be grateful for whatever they managed to get in this world.

"He's a lawyer," her mother would say. "He has a future. That's nothing to sneeze at."

"You've got security," her father would state in his basso profundo voice. "Everything else comes second. Make allowances for him, Molly. He'll come back again." Her father had walked out when she was eleven years old, and Lainie had welcomed him back six months later. It didn't work out any better the second time around, but that wasn't the point. Men made mistakes. Women forgave them. That was the way of the world.

But this was more than making a mistake. Robert had found true love—whatever that was—and he couldn't wait to leave his wife and unborn child behind in order to claim it. Besides, a man who planned to come back didn't take the mattress and box spring and feather bed and nightstands and lamps and area rugs.

If she'd needed proof that he didn't love her anymore, she had it in the echoing emptiness of her dream house.

Maybe it was time she called a lawyer.

THREE

Rafe grabbed a Whopper, fries, and a chocolate shake at the Burger King drive-thru on Route 206 then headed for home. The radio was set to an oldies station that broadcast out of Philly. He steered with one hand and managed his supper with the other while Smokey Robinson sang about shopping around.

Smart guy, that Smokey. Maybe if Molly Chamberlain had shopped around she wouldn't have ended up with a low-life bastard like the man she'd married. The guy was slick, Rafe had to grant him that. "Your references are good," the guy had said over the phone. "I want the best for my wife."

They met the next day at the diner on Route 1 and agreed on the price. "No contract to sign?" Chamberlain had asked, amusement evident in his well-educated voice.

"I work on handshakes," Rafe said.

The bastard laughed. "Then a handshake it is."

A handshake meant something back where Rafe came

from. It was a man's bond. Looked like things were different in Princeton. Chamberlain walked out on the deal the same way he walked out on his wife.

Nobody was about to nominate Rafe for sainthood, but there was no way in hell he would have walked out on the woman who carried his child. Hell, Karen had to push him out the door when the end finally came down. She'd had to lay out his shortcomings in black and white and blood red before he let her take Sarah and move on to a better life than the one he could provide. A bigger house. A newer car. A fatter bank account. All the things that mattered to her.

"It's better if you don't see Sarah," Karen had said the day she left him for another, better man. "She's only a baby. Why confuse her? It's not as if she'll remember you."

The sad thing was that he bought it. He let her walk out the door with his baby daughter. He told himself that the kid didn't need any complications, that old Jeff or George or whatever the hell his name was would be ten times the father he could ever be.

He even believed it for a while. By the time he got smart and started looking for his daughter, it was too late. Sarah had disappeared behind Karen's chain of marriages and name changes, and Rafe's limited resources hadn't been able to keep pace.

Karen wanted more than the endless Montana winters they'd both grown up with. She wanted more than life on a failing piece of land in the middle of nowhere. She said she wanted more for their daughter. Montana winters were as harsh and unforgiving as the land. Karen was a young, vibrant woman who yearned for bright lights and excitement and fun. And he let her go.

*So what makes you better than that Chamberlain bas-
tard?*

That was an easy one.

Nothing.

Chamberlain walked out on his wife and kid. Rafe
had let himself be pushed out. And maybe, if he was
being honest with himself, there was a part of him that
had been glad to go. He was tired of the fighting, tired
of sleeping on the couch every night because his wife
didn't want him in her bed. She curled herself around
the baby and shut him out as if he'd never existed. After
a while, he wasn't sure he did.

He didn't miss Karen. He missed the idea of her. He
missed knowing there was someone who gave a damn
if he lived or died. Not that Karen had ever cared, but
he'd been able to convince himself that she did, and for
a while that was enough.

Hard to do that when you came home every night to
an empty house.

Two empty houses if you counted Miriam's.

He polished off the last of the fries as he hung a right
onto the dirt road that led to the main house. Miriam
was down in Florida, where she spent most of her year.
The main house was closed and empty except for the
front rooms and the kitchen. Ginny, the housekeeper,
came in three mornings a week, but the place still looked
more like an abandoned warehouse than a home. Miriam
was the one who brought it to life.

He went in through the back door and whistled for
Jinx. A second later he heard the faint tinkling of a bell,
then, a few more seconds later, the huge black-and-white
cat was rubbing herself against his ankles. Miriam used
to take the cat down to Florida with her, but now that

Jinx was old and infirm, the vet suggested she'd be better off where she was.

"I should find her another home," Miriam had fretted before she left for Florida a few weeks ago. "You do enough for me, Rafael. I'm not about to turn you into a pet-sitter."

Rafe had mumbled something about letting the old cat live out her days where she was most comfortable, which had led to a sharp laugh from Miriam, who was pushing eighty-five and not about to do any such thing herself.

He checked the front rooms, listened for strange noises, then headed up the sloping backyard toward his house. Jinx shadowed every step he made. He had a few scars from a tangle with Jinx back in the old days, but they'd reached an accommodation that suited them both. Neither one of them liked being alone.

The old carriage house was set deep in the woods, and if you looked hard from the back door you could catch a glimpse of the Delaware River. The garage, a more recent addition, faced the main building. These days it was filled with furniture Miriam no longer wanted or needed. He'd been working on replacing bad siding on his house and the garage for six months now and, from the looks of things, he had another six months' work ahead of him. Six months . . . six years. It didn't much matter. One thing he had was time.

You'd think he'd be used to being alone after all these years, but he wasn't. There was still that moment after he opened the front door when he thought he heard the sound of music floating out from the kitchen, when he actually believed there was somebody waiting for him. Somebody like Molly Chamberlain, maybe, with that cascade of autumn hair and huge blue eyes and lush body pressed against his chest—

"Get over it," he muttered as he opened a can of cat food. Jinx meowed and wrapped herself about his ankles. When was the last time a woman did that? He crouched down and placed the dish in front of the old cat. Jinx was all over it before he stood back up.

Molly wasn't hungry, but she forced herself to make a scrambled egg. She carried her bright yellow sandwich plate and glass of milk upstairs to the den—the only room with furniture in it. She sat on the edge of the bed and looked out the window at the darkening sky as she pushed the lumps of egg around with her fork.

She had an appointment tomorrow with a lawyer who came highly recommended by three of her newly divorced acquaintances. Spencer Mackenzie had a fairly impressive list of clients and was generally considered to be a fair, kindhearted, honest man—all the things Molly had once believed her own husband to be.

She put the plate down on the nightstand. Her stomach was tied up in knots. She had a lump in her throat the size of a softball. The only thing she could manage to get down was a sip of milk.

Think of the baby, that voice inside her head warned. *You don't matter. The baby does.*

She forced herself to drink some more milk then shuddered as it slid down her aching throat. A person really could cry herself sick. She'd proved that after Rafe Garrick left and she faced what had happened to her. She'd gone out for the afternoon to see her doctor, and by the time she got home, her whole life had been turned upside down and inside out. She'd managed to pull herself together when she called Mackenzie's office, but the second she hung up the phone, the tears started again.

While she was making supper, Gail from across the street called her to try to apologize, but Molly wasn't in the mood to play the neighbor game. She stood by the answering machine in the kitchen and listened to Gail mouth meaningless platitudes, and she could barely hold back from smashing the machine with the bottom of her frying pan.

She was so filled with emotion she found it hard to breathe. Anger. Pain. Bitter disappointment. She wanted to hit something or somebody. Just ball up her fist and ram it into Robert's face. She wanted to wipe that phony smile off his face permanently. Knock out a few of those nice, even white teeth. Maybe make him feel one-one-hundredth of the pain she was feeling right this minute thanks to him.

The first stars appeared beyond her window, faint suggestions of light in the milky night sky. The Perseid meteor showers had been a disappointment this year. She'd sat out on her front step for hours, just looking up at the sky and waiting, but all she saw was a few faint streaks of moving light.

The baby moved restlessly inside her. She leaned back against the pillows and moved her hand over her belly in gentle circles. Funny how soothing touch could be. You wouldn't think the touch of your own hand against your own skin could be comforting, but it was. She'd always imagined it would be Robert's fingers splayed across her swelling belly, his mouth pressed against the taut skin, Rafe Garrick's mouth and tongue finding her center, teasing her until—

Heat blossomed deep inside her chest. Her face

burned with it. Robert's tongue never went anywhere it didn't have to go, and she'd never felt the loss. She'd never imagined it sliding up the inside of her thigh or exploring higher. Not in all the years they were together. Not once. Sex had never been the centerpiece of their marriage. Friendship was. Companionship. The joy that came from working together as partners with a common goal.

She sat up and reached for the cool glass of milk and pressed it against her forehead. She was surprised it didn't sizzle when it touched her heated skin. The searing image of Garrick's dark head buried between her thighs was almost enough to bring her to a climax, which was laughable since she couldn't remember her last climax. They'd been as infrequent in her life as four-leaf clovers and rainbows. She'd heard that something amazing happened to women in the second trimester. It had to do with increased blood flow and greater energy, and it made sex juicy and even more wonderful than before.

Which was terrific if you had somebody to share all of that wonder and juiciness with and you were the kind of woman who'd know what to do with it in the first place.

There was an enormous difference between being a sexy-looking woman and being a sexual one. She'd be a fool if she didn't realize she had the former down cold; it was the latter that had always eluded her. Some women sizzled naturally. Some simmered. Some could barely manage the occasional flickering flame. That was Molly. She loved being held, she loved pillow talk. If sex was how you got there, then she was all for it. Otherwise, she could easily live without it. And so could

Robert. At least, the Robert who'd lived with her.

Who could say? Maybe he made love morning, noon, and night with Diandra, the love of his life. Maybe she'd awakened something in him that Molly didn't even know existed. Did he kneel between Diandra's legs and stroke her with his tongue? Did he dip into her and taste her the way he'd never tasted Molly?

It suddenly struck her as a terrible shame that in all the years she'd slept next to Robert, they'd never once shared that deepest intimacy. He'd suggested it once with an insistent hand on the back of her head, but she'd refused. The thought did nothing for her, and Robert quickly put aside the notion.

She'd thought of that when Rafe Garrick swept her up into his arms. Maybe it had been the rugged strength of his body, the way she'd felt cradled and protected, or maybe it was just that she'd needed to feel a man's hands on her body—whatever it was, the image of her hair drifting across his naked belly had suddenly flashed in front of her in all of its Technicolor glory. She saw her hands sliding up his thighs, felt the dark nest of curls tickling her cheek, the way his erection leaped at the first touch of her tongue.

And then she saw the dark flare of something unknowable in his eyes and she pressed her face against his unfamiliar shoulder and prayed he couldn't read minds, because if he could, she'd have to join the witness protection plan—because there was no way she could ever look him in the eye.

Assuming she ever saw him again—which, all things considered, wasn't very likely at all.

•   •   •

Spencer Mackenzie was a good lawyer, but he wasn't a great one. At some firms, that wouldn't get you an office with a window. At Steinberg, Corelli, and Winterbourne, it got him a partnership before he turned thirty-five.

He didn't have the sharpest courtroom style. His attention to detail waxed and waned with the seasons. But when it came to generating billable-hours business, Spencer Mackenzie was your guy.

The one thing he had that the others didn't was connections. Old money, old family connections. His family was old guard New York, the land of Junior League balls, smoky wood-paneled men's clubs, handsome Fifth Avenue apartments that were handed down from generation to generation like the family silver. When you didn't work as hard as the other guy, you had more time to get out and socialize, and socializing was Spencer's strong suit. Growing up in his late brother's shadow, he'd learned to compensate for being second best in grades and potential by being fun to be around. Sometimes that proved to be more than enough. It was working for him at SC&W, and one day it might even work with his family. They might even forgive him for being the son who lived.

Last summer he'd driven up to Greenwich for a friend's wedding and he'd come away with three new clients. A lot of divorces in Greenwich. Apparently not even those Connecticut mansions could protect their residents from the cold winds of change. But it wasn't the state of marriage in the Nutmeg State that had stayed in his memory. It was Molly Kelly Chamberlain.

Over the years he'd gotten pretty damn good at picking out the likely candidates for divorce, and the beauteous Mrs. Chamberlain wasn't among them. That fact had depressed him for a good week.

She actually loved her husband. She'd looked at the guy as if he'd hung the moon. Nobody had ever looked at Spencer that way, and he'd felt a pain in his gut the first time he looked into Molly Chamberlain's big blue eyes and saw her husband's reflection looking back at him. As a rule beautiful women didn't unnerve him. His mother and sisters were renowned for their fine-boned, patrician good looks, that ice-princess Grace Kelly thing that set most men's imaginations into high gear. Most of the women he'd dated were cast from the same mold, and after a while he took beauty as a given. Only the lack of it made him sit up and take notice.

But there was something different about Molly Chamberlain. He'd zeroed in on it right from the first moment they'd met at Randall and Deni's wedding a few months ago. Instead of slow heat, there was fire. When he asked her to dance and his palm touched the bare skin of her back and found it cool, he'd started in surprise.

"Is something wrong?" she'd asked. He could still hear her voice, smoky and promising.

"This is a tango," he said. "It's been a hell of a long time since I tangoed."

"I can't tango either," she said with a throaty laugh. "We'll fake it."

She was tall and lithe, and they moved well together. He spun her into a turn, and her cloud of sweet red-gold hair fanned across his cheek as she moved back into his arms. Except for the wedding ring on her left hand, she was perfect.

"Mr. Mackenzie." He looked up to see his assistant Annie in the doorway. "Mrs. Chamberlain is here for her one o'clock. Want me to show her in?''

"Thanks, Annie. I'll do it.''

He grabbed his suit jacket from the back of his chair and slipped it on. He hadn't actually seen Molly Kelly Chamberlain since the day of the wedding. When she called yesterday afternoon and said she wanted to meet with him, he'd allowed himself ten seconds to believe it might be personal. Then he got real.

She was sitting on a plush leather chair in the waiting room, her long showgirl legs crossed, back straight, head held high. She had told him over the phone that she was pregnant, but you wouldn't know that by looking at her. She was all long curves and elegant lines. Despite her sober navy suit, she looked like an exotic flower set down among potted plants. He'd never wanted a woman more or stood less of a chance.

"Mrs. Chamberlain." He extended his right hand in greeting.

"Molly," she said, rising gracefully to her feet. She clasped his hand. Again the cool touch of her skin took him by surprise. He had the feeling she was the kind of woman who would always take him by surprise. "Thank you for seeing me on such short notice, Spencer.''

He liked the way his name sounded when she said it. "We'll talk in my office.''

He stepped to the right to let her pass. His hand rested lightly on the small of her back as he escorted her inside. He ignored his assistant Annie's curious glance. He wasn't a toucher. Everyone knew that.

"Coffee?" he asked as she sank into the deep blue armchair in front of his desk.

"Water," she said. Her hands rested lightly across her flat belly. "Caffeine's no good for the baby.''

He felt a surge of disappointment at the reminder that she was, in all the ways that mattered, unapproachable. "Water it is," he said, then filled a crystal tumbler with iced water from the pitcher atop the bar. He poured himself one as well.

"Thank you." She took a sip. Her lips were full and tinted a deep peach. She didn't even leave a lipstick mark on the rim of the glass. Her skin was fair and clear. No freckles for this redhead. The gods wouldn't do that to an angel. Her eyes were large and vivid blue, framed by thick dark lashes that cast shadows on her cheeks. She had an artist's hand with makeup, and he was connoisseur enough to appreciate the effort she put into looking the way she did. She even smelled incredible, like the beach at dawn. Women didn't get much better than this. If they did, he hadn't been living right.

He sat down behind his desk. He felt vaguely fraudulent. There was something about her that made him acutely aware of his shortcomings, both real and imagined.

"So what can I do for you today?" he asked, then looked on in astonishment as the beautiful Molly Chamberlain began to cry.

It was like watching the Mona Lisa cry, a deconstruction of serenity that shocked him to the core. He wanted to take her in his arms and kiss away those tears, every single goddamn one of them, but she was here as a client, and he knew the rules. He pushed a box of tissues across the desk toward her and waited.

"I'm sorry," she said when the tears subsided. "I don't know where that came from."

"You're going through a stressful time," he said, struggling to retain his professional equanimity in the face of such appealing disorder. She looked better now, tearstained and wretched, than most women looked on their wedding day.

"I must look terrible." Her hands fluttered about her face as if she wanted to shield him from the way she looked. She wasn't fishing for a compliment; she seemed genuinely embarrassed.

"You look beautiful." He hadn't meant to say that, but the words wouldn't be stopped. He consoled himself with the fact that she must hear those words a thousand times a day, from men in a better position to act on them.

She sniffed delicately into a tissue then met his eyes across the desktop. She looked almost grateful, but then again that could be his imagination. "You're kind," she said, not smiling. It was an observation, nothing more. "I appreciate it."

He waited while she took another sip of water and composed herself.

"It's my husband," she said at last. "He came to the house yesterday and took everything."

"He came for his belongings," Spencer said, making notes with the fat gold-nibbed pen that had belonged to his brother Owen.

"He came for more than his belongings," she said. "He took just about everything we owned. Furniture, lamps, books, you name it."

"Where were you when this happened?"

Her expression shifted. "At the obstetrician's office."

Spencer shook his head in disgust as the pen slid across the page. "Nice guy."

"He used to be," Molly said. "At least, I thought so until he fell in love with somebody else."

"Nice guys can surprise you."

"Well, he surprised me yesterday." She sat up straighter in the chair, and he watched, amazed, as she lost that vulnerable look and became the sophisticated woman he'd greeted in the waiting room not twenty minutes ago. "What can we do about it?"

"We could have done a lot more before the fact."

"That doesn't help me now, does it?" She said it quietly, with no particular degree of anger in her tone, but he felt her disapproval bone deep.

"No, it doesn't," he said. "You said on the phone that he canceled your credit cards."

"All twelve of them." She crossed her legs. He pretended not to notice. "There was six thousand dollars in the checking account when I emptied it this morning."

"Good move."

She inclined her head in acknowledgment. He found it hard to believe she was the same woman who'd burst into tears the second she sat down.

"What other assets do you have?"

"My clothes," she said. "My car. The house."

"Not the house," he said. "You own that jointly, don't you?"

"Yes, but—"

"The law is very specific about that. The house is a joint asset."

"My father gave us the down payment."

"As a loan or a gift?"

"A loan," she said.

"Good. Gifts come with no strings. A loan requires repayment. To your side of the family. That tips the balance in your favor."

"I don't really understand."

"Trust me," he said. "This is ammunition we can use."

"I hate the way that sounds."

"You'll hate it even more if you and your baby end up with nothing."

"That's what my neighbor said."

"Your neighbor's right."

"So what do I do now?" she asked.

"I need a list of everything that's missing. Some photos of the house before, if you have any. Some photos of it right now. Any witnesses who might have seen your husband loading up the moving van. We'll hire an investigator to find out what he did with the furniture. Then I talk to his attorney."

She looked disappointed. "I thought you'd talk to his attorney right now."

"We don't want to tip our hand." He hated that look in her eyes, as if he'd somehow failed to measure up.

"I'm more worried about how I'll pay my bills."

"You have the money from the checking account," he pointed out.

"Right," she said, meeting his eyes. "That should last me until the baby graduates high school."

There was no mistaking the sharp edge to her words. He had to change direction fast or lose the moment.

"I have some ideas." He glanced at his watch. "It's almost noon. Why don't we continue this over lunch?"

La Perroquet was a little jewel of a restaurant tucked into Palmer Square: whitewashed stucco walls, lots of flowers, a table for two outside in the enclosed garden. Early autumn sunshine streamed down on them, filtered through the leafy maple trees that had been around when

George Washington walked those Princeton streets.

"I used to do this all the time," Molly said as she closed her menu.

Spencer Mackenzie aimed one of his edgy grins in her direction. "Eat?"

"Lunch," she said, tapping his forearm lightly with the edge of the menu. "I am descended from a long line of lunching ladies. It's my birthright."

"We must be related," he said. "My mother's made a career of it."

She grinned back at him. "You're Jewish, too? With a name like Mackenzie, I would never have guessed."

"Kelly isn't a Jewish name," he observed.

"My mother's Jewish, my father's Catholic," she said.

"Must have been great around holiday time."

"Great and confusing. My lunching genes, though, come straight from my mother."

"Lunch crosses all social and religious barriers. The U.N. should hold peace talks over lunch. Then we'd get somewhere."

She laughed out loud for the first time in weeks. "I nominate you for secretary of state. You're very diplomatic."

"Not often enough. Ask my family."

"Tell me," she said. "Tell me exactly what your family would say about you." She felt suddenly light-headed, as if she'd been drinking champagne instead of iced water. How long had it been since she'd flirted with a man? She couldn't count back that far.

He told her a story about the time his mother went into labor at Tavern on the Green and ended up giving birth in the back of the family limousine en route home to Greenwich.

"I shouldn't laugh," she said, doing exactly that. "God knows where I'll end up giving birth."

"In a hospital room," he said, "exactly the way you have it planned."

"From your mouth to God's ear." She speared a leaf of romaine with her fork. "Right now I'm not sure how I'll pay the doctor's bill."

"That's what you have me for," he said. "I'll worry about bills. You worry about decorating the nursery."

She took a deep breath then met his eyes. "And who's going to worry about paying you?"

"That's how you know I'll do a good job," he said, that poster-boy grin making a reappearance. "It's in my own best interest."

"You sound like a lawyer," she observed with maybe a touch more sharpness than she'd intended.

"We're not all bastards," he said.

"You read my mind."

They settled into a discussion of the public's preconceptions about lawyers and doctors and used-car salesmen that lasted right through dessert. By the time Molly finished her cup of decaf and the last forkful of Key lime pie, she was feeling happier and more relaxed than she had since Robert told her he was leaving. *I like you,* she thought as he paid the bill. Probably more than a client should like her lawyer, but she wasn't going to worry about that now. He was witty, sophisticated, obviously born into money. He was the kind of man who could make a woman feel secure.

They stepped out into the afternoon sunshine. "Feel like walking?" he asked.

"Why not?" she asked. "There's no place I have to be."

"You don't remember me, do you?" he asked as they strolled to the corner of Nassau Street and the Square. "We've met before."

"That's impossible," she said. "I'm sure I would have remembered." He'd come recommended by two neighbors and the woman on the next StairMaster at the gym.

"Deni's wedding last year," he said. "We did a tango."

She stopped and stared at him. "That was you?"

"None other."

"I stepped on your foot three times."

"Four," he said. "Not that I was counting."

"I owe you an apology," she said as they started walking again.

"I'll settle for another tango one day."

She placed her hands on her stomach. "My tango days are over for a while."

"I'm a patient man," he said, meeting her eyes. "I'm willing to wait."

It felt good, walking down the street with a handsome man by her side again. And he *was* handsome. Why hadn't she noticed that the night she danced with him at Deni's wedding? Of course, she'd been married then and totally in love with Robert. She probably wouldn't have noticed if he'd been Redford in his prime.

She'd also noticed the way he took her arm again when they crossed Nassau Street, then held onto it a little longer than absolutely necessary. They both pretended nothing had happened, but she knew that he knew she'd been aware of the possibilities hidden in that touch. It was the kind of touch she understood, and her response was familiar and comforting. Nothing like the wild burst of flame she'd felt just thinking about Rafe Garrick.

They walked down to the U Store, and she noted the upscale cosmetics on display in the window. "No money troubles in Princeton," she remarked, unable to keep the edge of bitterness from her voice.

"You'll be fine," Spencer said, touching her hand for the briefest moment. He reminded her so much of Robert, the Robert she'd fallen in love with and married. Her easygoing, companionable partner.

"Short of robbing a bank, I don't see how. I'd go back to working full-time, but the doctor thinks the daily commute to Manhattan would be risky right now. I've taken on as many manuscripts as they'll give me." She'd explained that so often lately she could do it in her sleep.

"Be patient," he said. "It will all work out."

She wanted to ask him how he could be so sure, but the sun was shining, he was giving her one of those smiles, and besides, would it kill her to believe he might be right?

A battered red pickup truck was parked in front of her house when Molly got home. "There's nothing left," she muttered grimly. Not unless they were there to steal the carpeting. Reality had hit her right between the eyes on her way home. She'd been so dazzled by Spencer Mackenzie's warmth and concern that it hadn't occurred to her that he'd yet to offer one solid piece of advice.

The one thing she didn't need right now was to bump up against one of Robert's thieving pals. Or, even worse,

Robert himself. Although the odds of seeing Robert in a pickup truck were a million to one.

There was nobody in the vehicle. That didn't surprise her. The thief was probably inside trying to pry up the nails on the wall-to-wall. She parked the Jeep in her driveway and was about to climb out and track down the perpetrator when Rafe Garrick rounded the side of the house. He had a loose, long stride that reminded her of the cowboys she'd seen in the movies when she was growing up. Broad shoulders, narrow hips, long legs— she had to battle down the surge of heat building inside her chest.

"Hello again," she said, walking toward him.

He nodded at her. "I was checking out your back- yard."

Her brows drew together in a frown. "Do you mind if I ask why?" She didn't like the idea of a stranger, a man, poking around her home when she wasn't there. Especially one who made her feel like a stranger in her own body.

"The fence needs repair, your deck's rotting out, and your lawn's the worst one for miles around. And that's just for starters."

"Aren't you the bearer of glad tidings," she said, bristling at the implied criticism.

She noted the tight look of his jaw. She didn't partic- ularly care if she'd insulted him. He was a stranger. He had no right to be there uninvited.

"I'm here to help you," he said.

"Who asked you?"

"I have your money. It's the least I can do."

"No, the least you can do is respect my privacy. No- body asked you to prowl around my house."

"I wasn't prowling."

"You weren't invited."

He looked at her for a good three or four seconds. "You're right," he said. "I wasn't."

"I thought you were here to take the carpeting."

His expression softened. It annoyed her to even notice. She didn't care about his feelings. His feelings were irrelevant. This was about the sanctity of her home. She didn't have much else left but she still had the right to pick and choose who spent time there.

"Why would I take your carpeting?" he asked. His voice held a faint note of amusement.

"Why would Robert take my furniture?" she tossed back at him. "It's all I have left, therefore it's the next to go."

"I don't want your carpeting."

"Good," she said, beginning to soften a bit herself. "Because I'm not in the mood to fight you for it."

"Fighting's good," he said.

"If you win, maybe."

"What does your lawyer say?"

"He says I shouldn't worry."

"He'll do the worrying for you, right?"

Heat rose up her throat and into her cheeks. "Yes," she said. "That's exactly what he said."

"Bastard."

"He's actually a very nice man."

"Great," he said. "So what's he doing to protect you?"

"He outlined a few things," she said. "Not that it's any of your business."

"You'd better make it *your* business," he said. "Lawyers are crooks."

"I don't think Spencer's a crook."

"Spencer? You call him by his first name?"

"Why wouldn't I?" She was growing tired of the sparring. "He calls me by my first name."

"Is there something between you two?"

"This is about you," she said, "not me. You have no right to be here. I don't appreciate having a stranger on my property. You should have called."

"I don't have your phone number."

"Try 555-1212. I hear they specialize in phone numbers."

"I did. You're unlisted."

"You're right," she said. "I forgot that."

"I could've written you a letter." An edgy smile lifted the left corner of his mouth.

She refused to acknowledge either the smile or where she'd imagined that mouth exploring the night before. "You know I can't afford to hire you," she said.

"You can't afford not to hire me."

"How do you figure that?" She'd seen her bank book. He hadn't. She couldn't afford to hire a mouse.

"You're already out the money. You might as well get something for it."

She looked at him closely. If there was an ulterior motive behind his words, he hid it well. "Come in," she said after a moment. "I'll give you some iced tea, and we can talk." She laughed bitterly. "We can't sit but we can talk."

"We can sit," he said.

"On the stairs, yes," she said.

"We can do better than that." He motioned for her to follow him back to his truck, where he pulled back the canvas covering. "A few things you might be able to use."

"Chairs!" she said, astonished.

"And a table, a few lamps. I can get you a sofa by Sunday afternoon."

"I can't believe you did this."

"No big deal," he said, grabbing one of the upholstered chairs and lifting it from the truck.

"It *is* a big deal," she said. "I don't have the money for this."

"Just say thanks," he said, starting up the path to the front door.

"I can't say thanks because I can't accept this."

"Are we going to waste time on this or can we just cut to the final scene?" He didn't break stride. "I owe you a shitload of money. I don't have it to give back to you. This is one of the ways I can pay down the debt."

"I don't know—"

"You're pregnant," he said. "You're going to get more pregnant. If you can't take this stuff for your own sake, think about the baby. Call it a loan if it makes you feel better."

His words hit her hard. This stranger cared more than the baby's father. She found herself softening.

It made perfect sense when she thought about it. He'd pocketed a fair chunk of change for work he wouldn't be doing, and she could see he was the kind of man who couldn't live easily with that. Still she felt vaguely disappointed and wasn't sure why.

She walked ahead of him and unlocked the front door.

"Where do you want it?" he asked as he stepped into the foyer.

"The living room," she said. "Near the window."

"Not bad," he said. "Good thing you have white walls. Everything goes with white."

Almost everything, she thought. The green-and-white plaid club chair might be pushing the envelope, but she didn't say anything. She was grateful to have something other than the floor and the staircase to sit on.

"Go do what you have to do," he said. "I'll bring in the rest of the stuff."

"How about that iced tea?"

"Sounds great."

He worked like a dog, dragging chairs and tables and lamps into her previously empty living room. By the time he was finished, her living room and dining room looked positively livable. They weren't going to make the pages of *Architectural Digest* but they were cozy and comfortable, and she was embarrassingly grateful.

By the time she brought out a tray of peanut butter and jelly sandwiches and a pitcher of iced tea, he was sprawled in the green-and-white chair with his eyes closed.

An odd feeling came over her. She didn't know the first thing about the man. She couldn't even remember his name. Yet there he was, sleeping in her living room on furniture he'd dragged in on his extremely broad back and shoulders. Yes, she'd noticed his body. She'd have to be dead to miss those powerful forearms and huge football player's hands. He was as tall as Robert and around the same age, but that was where all similarity ended. There was nothing familiar about him, the way there was with Spencer. His accent, the way he walked, that faraway look in his eyes—he wasn't like anyone she'd ever met.

For one thing he hadn't even tried to make a pass at

her. He treated her the way you'd treat a maiden aunt, with respect and a certain distance. Most men she met made at least a token effort at flirtation, even if it was nothing more than a twinkle in the eye or a smile of recognition. She'd been fending off advances since she bought her first bra. It was as natural to her as breathing. What wasn't natural was being overlooked.

Not that she was complaining. If the man was going to be working around her house, it was better for both of them if he found her as appealing as poison ivy. Still, it seemed odd. Robert's defection had badly damaged her self-confidence. When she washed her face in the morning, she found herself staring at her reflection in the bathroom mirror, trying to see herself through Robert's eyes, trying to understand why he'd left.

Because it had to be her fault. Happy husbands didn't leave their wives. It was that simple.

She placed the tray down on the small end table and tried not to notice the way the right-hand corner had been chipped away over the years. The table was a lovely burnished walnut that had probably seen many years of use. She touched the dent with her index finger, then ran her hand across the scarred surface. The wood felt soft inside and smooth. Not at all what she'd expected. She stroked it lightly, wondering at its velvety texture, the faint scent of lemon and wood.

She'd never lived with used furniture before. Her mother had always prided herself on owning fresh-from-the-factory furniture that had no history but the one they created for it. There was something lower class about old furniture, her mother believed, as if the ghosts of the past could reach out and pull her back to old ways and old times. Even when Molly and Robert were starving students, their furniture had been brand-new. Nobody else's broken dreams or sorrows had ever touched it.

It hadn't made a difference, though. Not for her mother and not for Molly.

FOUR

❧

Rafe opened his eyes to find Molly Chamberlain watching him. She was sitting in the maple rocker he'd found a year ago when he first moved to the area. The sight hit him like a kick in the gut. It was the one thing he'd brought that hadn't belonged to Miriam. He'd been hauling away junk from one of those pricey mansions up around Alpine when the rocking chair caught his eye— soft maple, badly scratched and gouged, but curved into a shape sweet enough to make you cry. He worked on it at night when he couldn't sleep, when the old demons rose up in the moonlight to remind him he was nothing, had always been nothing, would be nothing all the days of his life.

He'd worked hard on that rocker, sanding, smoothing, carefully healing the ugly battle scars and wounds. He stained it, waxed it, set it near the window in his carriage house. He didn't use the rocker. He didn't try to sell it. The rocker sat there, day after day, waiting.

Long ago, when he and Karen first got married, he'd

bought a rocking chair. It wasn't much of a chair, a cheap K-mart job with brittle wood and a cotton cover, but it held a lot of dreams. "I'll put it by the fireplace," he'd said to her. "You can nurse the baby there." Karen was four months gone at that point and angry. She'd turned away without a word. Nobody had ever used that rocking chair.

The sight of Molly Chamberlain in this refinished wonder unsettled him all the way to his core. There was something deeply right about the sight of her sweetly pregnant body cradled in the chair's curves and hollows. He felt as if he held her in the palms of his hands. Late-afternoon sunshine spilled through the window and made her hair shine coppery gold. Autumn leaves, he thought, spun through with gold. Her clear blue-eyed gaze was focused directly on him. She had this way of looking at him, as if she could see past his defenses.

He knew that was crap. It had to be. The only thing she wanted to know about him was why he was asleep in her living room.

"Damn," he said, dragging his hand through his hair. "Sorry about that."

"Don't apologize," she said. "Obviously you were exhausted."

"Lazy," he said. "At least that's what my pa used to say." Between swings of the belt buckle. *Lazy fucking good-for-nothing bastard . . . move that bony ass of yours outside and earn your damn keep . . .* He could still hear the words, all these years later.

Her gaze didn't flicker. "How long has it been since you had a decent night's sleep?"

"Hell," he said on the edge of a laugh. "A week. Maybe two. I don't need much sleep."

She tilted her head slightly to the right, and a shaft of sunlight against the red-gold curls came near to blinding him. "You need more than you're getting."

"There's a lot you need, too."

She looked down at her hands, and he saw the way her whole body started to close in on itself like a morning glory come first light. Was she blushing? He didn't know women still did that.

"That's not how I meant it," he said. "I'm talking about the yard."

"I know," she said, recovering her poise. "You were right about this place. It's falling apart."

"I didn't say it was falling apart. I said it needs tending." She needed tending, like a beautiful lost garden—

"It needs more than tending. It needs a complete overhaul." She leaned forward, her tangle of curls tumbling over her shoulders. "I'd like to take you up on your offer."

A second passed while all the offers he might have made flashed through his mind. But there was only one she knew about. "You want some yard work."

She nodded. "Yard work, deck repair, whatever you think is fair compensation."

"You'll get your money's worth."

"I trust you," she said, then held out her right hand.

He clasped it in his. Her fingers were long and slender and strong. Her handshake was firm. He wanted to turn her hand palm up and trace circles with his tongue.

"This is great," she said, sitting back in the rocking chair. The curve of her bottom fit the curve of the seat as if fashioned by the hand of God. "We both get what we want from it."

Not by a long shot, he thought. *Not even close.*

• • •

Rafe returned the next day and mowed the lawn front
and back. Molly weeded the flower beds and did some
pruning, but fatigue swept over her before long, and she
retreated inside. The truth was, the sight of him working
in her yard unnerved her to the point where she didn't
know where to look or for how long. The urge to drop
to her knees in worship was almost unbearable. Much
easier to hide out in the kitchen where she could pull
down the shade and tell herself it was to keep out the
sun.

Besides, who needed the sun when she had her imagination to keep her warm. All she had to do was think
about the way he looked, barechested and sweating in
the sun, and she was on fire. Pulling down the shade
didn't help. She wasn't even sure a cold shower would.
She hoped he was a fast worker because she wasn't sure
how much of this she could stand.

She'd lived the last thirty years of her life without a
single sexual fantasy, and now, when she was pregnant
and alone, she couldn't close her eyes without feeling
Rafe's hands on her breasts, his muscular legs covering
hers, his mouth open and wet and hot—

Craziness, that's what it was. Wasn't she in enough
trouble as it was without adding sex to the mix? Her
hormones had never given her any trouble before, and
she wasn't about to let them get the upper hand now.

They worked out a schedule. He would keep the lawn
mowed between now and the end of the growing season.
He'd take care of leaves. He'd repair the deck, take
down the trees that had been damaged in the last big
thunderstorm, then move inside to handle some of the
odds and ends that needed doing. Maybe by the time he

moved inside, she'd be used to having him around.

If not, she'd have to consider moving.

She didn't have to see him to be aware of his every move, every gesture. He was so unlike the other men in her life that she wondered if he was even part of the same species. He took up more space, for one thing. He was taller, broader of shoulder, more dazzling. There, she'd said it. He dazzled her. She feasted on the sight of him. She wondered what he would think if he knew the way she dreamed about him, the things they did in the half light of dawn as she hovered between sleep and wakefulness.

This morning she'd woken up to find her hand between her legs.

You can blush when you're alone. She knew that now for a fact.

He tapped on the back door around four o'clock.

"I'm finished for the day," he said, wiping his forehead with the edge of his T-shirt. "I have a construction job tomorrow morning at the hospital but I'll be back by three to start work on those trees."

"You don't have to come by at all tomorrow," she said, noting the dark circles under his eyes. "Why don't you give yourself an afternoon off?"

"I have too many afternoons off," he said. "I'll be here by three."

It turned out she could set her watch by Rafe. If he said three, he was there at 2:59. If he said nine in the morning, you could bet he'd be there before *Good Morning America* signed off. She made sure he had coffee and cold drinks and cheap sandwiches. More than once she invited him in so he could escape the Indian summer heat, but each time he refused.

And each time he refused, she breathed a huge sigh of relief. He made her uneasy in a way she couldn't define. He was never anything but businesslike, even a bit distant. He thanked her for the drinks and sandwiches and ate them alone out on the back deck. It never occurred to her to take her own lunch out there and join him. They lived in very separate worlds, and it was better not to mix the two. At least that's how she read his body language when she was around him. Maybe he didn't like her or couldn't stand her perfume or was afraid she'd talk his ear off about her almost ex-husband and her baby-to-be. Maybe he sensed she was lonely. That was usually enough to send most people packing.

Funny how she'd thought getting married would put an end to being lonely. When she met Robert on their first day of high school, she'd believed she'd found her soul mate. Her best friend. The man she'd grow old beside. She'd never known anyone with ambition before. Her fractured family was a mix of opportunists, dreamers, and hard-luck cases with a private income. Not Robert. He was descended from a long line of achievers. He knew exactly what he wanted from life and how to get it and he swept Molly up in his tide of enthusiasm. *We're in this together,* he'd said. *We're a team.* Okay, maybe he hadn't said it in those words exactly, but he'd said it. Why else would she have signed on for life?

Sometimes she ate her lunch standing up at the kitchen counter so she could look out the window and admire the way his black hair gleamed almost blue in the noon sun. She told herself she ate at the counter because it was faster and easier, but that wasn't the truth.

She liked the way his hair looked in the sunlight.

She felt a little guilty about it. Not enough to stop watching him from the kitchen window, but enough to make her remember how hard she'd been on men who enjoyed watching her. Maybe that was part of the lure: Rafe Garrick didn't give her so much as a second glance. She'd rarely met a man who didn't react to her physical appearance in some way, and it unsettled her. Even Robert, at the end, had paid tribute to her looks. "You're a beautiful woman, Molly," he'd said as he walked out the door. "You won't have any trouble finding someone else."

Assuming the day would come when she actually wanted someone else.

Two weeks went by, and she'd heard from Spencer Mackenzie three times since their first meeting. He never had much of anything to tell her. For some reason that didn't seem to matter to either one of them. They fell into easy conversation as if they'd known each other for years. In some ways they did. They knew many of the same people, had vacationed at the same places as children. They spoke a certain shorthand that needed no explanation. She and Robert had talked like that, in half sentences and coded phrases. She hadn't realized how much she'd missed it. Spencer had achieved the life her own husband had been aiming toward. She knew that life. She'd been part of it. Robert's dreams had been her own, and his success would have ultimately made her dreams possible. She would have had the family she'd always wanted.

Of course, she didn't say any of that to Spencer. She knew better. If you ever wanted to know what divided the elite from the just plain rich, it was how they handled emotion. That was where her parents always got it wrong. They never could manage to tamp down all of those unruly feelings that kept spilling over at the most inopportune moments.

So she kept her emotions to herself. She still regretted crying in his office that first afternoon. He must be accustomed to it, working on as many divorce cases as he did, but she wished she could reach back and erase the tape and start over again.

You cried in front of Rafe, too. Why doesn't that bother you?

Rafe's emotions were even less on display than Spencer's, and yet she hadn't felt the same degree of regret over her loss of composure. Embarrassment, yes, but not regret. They'd never had anything close to a real conversation. *Want some iced tea? Yeah, leave it on the back step. Sure hot out today, isn't it? Yep, it sure is.* They ate their sandwiches not fifty feet away from each other every single day of the week and they never once had lunch together. He sat outside under the maple tree while she sat inside at the secondhand card table he'd found for her but never shared.

She wouldn't have thought twice about asking Spencer to join her, even for pb&j. Everything with him was easy and natural, as if she'd been there, done that, many times before. Everything about him was comfortably familiar. She understood his sense of humor, the way he phrased his sentences, even the way he paused before he answered so he could frame his response to its best advantage. That was the lawyer in him, and she understood. Robert had been like that, too, the good Robert. The one she'd married.

None of it made any sense, which only proved that she was still a long way from looking for serious male companionship. No matter what her body told her whenever Rafe Garrick was near.

Molly made a trip into Manhattan to touch base with her contacts at her old publishing house and to gather up as many slush-pile manuscripts as she could carry home. Over lunch with an associate, she pitched the idea of trying her hand at cover copy and got the go-ahead to send in some samples. Buoyed by the hope of additional income, she played with some concepts on the train ride home and was feeling happier than she had in months when she pulled into her driveway. The extra work wouldn't bring in close to as much money as she needed, but it was a start.

She was surprised to see that Rafe's truck was still parked at the curb in front of her house when she got home. She glanced at her dashboard clock. It was nearly six. He'd never stayed this late before. Usually he juggled two or three different jobs on a given day, and one of them always started around dinnertime. She went inside, tossed her packages on the kitchen counter, then opened the back door. The sight in front of her stopped her cold.

"The deck's gone!" she exclaimed, staring at the pile of splintered redwood.

Rafe was busy down at the far end of the deck, prying up nails with the business end of a claw hammer. "My other job canceled out on me. I figured I'd get started on this before it got too late in the year."

"You tore down my deck!" The yard looked as if a tornado had touched down west of the kitchen window.

"No choice," he said. "The wood was too far gone. You have termites."

"Don't say that!" She clapped her hands over her ears. "I really don't want to hear that."

"I don't want to say it, but the fact is, you'd better have the house checked."

"I can't afford termites and I can't afford a new deck," she said, feeling her heartbeat accelerate dangerously. "I can't even afford the nails, much less the lumber."

"You worry too much." He looked up at her. A minor grin tilted the ends of his mouth. "Anybody ever tell you that?"

Her hands cupped her belly in what had become her default gesture. She wished she had a suit of armor to protect her from grins like that. "I can't sell the house without a deck."

"You're selling the house?"

"I'm thinking about it."

"Too big for you?"

"That's part of it." Too big. Too lonely. Too filled with broken dreams.

"When?"

"I don't know exactly. After the baby arrives, I would think." She arched a brow in his direction. "You've asked me a half dozen questions in thirty seconds. That's more than you've asked me in the last three weeks."

"When I need information, I ask. When I don't, I shut up."

"Obviously you're not from New York," she observed.

His grin grew more pronounced. She took note of the crinkles around his dark blue eyes and the vertical slash of a dimple in his lean right cheek. "Montana." One word, uttered with a slightly ironic spin.

"Montana!" She found herself smiling back at him. A cowboy! That explained a lot. "I've never met anyone from Montana before."

"So will you quit worrying about the deck?" he asked. "It'll be long done before the baby comes."

She had to force herself back to the issue at hand. The notion of a Montana cowboy in her own backyard was more interesting than a deck. "Unless you have your own lumberyard, I don't see how."

"I have a stack of pressure-treated lumber in my shed."

"You have a shed?"

He nodded.

"Does that mean you have a house?" She'd imagined him living in a small apartment somewhere. Maybe in Philly or down near Trenton.

"A fixer-upper," he said, prying up another one of the two-by-fours.

"Where?"

"Up near Stockton."

"On the river?" The Delaware wound its way between New Jersey and Pennsylvania. Stockton was on the New Jersey side. Once upon another lifetime, she and Robert had spent a weekend at a B&B near Stockton. He'd studied for the bar exam while she wandered the town alone.

"Close enough to flood."

"What's your house like?"

"Nothing like yours."

"I'll bet you can afford your house. That's more than I can say."

"Did you tell your lawyer you need help?"

She felt her face redden. "Of course I told Spencer. I tell him everything."

"So what did Spencer say?"

She hesitated. "He said I shouldn't worry."

Rafe grunted. She wasn't sure if it was a commentary or he'd bumped himself.

"There isn't much he can do for me right now," she explained, eager to keep Spencer in a good light. "He's asked Robert's attorneys to take care of my bills, but they're dragging their feet."

"Hand me a screwdriver, would you?"

She reached for one in the huge metal tool chest on the ground next to her and tossed it to him.

"I need a Phillips."

"Why didn't you say so?"

"I figured you knew."

"I didn't," she said, plucking a Phillips from the jumble of tools. He caught it in his left hand.

"How bad are your finances?" he asked.

She decided not to pull her punches. "Terrible," she said. "I can last another two months and then I'm out of luck."

He rocked back on his heels and met her eyes. "And you're willing to wait for your lawyer to make things better."

"I don't see where I have a choice."

"If you don't see that you have a choice, you've got a bigger problem than not being able to pay your bills."

He turned back to what he was doing, leaving her standing there with a firestorm of snotty responses burning up her brain. Better to keep her mouth closed until he fixed the deck.

She stalked back into the house and prowled around the kitchen. Soup sounded terrible. She was sick to death of peanut butter sandwiches, and if she ate another egg she'd turn into a chicken herself. Nothing appealed to her. She couldn't settle down. For a second, she considered picking up the telephone to call Spencer, then decided against it.

She hated to admit it, but Rafe was right. This was her choice, not Spencer's. Taking in a boarder wasn't a perfect solution, but right now it was the only one.

FIVE

—◦◦◦—

By the time she was halfway through her first week of residency, Jessy Wyatt knew she'd made the biggest mistake of her life by coming to Princeton. Most of her colleagues were Ivy League–educated children of privilege whose lineages could be traced all the way back to Plymouth Rock. She could hold her own in the hospital, where medicine was the common tongue, but once she stepped outside, she was lost. She didn't understand their references or their jokes. And she could tell they didn't understand what she was doing there, which made them even because, at this point, neither did she.

There were times when she felt she'd be more comfortable on Neptune than she was there in the heart of central New Jersey. Not even her internship in Dallas had prepared her for this, and Dallas had been a major culture shock for her at the time. At least in Dallas she'd had someone to talk to.

"We're going over to Marita's Cantina," one of the other residents said, poking her head into the doctors' lounge, where Jessy was slumped over a cup of coffee. "Why don't you join us, Jessy?"

Jessy pretended to stifle a yawn. "I'm going to nap," she said, trying to look tired. "But y'all have fun."

The resident, a light-skinned black woman, grinned. "Y'all? This is New Jersey, girl. Better work on that."

That and everything else, Jessy thought as the woman went off to join the others. She didn't dress right, talk right, fix her hair right. Everything about her was as wrong as it could possibly be. Her exhaustion wasn't helping matters either. She'd been sleeping in the doctors' lounge, using their bathroom and shower when nobody was around. Nobody had prepared her for the prices in Princeton. The used car she'd bought at a lot near Trenton had almost depleted her savings. Rents were outrageously expensive. It would take months until she could afford a place of her own, but she had the feeling that no longer mattered. If anyone found out she was living at the hospital because she was too poor to live anywhere else, her fate would be sealed.

Two silver-haired male doctors strode into the lounge. They wore standard-issue white coats, but there was nothing else standard-issue about them. They were both tall and lean, the kind of men you'd find on a country club golf course or tennis court. If they noticed her sitting there at the table, they gave no indication. She was part of the furniture to them. Surgeons, she thought, watching the way they used their hands in conversation. God-complexed, life-giving surgeons who viewed the world from Mount Olympus.

She wondered what they would think if she emerged from the bathroom in her favorite pale blue nightgown and terry scuffs. Would they notice her if she curled up on one of the vinyl bench seats near the coffee machine? Would they lower their voices when she lowered the lights and tenderly cover her with a privacy drape?

She gathered up her things and, with a nod to the two men, left the lounge to find a new place to live.

"You really don't have to do this," Molly said to Spencer for the fourth or fifth time that hour. "This is service above and beyond."

"You know my feelings on this, Molly," Spencer said with that easy grin of his. "I think you're making a mistake, but the least I can do is help you see it through."

"I'm not that apprehensive anymore," Molly lied. "She sounds like a perfect tenant." Young, single, a resident at the medical center. She'd probably never be home. *And a stranger, Molly. Don't forget that important fact.* She was reduced to letting strangers live with her for money.

"You're a lousy liar."

"You noticed," she said. "And here I thought I was getting better at it."

"I know this isn't a perfect solution," he said, moving a little closer to where she stood by the living room window. "I would do anything to settle the divorce in a timely fashion for you."

"I appreciate everything you've done, Spencer," she said quickly, afraid she'd offended him. "I hope you realize that." Once he'd come to terms with the fact that she meant what she said about taking in a boarder, he'd taken over the process of advertising for and screening tenants. Actually his assistant did all of the hard work. Spencer had simply met with Molly and helped guide her through the stack of papers and references. The final decision had been hers.

He was saying something about the rental agreement, but his words danced right over the top of her head.

"I trust you," she said, waving her hand in the air. "I know you'll protect me."

"That's my job," he said.

She looked over at him, wondering if that was all it was. Lately her imagination had been running away with her. It was so easy to pick up the telephone and pour out her heart to Spencer. He lived the life Robert had been striving toward: successful lawyer at a successful firm with money and perks at his disposal. His family had been pressing him to marry and produce a few Mackenzie heirs, but, as he'd told Molly last night over dinner, he wasn't in a rush. "When I do it, I want to do it right," he said to her as the waiter brought them their entrées. "I've seen what happens when it goes wrong."

So have I, she thought. She was living it. A man like Spencer would be very careful when he picked a wife. No mistakes for him.

"I think I'll pour us some iced tea," she said, determined to banish the unpleasant thoughts from her mind.

"You stay put," he ordered. "Jessy will be here any minute. You should be the first person she meets."

"We're not looking to bond with each other," Molly said in a dry tone of voice. "She doesn't have to imprint on me like a duckling."

His laughter caught her by surprise. Her best remarks usually got no more than a smile from him.

"I'll get the iced tea," he said. "You work on your attitude."

She thought of something smart to say but decided

against it. It was enough she'd made him laugh once today. She wasn't about to push her luck.

Rafe was mowing the front lawn when he heard the sound of laughter from Molly's house. He felt like steering the mower right into the guy's shiny black Porsche.

When you grew up in the middle of nowhere the way he had, you learned to rely on your instincts, and his instincts told him Spencer Mackenzie was no good for Molly Chamberlain. The second the guy pulled his fancy sports car into the driveway, Rafe found himself battling the urge to ram his Chiclet-white teeth down his throat. No particular reason. The guy didn't ignore him the way another rich guy might have done. No, Mackenzie was too smooth and polished for that. He gave Rafe a friendly, hail-fellow-well-met hello then strode up the walkway to the front door as if he owned the place.

Rafe wanted to deck him.

No reason. He just hated the guy on sight.

He'd hate any man who made her laugh.

Jessy found Princeton Manor Estates with no trouble. She rolled to a stop at the gates and gave her name to the serious young man in uniform. He made a production of checking a list, frowned, then made a telephone call. She watched as he mumbled something, nodded, then waved her on. She forced a pleasant smile and a thank-you. Her Southern background wouldn't let her do anything else. He probably thought she was a cleaning woman from a not-very-successful service. Not that she blamed him. Her car was older than he was.

She glanced down at the map Mr. Mackenzie's secretary had faxed over to her at the hospital. A right on

Rosebud Ridge, a left on Marigold Drive, a quick series of rights on Amaryllis and Lilly, and that should bring her to the base of Lilac Hill. She wondered how anybody found their way around Princeton Manor. The roads curved and meandered like lazy Mississippi streams with no particular destination in mind. The houses were all enormous. They looked more like small hotels than private homes. Saabs and Porsches napped in the driveways. The lawns were manicured to golf-course perfection.

And the flowers. Flowers bloomed everywhere Jessy looked. Lipstick-red geraniums, pale blue snowballs, and wild, boisterous impatiens, tumbling red over white over pink. *You'd love it here, Mama,* she thought as she turned right on Amaryllis. This was everything Jo Ellen had ever wanted. A big fancy house with a flower garden front and back. ''You'll have all the things I never did, honey,'' she'd said to Jessy more times than she could count. ''You'll be somebody . . . You'll be a doctor.''

Lilac Hill was well named. Lilac bushes thrived everywhere she looked on the gentle rise of land. The houses were even larger than the ones on Amaryllis and Rosebud. Jessy couldn't help but wonder why someone with this kind of money would be looking to take in a boarder.

Not that she was complaining. The rent was more than reasonable, it was close to the hospital, and meals were included. Maybe Mrs. Chamberlain was a lonely old widow who just wanted to know there was somebody else in the house. The idea appealed to Jessy. She liked old people. She probably should have gone into gerontology instead of gynecology. She hoped Mrs. Chamberlain was a blue-haired eighty-year-old matron who liked to knit and read romance novels and talk about the old days. Someone who wouldn't judge her by her accent or her bloodline.

The Chamberlain house was at the top of the rise. It looked like every other house in the subdivision, only more so. A guy in jeans and a T-shirt was mowing the side lawn. He watched as she parked her car on the street and climbed out. She started to lock the door then realized how totally ridiculous she was being. The landscaper probably owned a better car than she did.

She ran a quick hand over her tightly braided hair. A few of the other residents at the hospital wore their hair this way, and she'd noticed how neat and professional they always looked. Too bad the effect on her was more schoolgirl than professional. She slipped her huge totebag over her shoulder then started up the path that led to Mrs. Chamberlain's front door.

The landscaper stopped mowing and watched her progress. She knew she walked like what she was: a kid who'd grown up barefoot and still hadn't made her peace with shoes. Why didn't he go back to cutting the grass and leave her alone? She shot him a look. He didn't even have the brains to seem embarrassed. What he seemed was too darned curious for his own good. Thank God it was autumn and pretty soon there'd be no need for a landscaper to come by and mow lawns and spy on people.

Back home people did things like that, nosying all over the place, trying to peek through windows and eavesdrop on phone calls and read someone else's mail. She would have figured Princeton folk were too sophisticated for that kind of white-trash nonsense. *Goes to show how much you know, Jessy Ann Wyatt.*

She climbed two steps to the front porch. She'd never seen a brand spanking new front porch before. All the front porches she was familiar with were rickety and old, with wood worn thin and smooth by years of footprints and gliders and rain. Nothing like this spit-and-polish wonder. More than the fancy cars or the fancy people, this fancy porch was enough to make her turn tail and run away as fast as she could. She didn't belong here any more than her daddy belonged in the Lincoln bedroom at the White House. Some things just weren't natural.

But it was one o'clock, and she was still her mama's girl, the one who was brought up to be on time and keep her promises. She reached out and pressed the doorbell. From somewhere deep inside the house, she heard the sound of Westminster chimes. She'd been to church services in Dallas that had less music than that.

What are you doing here, Jessy girl? This ain't no place for you. You should've stayed home where you belong, with your own kind.

Now, what was her daddy doing, talking to her like that? She'd left him behind in Mississippi. He'd probably forgotten all about her before her plane even taxied down the runway. It was her own insecurities speaking, that's all, reminding her that she'd never be one of them, no matter how good a doctor she was.

Why wasn't Mrs. Chamberlain answering the door? Maybe the old woman had peeked out the window, noticed her old car, and changed her mind about the whole thing. Which was just fine with Jessy because the doctors' lounge was beginning to look like the best place in town. She turned and was about to start down the porch steps when the front door swung open.

"Jessy Wyatt?"

Jessy stopped, took a deep breath, then turned around. A tall, downright gorgeous woman with a mane of light auburn hair stood framed in the doorway. She wore a loose turquoise dress, strappy sandals, and huge gold hoop earrings. She looked like an upscale gypsy.

"You are Jessy Wyatt, aren't you?" The woman's voice was husky, her tone amused. She sounded like one of those women on television who sold cars and sexy lingerie with a wink and a smile.

"I'm Jessy Wyatt." Jessy knew exactly how she sounded. Like white trash with an education. "I have an appointment with Mrs. Chamberlain."

"I know," said the woman. "I'm Molly Chamberlain." She might as well have said Cleopatra.

"Jessy Wyatt."

"You said that before." She frankly assessed Jessy with curious blue eyes. "Are you sure you're really a doctor? You look about twelve years old."

"I'm twenty-nine."

"You don't look it."

"I will when I'm forty."

Molly Chamberlain's laugh was full-bodied and lusty, not at all what Jessy would have expected from such a perfect-looking woman. "So are you going to stand out there on the porch all day or are you going to come inside?"

"Where I come from, we wait to be invited."

Molly's dark, perfect brows arched slightly. "Well, honey, you're in New Jersey now, and we don't stand on ceremony." She opened the door wide and motioned Jessy inside.

There was something about Molly's words, or maybe

it was the way she said them—friendly, challenging, faintly sarcastic. Whatever it was, the combination got under Jessy's skin and gave her confidence. She brushed past the woman and stepped into the foyer, half dizzy from the combination of Shalimar and central air conditioning.

"You have an accent," Molly said.

"So do you," Jessy said, beginning to enjoy the byplay.

"Alabama?"

"Mississippi," Jessy said. "Near Jackson."

"I wish I sounded like you," Molly said. "My husband—" She stopped. "Damn it. I've got to stop doing that."

"Stop doing what?"

"Talking about my husband. He's gone. I have to get used to it."

"I'm sorry," Jessy said. A widow. That explained everything. "How long has it been?"

"Eight weeks."

Jessy tried to keep her expression bland. Back where she came from, widows didn't wear bright turquoise minidresses eight weeks after they buried their husbands. "Was it sudden?"

Molly snapped her fingers. "Like that. One day he was here, the next he was gone."

"You must still be in shock."

"Tell me about it." She rested her graceful hands on her belly.

For the first time Jessy noticed the swell behind the loose-fitting dress. "Are you pregnant?"

"I just started my fifth month."

"I'm an OB-GYN."

Molly looked at her, then started to laugh again. "I guess we're a match made in heaven."

"Looks like." She seemed awfully cheerful for a new widow, but that was none of Jessy's business. She could tapdance on top of her ex-husband's grave, and it still wouldn't be any of Jessy's business.

"Let me show you your room. Spencer went to get us some iced tea. I don't know what's taking him so long."

Spencer? Jessy wasn't the backward country hick she'd been a few years ago, but this was too sophisticated for her. Damn but these Princeton Yankees did things different. She was about to say that sure, she'd love to see her room, but a man's voice interrupted her.

"You ran out of ice. That's what took me so long."

Jessy turned in the direction of that voice. She couldn't have done anything else. That was the voice she heard in her dreams.

"Spencer!" Molly Chamberlain sounded downright delighted. Her dead husband must be spinning in his grave. "Come in and meet Jessy."

Jessy's palms started to sweat. She was no more than ten feet away from the front door. Maybe she should make a run for it. But that voice, that sexy wonderful voice, called out her name, and she heard him walk closer. She turned around, and at 1:23 P.M., Jessy Ann Wyatt fell in love.

It happened that fast. One second she was her normal solitary self, and the next her hopes and dreams had a focus. All her life her dreams had had her mama Jo Ellen's name on them. Class valedictorian, full scholarship to Duke, her years in Dallas—they were all her mama's hopes for her daughter's future.

But this dream, this man, was Jessy's alone. She'd imagined him every night of her life since she was old enough to know that boys and girls were different, and now that he was standing there in front of her, she couldn't remember her name.

"Jessy." Molly Chamberlain's voice tugged at her sleeve. "I'd like you to meet Spencer Mackenzie."

"Jessy and I already know each other," Spencer Mackenzie said as her right hand disappeared into his.

Say something, you fool. Don't go staring at him like he's a plate of barbecue and you've been starving for a week.

"We do?" she managed. She'd never seen hands like his before, large but graceful, the kind of hands you'd imagine sliding across the keyboard of a grand piano. The kind of hands she'd imagined sliding across her body even though she almost never had time to think about things like that. *Get a grip on yourself, girl. Like he'd notice you with Molly Chamberlain standing right next to him.*

"I arranged this for you," he said as he released her hand. It took all her self-control to keep from begging him to hold onto her forever. "We talked about the terms of the lease."

Actually it was his secretary who had talked to her and sent on the paperwork, but if he wanted to believe they'd spoken, she wasn't about to tell him otherwise.

"Thank you," she said, wondering if he realized her palm was sweating. If he did, he was too much of a gentleman to let on.

"So how do you like it?"

"I like the foyer just fine," she said.

"I was about to show Jessy her room," Molly said.

"Unless you'd rather do it while I make us some sand-wiches."

"You don't have to make me anything to eat," Jessy said. The thought of being alone with Spencer Macken-zie made her feel faint. "I had something at the hospital cafeteria before I came here."

"I've eaten at that cafeteria," Molly said, rolling her eyes in comic dismay. "I promised room and board and I'm a woman of my word."

"I know this place better than Molly does," Spencer said to Jessy. "I'll give you the grand tour."

I'll just bet you know this place, Jessy thought as she saw the way he looked at Molly as she glided from the room. Jessy had seen a lot of pregnant women in her day, and she'd never once seen one capable of gliding past the third month. There was a lot to hate about Molly Chamberlain: her big house, her pregnant belly, the Greek god who kept stealing glances at her when he thought no one was looking. She wasn't sure she wanted to live there with a woman who made her look even plainer than nature had managed to do.

But then who was she kidding? In a million years she wouldn't stand a chance with someone like Spencer Mackenzie. The Molly Chamberlains of this world had them all sewn up.

SIX

~~~

I don't like you, Molly thought as she watched Jessy Wyatt eat a tuna salad sandwich. *And I don't think you like me too much either.* She'd gone out of her way to be scrupulously sweet and polite to the young doctor, and so far she'd been rewarded with sidelong glances and monosyllabic comments delivered with a faint edge hidden beneath the Southern syrup.

Jessy Wyatt was a plain little thing with long light brown hair that fell between her shoulders in a messy braid. She wore beige cotton trousers and a pink T-shirt that drifted loosely over her small breasts. One bra strap peeked out from the boat neckline. Her sneakers were worn and white. She carried a pager clipped to her woven belt and an enormous tote bag that looked like it weighed as much as she did. The thought of her examining patients and delivering babies was almost laughable. She didn't look old enough to menstruate.

You're being a bitch. So what if she's not what you were expecting. You needed a boarder and you've got one. She hadn't advertised for a friend, just someone to share the house with her. As long as she and Jessy didn't come to blows, they'd be okay.

"Need more iced tea?" she asked, pushing the pickle around on her plate with the back of her fork.

"More sugar would be nice," Jessy said. Her tone was polite, but Molly heard a note of censure beneath it.

"Sorry. I always make it without sugar."

Jessy looked down at her plate but not before Molly saw the faintest beginning of a smile on her lips. "We like it real sweet where I come from."

Molly pushed the sugar bowl across the kitchen table. "Help yourself," she said. "I don't use sugar."

"I inhale it," Jessy said.

"And you're still skinny." Molly's fingers tightened around her glass. "Aren't you lucky."

"I can eat anything I want," Jessy said, spooning sugar into her glass with abandon. "Butter, ice cream, chocolate, steak—"

"I can see why you're not a cardiologist."

Jessy's head shot up, and she looked over at Molly. "Are you insulting me?"

"Of course not," Molly said. "Just making an observation."

"I'm a good OB-GYN."

"Did I say you weren't?"

"You're looking at me like I'm somebody's kid sister home from school."

"Can you blame me? You look about twelve."

"Thirteen," said Jessy. "Fourteen on a good day."

Damn it. She had a sense of humor. Molly always had a hard time disliking people who could make her laugh.

"Listen," she said, pushing away her sandwich plate with both hands, "I think we got off on the wrong foot somehow."

Jessy said nothing. Her deep-set brown eyes remained level and unrevealing.

"I'm going through a rough time right now," Molly said. She waited for a response. Jessy continued munching on her sandwich. What was wrong with the girl? Didn't she recognize a cue when she heard one? This was when Jessy was supposed to say don't worry . . . I understand . . . no problem. Instead she chewed her tuna on rye and watched Molly as if she were a specimen on a laboratory slide.

Molly regrouped and tried again. "My husband left me in a difficult situation. I never thought I'd have to rent a room to a stranger, but then I never thought I'd be having a baby alone either."

"I'm not looking for friendship," Jessy Wyatt said, "if that's what you're afraid of. I'm pretty self-sufficient."

"Actually that's what I was hoping for," Molly said, oddly stung by the young woman's blunt words. "I want this to be businesslike and uncomplicated for both of us. The fewer entanglements, the better."

"I'm glad we understand each other." Jessy's accent wrapped itself around her words, softening their impact. Molly found herself with a newfound respect for the Southern woman. You could get away with a lot with an accent like that, much more than you could when your speech was laced with the Hudson River.

"I don't want you to think that just because I'm pregnant and you're an ob—" She didn't need to finish the sentence. It was self-explanatory.

"Good," said Jessy, "because I wouldn't ask you for a free room or use of your car."

Molly felt heat rush to her cheeks in response. "I'm not trying to start an argument," she said. "I'm trying to bypass trouble."

"I know that." *Ah know that.* "So am I." *So am Ah.*

"Then we understand each other."

"Perfectly."

It was like dealing with a man, Molly thought. Jessy Wyatt didn't give up one more word than absolutely necessary, and the ones she gave up seemed to cause her physical pain. If she had been looking for friendship from her boarder, she would have been sorely disappointed.

You knew without asking that Jessy Wyatt would never let a man catch her by surprise the way Molly had. She was too smart and independent for that. She would have known Robert was falling in love with another woman before he did. You could see it in the way she carried herself, almost daring the world to try to block her progress.

"So when do you start your own practice?" Molly asked, trying to ease them both into more conventional conversation.

"Around the millennium," Jessy said. She spooned more sugar into her iced tea. "I'm just starting my residency."

"Oh." Molly refilled her own glass of tea from the bright red pitcher in the center of the table, then topped off Jessy's glass as well. "So you'll be in Princeton awhile."

"Depends," said Jessy.

"On what?"

"On what Princeton has to say about that."

"I don't follow."

"I'm not sure I fit in."

"That's all that's worrying you? Let me put your mind at ease: Nobody fits in except the natives."

"And you know because you are one."

"Me?" Molly laughed out loud. "Honey, you've got that all wrong. I'm no more a part of this place than you are."

"You look like you belong."

"So could you if you dressed differently." She sipped her tea then added a lemon wedge. It floated atop the perfect little ice cubes like a yellow crescent moon. "But there's a big difference between looking as if you belong and really belonging."

"Tell me something I don't know."

"I can tell you this," Molly said. "If you don't change your attitude, you won't stand a chance."

"My attitude?" *Mah attitude?*

"That chip on your shoulder is bigger than your accent."

"I don't have a chip on my shoulder."

Molly smiled and took another sip of iced tea. "Whatever."

Jessy pushed aside her sandwich plate and leaned across the table. "What makes you think I have a chip on my shoulder?"

"Forget I said anything." Molly offered a bland smile. "I'm always sticking my nose where it doesn't belong." *I could shoot you, Spencer. Couldn't you have found me someone who actually likes me?*

"No," said Jessy, her expression growing more intense, "I really want to know why you said that. Nobody's ever said that to me before."

Molly didn't bother to hide her surprise. "I would think you'd hear it hourly."

Jessy pushed back her chair and stood up. "I don't much like being insulted."

"I don't blame you," Molly said. "Nobody does."

"So why did you do it?"

"I didn't insult you. I'm trying to help you. If you're going to live here with me, you might want to pretend it wasn't a punishment."

"I think you're the one with the problem," Jessy said. "I'm real sorry your husband died, but don't go taking it out on me."

"Hold on a minute," Molly said, rising to her feet. "You want to say that again?"

"I'll say it as many times as you want me to," Jessy shot back. "Just because your husband died and you have to take in strangers—"

"My husband didn't die," Molly broke in.

Jessy's eyes widened. "Oh," she said, cheeks reddening. What was that all about? "I didn't realize. Is Spencer—"

"Spencer's my lawyer. My husband walked out on me two months ago."

Jessy tried to concentrate on what Molly was saying, but the sound of her own relief overwhelmed everything else. Actually, relief sounded an awful lot like a heartbeat sliding toward arrhythmia, and it took a few deep breaths to bring it back to anything approaching normal. For one terrible moment she'd thought Spencer and Molly were married. She knew it was irrational. Spencer

Mackenzie's wife wouldn't be taking in boarders. You only had to look at his beautiful clothes and perfect hair to know that. Still, when Molly said she wasn't a widow and then mentioned Spencer's name, Jessy's heart came close to breaking.

She wouldn't have thought it possible. Human hearts didn't break from emotion, especially not over someone just met. Everything she'd learned in med school pointed her away from such a belief. But none of that explained the way her heart had felt, as if someone had dragged a big rig across her chest.

Relief wasn't much better. She felt giddy and disoriented. She understood maybe every fourth word Molly uttered.

"Are you listening to me?" Molly demanded. She sounded exasperated, and Jessy couldn't blame her. "I just told you my whole story, and you haven't said a word."

"Sorry," Jessy said. "I was thinking about a patient." She doubted Molly believed her, but it was the best she could do. *Husband left . . . younger woman . . . took everything.* She hoped that covered the highlights. "So you're getting a divorce?"

Molly shot her a skeptical look that might have sent another woman running for cover. Jessy, however, was made of sterner stuff. At least, she pretended to be. "I'm getting a divorce. I'm having a baby. I can't afford to keep this house and I can't afford to sell it."

"Which is where I come in?"

"Exactly."

"I was sleeping in the doctors' lounge," Jessy said. "I couldn't afford an apartment in town. Finding this"— she gestured broadly—"is a godsend." And finding

Spencer Mackenzie was a downright miracle.

They considered each other for what seemed like forever. *You said too much, girl. Now she knows you're white trash and she'll send you packing.* It was one thing to be left high and dry by a no-good husband. Everybody understood it wasn't your fault. They knew you were used to better. For Jessy, this was the best it had ever been. She had no doubt they knew that, too.

"So what do you think?" Molly asked, folding her arms across her slightly rounded belly. "We don't have a whole lot in common. Do you think this can work?"

"Like you said, we don't have to be friends. We just have to live together."

"Talk to my husband," Molly said with a quick smile. "He'll tell you how good I am at that."

"I'm willing if you are."

Molly extended her right hand toward Jessy. She clasped Molly's hand and met her eyes. To her surprise she saw kindness in them and understanding and something that just might be the start of respect.

Rafe pushed the mower up and down the length of the backyard. The vertical blinds were open, and he could see Molly at the kitchen card table. She sat opposite the skinny little brown-haired woman he'd seen getting out of the faded green Chevy Nova. They didn't look too happy. The skinny one was bent over her plate while Molly looked as if she wished she were anyplace but where she was. She had this habit of pushing food around with her fork, like a little kid hiding the peas beneath the mashed potatoes. He was learning all of her habits. He knew that she always rinsed dishes before putting them in the dishwasher, that she drank milk from a dark blue glass wineglass with a fragile stem, that the sweet curve of her body as she bent down to bring in the morning newspaper was the essence of beauty that had eluded poets for centuries. He didn't even like poetry, but somehow he knew this.

He usually grabbed his lunch under the big maple tree opposite the sliding doors. It was a great spot. He could lean against the trunk and watch her moving around the kitchen while he polished off a hero and a can of Coke.

He'd never seen a woman move the way Molly Chamberlain did. She didn't so much walk as glide, a supple, sinuous movement that rippled behind his eyes late at night when he couldn't sleep. He saw other wonders on those sleepless nights. Molly Chamberlain moving beneath him—her hips arching to meet his, her eyes closed, her full round breasts softer than a whispered dream. Some mornings he couldn't meet her eyes because he was sure the moment she looked at him she'd know what he'd been thinking.

Assuming she ever looked at him at all.

The lawyer appeared in the kitchen. He said something, and the two women laughed. Polite laughter. It had to be. He'd never met a funny lawyer and he doubted if that Porsche-driving specimen would be the first.

Molly pushed back her chair and stood up. The lawyer was at her side instantly, offering her a hand even though it was clear she'd already managed the feat on her own. She smiled up at the lawyer, looking more at ease, more comfortable than she ever had with Rafe. He knew that look. It was the same one Karen had used on every man but the one she was married to.

They almost looked like a family in there. There was

something about Molly and the lawyer that seemed pre-ordained. She was the kind of woman who was meant to have certain things in life: a big house, a nice car, an expensive husband. Somebody like the guy in the fancy suit who was dancing attendance around her.

The sight bugged Rafe. It gnawed at his gut like a handful of jalapeños. Ever need proof which way the wind blows? Try being on the wrong side of Molly Chamberlain's window.

At first Spencer thought Jessy Wyatt was being polite. The last time anyone had listened so intently to one of his stories was when he was trying to explain to an irate judge why his client had decided a trip to the Bahamas was more important than showing up for her hearing.

Molly usually paid fairly close attention to his stories, but her attention was wandering. She seemed more interested in glancing out the sliding doors to watch the help mow the lawn.

No, it wasn't his story that was captivating the lady doctor.

He was tempted to glance down and make sure his fly was zipped, but Jessy's eyes hadn't dropped from his face. He was accustomed to a fair amount of attention from the opposite sex. The lingering glance. Perfectly aimed half smile. A touch so soft you might have imagined it.

But this was different. She wasn't flirting with him. She was declaring. The invitation was there. No doubt about that. But it was more than that. Her serious face was turned up to him like a flower, one of those scruffy orange lilies that grew along fences and at the side of the road. The kind he usually didn't notice unless some-body pointed them out.

He wouldn't have noticed Jessy Wyatt in a crowd. Hell, he wouldn't have noticed her now with Molly Chamberlain sitting across the table from her, looking burnished and ripe and beautiful, except that she made it impossible for him to look away.

He tried to turn it around and aim it back at her. "When will you be moving in, Jessy?"

She took a sip of iced tea then smiled at him. Her lips were wet and glistening. Her teeth were small and white. She looked almost pretty when she smiled. "Tonight," she said, the word rising up on a Southern wave.

"If you need help with your belongings, I can rec-ommend a good local moving service."

Her eyes crinkled as her smile widened. "I can pack my belongings in my suitcase and have room to spare for the complete works of Shakespeare."

He didn't know what to say to that. Most people of his acquaintance had more stuff than they could fit in a town house and summer place in Cape May. He'd need three trunks just to pack up his law books. His clothes would take another three. That thought had never made him uncomfortable before, but it did now.

The lawn mower sat in the center of the backyard like an abandoned car. One second Rafe had been pushing it up and down the slope, the next second he was gone. Maybe he'd had enough, Molly thought, tapping her fork lightly against the side of her plate. Maybe he had better things to do than pay off a debt to the wife of the man who'd backed out on the deal. She wouldn't blame him one bit if he'd packed it in and she never saw him again.

Jessy's voice danced around the edges of her thoughts. There was something vaguely familiar to the lilting tone. Jessy was flirting with Spencer. The realization hit her right between the eyes.

Molly looked at her across the table and saw nothing out of the ordinary. Jessy's plain face was expressionless, save for a smile that caused her brown eyes to almost disappear. Someone should have told her not to smile that way. She'd be a mass of crow's feet before she turned forty. Spencer stood perfectly straight with his back to the refrigerator. He looked like an advertisement for extreme discomfort. Poor Jessy. She was so far from being Spencer's type that it made Molly feel almost sorry for her.

It hadn't taken long for Molly to get a good sense for the type of woman who appealed to Spencer Mackenzie: beautiful, socially acceptable, and temporary. He was great company, but a woman would be very foolish to fall in love with him. Not that Jessy Wyatt was in love with him. She'd known him less than two hours. You could barely get a good case of lust started in two hours.

As if on cue, Rafe appeared in the doorway. "Sorry to interrupt," he said, although he didn't look sorry at all. He looked downright annoyed. "A messenger dropped this off for you."

"A messenger? Are you sure it wasn't FedEx?"

"I know the difference between FedEx and a messenger." His tone was flat, but she thought she caught a sharp edge to his bland words.

She felt her cheeks go red. She hadn't meant to embarrass him.

He crossed the room and handed her a flat, bright red envelope with a wide snow-white label pasted neatly in the center.

"Mr. and Mrs. Robert Chamberlain." She shook her head. "Somebody hasn't been keeping up with local gossip."

Spencer extended a hand to Rafe.

"Spencer Mackenzie," he said.

Rafe hesitated just long enough to make Molly wonder if he was going to ignore Spencer entirely. "Rafe Garrick."

The two men shook hands.

"I'm Molly's lawyer," Spencer said.

"I cut her grass," Rafe said.

Spencer nodded. "You're doing a good job."

"Thanks," said Rafe.

Molly winced. Somehow he'd managed to make "Thanks" sound like "Go to hell."

She slid her index finger under the bright red flap. "This isn't a fancy way of serving a subpoena, is it, Spencer?"

His handsome face darkened. "I wouldn't think so. Maybe you should let me handle this."

"I'm only joking," she said, waving him away. She ignored the smirk on Rafe's face. So what if Spencer didn't have a great sense of humor. Humor wasn't everything.

Jessy didn't try to mask her curiosity. She leaned forward, elbows on the table, and rested her chin in her palms. "Maybe you won the Publishers Clearing House sweepstakes."

Molly arched a brow. "The Prize Patrol isn't parked out front."

"Maybe they're around the corner," Jessy said, deadpan. "Ready to pounce."

"They better have an ambulance, too," Molly said as she reached into the envelope, "because I'll need resuscitation."

The men were quiet. That didn't surprise Molly. Men were invariably puzzled by female byplay. They probably thought she and Jessy were fighting, which Molly found hilarious since their handshake had practically been a declaration of war.

"So what is it?" Jessy asked.

Molly drew in a breath. "Tickets," she said after a moment. She looked up at Spencer. "For the Historical Society dinner dance."

"Two hundred a pop," Spencer said. "Robert must've been feeling guilty."

Molly fanned the four tickets between her fingers like a winning poker hand. "Think I could scalp these at the door?" Spencer's patrician jaw sagged. "I'm only kidding," she said quickly. "I know Princeton matrons aren't supposed to scalp tickets to a charity dance, but I don't think there's a law against giving them away."

She had their attention now. Rafe, Spencer, and Jessy were all staring at her as if she'd lost her mind.

"Here," she said, holding out the tickets. "Pick one."

Jessy leaned forward and plucked a ticket from the group. "Thanks," she said, dipping her head in Molly's direction. "Think they'd mind if I wore jeans?"

Spencer bent down and selected a ticket. "I'll pay you for this," he said.

"Try it and I'll find another lawyer." She smiled grimly. "These tickets are on Robert."

That left Rafe. He was leaning against the doorjamb, arms crossed over his chest. He looked amused, a little disapproving, extremely sexy.

"There's one ticket left," she said, feigning a casual self-confidence she didn't feel. "You might as well join us."

"Thanks," he said, "but I'll pass."

"Of course you won't pass," she said, aware of Jessy and Spencer's rapt interest in their byplay. "This is an exclusive group. You're part of it. There's a ticket here with your name on it."

His jaw tightened. She saw it happen. She'd read about it a million times, but this was the first time she'd witnessed the phenomenon. Impressive, she thought, and more than a little bit off-putting. He wanted that ticket as much as he wanted a case of chicken pox. Maybe even less. Which made her want him to have it even more.

Their eyes met, and everything else fell away. Who was she kidding? The only thing she wanted was Rafe.

SEVEN

❧

Jessy went back to the hospital after lunch to gather up her belongings. She'd stuffed most of them in a pair of lockers off the doctors' lounge. The rest she kept in the trunk of her car. It had been sweet of Spencer Mackenzie to offer the name of a moving company. If he'd offered himself as moving man, she would have said yes in a New York minute, even though a child could have carried everything she owned and then some.

Did he have any idea how she felt about him? She hadn't tried to hide it. Molly Chamberlain was wondering about it. Jessy saw it in her eyes across that sad little kitchen table that would have looked more at home in her mama's house than in the middle of that fancy Princeton mini-mansion. Of course, that mini-mansion wasn't worth spit in a bucket if you couldn't pay the mortgage.

Spencer was Molly's lawyer. That much Jessy knew for a fact. What she couldn't figure out was how they felt about each other. She'd listened to them talking in

Molly's kitchen, and it was like listening to foreigners. Only this time it was Jessy who was the foreigner.

They seemed to know the same people, the same references, the same jokes. Molly could finish Spencer Mackenzie's sentences, same as he could finish hers. Maybe they were old friends, Jessy thought. That would explain it. She didn't want to think they were anything more than that, because she loved him. She knew it was crazy to even think such a thing, but there wasn't a doubt in her mind. All her life she'd waited for this moment, wondered where she'd be when it happened, who the man would be, and now, today, right there in central New Jersey, it finally happened.

She loved everything about him. The sound of his voice, a mellow baritone that made her shiver. He had clear gray eyes like polished silver. His dark blond hair was perfectly cut, kept just long enough to make her yearn to run her fingers through it. His jawline was strong and well defined. Straight nose, gorgeous mouth. Even his ears were perfect. She'd never seen anyone like him before. Not even in her dreams.

She left her car on the upper level of the parking structure and bypassed the elevator. She raced down the stairs then hurried across the lot near the ER and into the hospital. A woman in a red suit was doing business at one of the pay phones to the left of the door. Her notebook computer was open on her lap, and a leather-bound organizer rested on the small shelf beneath the phone. Saleswoman? Patient? Visitor squeezing in some work between bedside vigils?

Jessy toyed with the possibilities as she emptied her lockers and stuffed everything into a Macy's shopping bag. She loved wondering about people, trying to figure out who they were and why they did the things they did. Back home everyone had been cut from the same bolt of cloth. They dressed the same, thought the same, went to the same schools and churches, and married each other's cousins.

She'd been planning her escape from the day she was born. She liked to think she'd come out of her mother's womb with her bags packed. Her daddy never quite understood why, not even on the day she finally left for good.

"You stick with your own kind up there," he'd said as they drove to the airport six weeks ago. "Nothing but Jews and Communists in New York, if you ask me."

"New Jersey, Daddy," she'd said with a look toward Jo Ellen. "Princeton's in New Jersey."

"New Jersey, New York. Same damn thing if you ask me." Jim Wyatt's eyes glittered with fifty-five years of suspicion. "Nothing but a bunch of Communists up there. Nigger-loving, Jew Commie bastards."

It didn't matter to Jim Wyatt that Communism had been dead for nearly a decade. Old hates were good hates, and he clung to them the way other men clung to their recliner chairs and remote controls.

Jessy was through trying to make him see the light. This time tomorrow she'd be walking down one of those picture-postcard Princeton streets, breathing that rarified air, acting like she belonged there. No more of her daddy's rants about Jews and Communists and blacks when it was really his own pathetic lot in life that had him so all-fired mad at the world.

"Now, you let the girl alone, Jimmy." Her mama's voice was soft and apologetic, but Jessy knew there was a core of steel inside the woman. If it hadn't been for

Jo Ellen's determination, Jessy would have ended up married to Danny Watson, dying a little more every day. Jo Ellen's ambition had been the fuel that got Jessy through med school. "She's going up there to be a doctor. She doesn't have time to be worryin' about your nonsense."

Daddy's lips thinned so flat they almost disappeared. "You won't think it's nonsense when we're all speaking Spanish."

Jessy couldn't help it. She burst out laughing. She didn't meet Jo Ellen's eyes because she knew her mama couldn't so much as crack a smile, or the wrath of God would fall on her narrow shoulders. As it was, Jim Wyatt would be all over his wife with angry words and accusations the minute Jessy's plane taxied toward the runway.

"They're callin' my flight, Daddy! I'll write soon as I'm settled." Jim didn't say much of anything, just stood real still as she kissed his cheek. Whatever he was feeling, he kept it all buried inside himself. He hated much better than he loved, her daddy did, but that wasn't her problem anymore. "I'm gettin' the car," he said to her mother. "You be out front, Jo Ellen. I'm not waitin' around all night for you."

Her mama nodded, but her focus was on Jessy, same as it had been since the day she was born. All of her mother's unanswered dreams were wrapped up in her little girl, the one who was going to make those dreams all come true. Jo Ellen's eyes were wet with tears, but Jessy knew her mama was too proud to let them fall in public. Oh, she'd cry later on. Probably in the shower, with the door locked and the water running so nobody could hear her. That was the way she'd cried when she'd heard her sixteen-year-old baby was carrying a baby of her own.

"It's for the best," Jo Ellen had said, smoothing Jessy's choppy light brown hair with gentle fingers. "Giving that baby away is the right thing to do." That was back when Jessy still believed those gentle fingers could hold back an army of hurt. "You have your whole life ahead of you, Jessy. Don't let your dreams slip away."

Jessy had been in line for a scholarship to Duke. Premed. Everything her mother had ever wanted for her. If she kept the baby, she could kiss all of those dreams good-bye forever.

Her daughter was taken from her womb, cleaned up, and presented to her new parents. Little did they know Jessy's heart went with her.

Now here she was, in faraway Princeton, living her mother's dreams for her. She'd graduated at the top of her class. She'd performed flawlessly as an intern. Her residency at Princeton was a major coup.

"You've got to be the best," Jo Ellen had said to her at the airport. "That's the only way out."

I am *out,* Jessy had wanted to say, but she knew Jo Ellen wouldn't hear her.

She was a good doctor but she'd never be a great one. Technical expertise without passionate commitment would keep her from achieving the top rung of success. Her dreams were smaller—and in some ways much harder to come by. She wanted someone to love her.

She wanted Spencer Mackenzie.

The doctors' lounge was filling up. She tossed the last of her things into her bag then closed both lockers. She was on duty tonight, which meant she had just enough

time to drive back to Molly Chamberlain's house, un-
pack, shower, then drive back to the hospital.

Quickly she checked her reflection in the mirror. Big
mistake. It didn't seem to make much of a difference.
She looked like something the cat dragged in, with her
braid unraveling and the dark circles under her too-small
eyes and the pallor that pegged her as a first-year resident. At least it was only pallor. As an intern, she'd
looked downright cadaverous. But, no matter how you
looked at it, she was no match for Molly Chamberlain.
The thought of seeing Molly first thing every morning,
sometimes even before her first cup of coffee, was
enough to make her reconsider. Maybe sleeping in the
doctors' lounge for the next few years wasn't such a bad
idea after all.

She must have been crazy to think Spencer Mackenzie
would ever notice her with Molly around. For a couple
of minutes there, she'd actually almost convinced herself
that she had a chance. In theory she looked like a con-
tender: she was single, a doctor, and not pregnant with
another man's child. The only thing Molly had going for
her was beauty.

Too bad Jessy didn't have anything that could compete with it. Men didn't stop in their tracks because
you'd maintained a 4.0 GPA or because you graduated
magna cum laude or because you finished at the top of
your class in med school. They didn't give a damn about
any of that. All they cared about was the way you
looked. And that's where Molly Chamberlain had it all
over Jessy. She didn't seem to have anything else going
for her, at least nothing that Jessy knew about, but what
she did have was more than enough. As far as Jessy had
been able to determine, Molly had been the classic rich

guy's wife with the Jeep and the fancy house and the baby on the way.

No career. No skills. Just beauty.

It was always enough. Maybe the men didn't always stay as long as you wanted them to, but they stayed for a while. Jessy couldn't even get them to notice she was alive. She wasn't ugly. Ugly could be interesting. Lots of models were downright ugly in person but turned into goddesses through the camera's loving eyes. Jessy was plain. Brown hair. Brown eyes. Nothing features. Her body was spare and straight. She could walk naked into a room, and nobody would know she was there. Not if Molly Chamberlain was anywhere in the vicinity.

Spencer stayed awhile after Jessy left.

"Let me put up a pot of coffee and fix you a sandwich," Molly said. "You must be hungry."

"Just coffee, thanks," he said. "I grabbed something to eat before I drove out here." He took a seat at the card table set up near the sliding doors.

She turned to Rafe, who was still standing in the doorway. "I don't suppose you want anything," she said. She'd already watched him eat lunch out there under the tree. It was the highlight of her day.

"The sandwich sounds good," he said, his expression studiedly neutral.

"To eat outside?" She didn't know why she bothered to ask. He always ate outside. That was their unspoken arrangement.

"I wouldn't mind getting out of the sun."

The statement was innocuous enough. Indian summer had arrived, and a full, blazing October sun beat down with mid-afternoon ferocity. She couldn't blame him for wanting to be inside, but there had been plenty of other hot sunny days. Why did he pick this one to come inside?

"Fine," she said, turning away. "You and Spencer can talk football while I get everything ready."

Rafe didn't sit down the way he was supposed to. Instead, he followed her into the working part of the kitchen.

"The table's over there," she said, gesturing across the room to where Spencer sat patiently.

"No reason you should do all the work." He was close enough that she could catch the smell of sun and warm skin. The combination made her dizzy with longing, and she took a step back.

"I think I can handle it myself."

"I'll get the plates." He reached into the cabinet over the sink and took down three flat white sandwich plates.

"How did you know where I keep the plates?" she asked.

"Lucky guess," he said, and placed them down on the counter.

He's watched me, she thought. The idea delighted her.

"Need some help?" Spencer called out from the other side of the room.

"I've got everything covered, Stuart," Rafe said.

"His name is Spencer," Molly said quietly.

Rafe grinned. "Whatever."

Poor Spencer, she thought as she put coffee beans into the grinder and pressed the On button. She hoped he wasn't as easily maneuvered in the courtroom as he was in the kitchen.

•   •   •

Molly had to hand it to Spencer. He gave it his best shot, but Rafe outwaited him.

"Too bad I have a four o'clock appointment," Spencer said as he shrugged back into his suit jacket. "I would've liked to spend the afternoon with both of you."

Rafe's face was a study in innocence. "Damn shame," he said as he poured an avalanche of sugar into his coffee cup. "Those court stories are riveting."

Molly fought down the overwhelming urge to kick him in the shins. Spencer had been nothing but gracious and friendly to Rafe. He deserved better than this low-grade sniping.

"I'll call you tonight," Spencer said to Molly as she walked him to the front door. "Why don't I drive us to the dance next week?"

"You don't have to do that," she protested, acutely aware of Rafe's interest. "That ticket comes with no strings."

"I want to," he said, then smiled. "No strings." He paused a moment. "Tell Jessy she's welcome to join us."

Molly wasn't sure if she was grateful or disappointed. She wasn't looking for a date with Spencer—at least she didn't think she was. Sharing a ride with Jessy was no big deal at all.

"Don't worry," Rafe said when Molly returned to the kitchen. "She's not his type." He leaned back in his rickety folding chair and extended his legs in front of him. She tried not to stare, but it wasn't easy. Up until that moment she hadn't realized just how much she liked long, muscular legs on a man.

She poured herself a glass of decaf iced tea and leaned

against the kitchen counter. "What's that supposed to mean?"

"You didn't see the way she was looking at him?"

She took a sip. Jessy was right. It did taste better with sugar. "How was she looking at him?"

"Like she wanted to jump his bones."

She choked on her tea. "That's ridiculous!" she sputtered. "They just met."

"What does that have to do with anything?"

What indeed, she thought, as that familiar heat gathered low in her belly. This was dangerous territory. "Let's just say I don't think Spencer is her type."

"Whose type is he?" Rafe asked. "Yours?"

"Actually he reminds me a lot of my husband."

"Your ex-husband."

"We're not divorced yet," she reminded him.

"Hook up with someone like Mackenzie, and the only thing that'll change is your last name."

"Is that a bad thing?"

"Depends what you're looking for."

"Nothing," she said, meeting his eyes. "I'm not looking for anything."

"You're sure about that?"

She placed her glass down on the counter and pushed her hair off her face with the back of her left hand. "I think you've used up your quota of questions for the day."

His eyes held hers, and something inside her heart shifted. She tried to will it back into place, but it wouldn't go. "Here." He reached into the front pocket of his denim workshirt and pulled out the dinner dance ticket. "Nice idea, but I won't be using it."

She felt a simmering combination of anger and disappointment. "Put it in your scrapbook," she said. "I have no use for it."

"No friend you could invite?"

"I thought that's what I did."

"We're not friends," he said. "We're not even close."

"You're right," she said, ignoring the heat moving over her breasts and up her throat. "I was being polite."

"So was I," he said, then turned and strode from the room.

Now, what was that supposed to mean? She heard the front door open then slam shut. Who would have figured him to be so literal? She didn't mean "friend"; she meant "acquaintance." Of course they weren't friends. Jessy Wyatt wasn't her friend either.

Spencer was, though. She enjoyed his company, his conversation. He knew when to talk and when to listen. Being around him was safe and familiar. She knew who she was when she was with Spencer.

Rafe finished mowing the yard then concentrated on hammering nails deep into hapless planks of pressure-treated redwood. Nothing like pounding nails to get rid of a man's aggressions. Maybe by the time he finished the deck, he'd have it under control again.

He'd come close to making a total fool of himself back there in Molly's kitchen. If she'd shown him the slightest encouragement, he would have dropped to his knees in worship. That was how far gone he was. He barely knew her and he worshipped her. She came to him in his dreams, and those dreams carried him through each day.

That ticket was burning a hole in his pocket. How in

hell was he going to sit there and watch another man cradle her in his arms, breathe the sweet smell of her hair, feel her heart beating against his chest. That was how it started, and he'd have to sit there and watch as Mackenzie got her to lower her defenses. It wouldn't be much of a stretch. She already trusted the guy—he was her lawyer. He was helping her get free of a bad marriage. He probably knew as much about her as she was willing to share with anybody.

He swung the hammer in a wide arc and brought it down squarely on his thumb.

"Son of a bitch!" He dropped the hammer and popped his thumb into his mouth.

"You should be more careful."

He turned around and saw Jessy Wyatt standing there looking concerned.

He grunted something and turned away. Just what he needed: an audience for his stupidity.

"Let me take a look."

"Nothing to look at."

"You hit yourself pretty hard."

"Nothing I haven't done before."

"You don't like me much, do you?"

That got him to turn around. Her plain face looked even plainer in the late-afternoon sun, and he found himself feeling sorry for her. She didn't stand a chance against Molly's fiery beauty. No mortal woman would.

"Where'd you get that idea?"

"Call it female intuition."

"I didn't think doctors went for that kind of thing."

"This doctor does."

"You might want to work on your game face, Doc."

He aimed his battered thumb toward the kitchen where

Molly was fixing supper. "You gave yourself away in there before."

"I don't know what you're talking about."

"The lawyer."

"Spencer Mackenzie?"

"That's the one. You don't stand a chance, Doc. You might as well know that going in."

Her plain face took on color, and she glanced toward the kitchen window. He followed her gaze. Molly was doing something at the sink. Her head was bent low. Her cascade of hair covered her lovely face. She must have sensed they were watching her because she looked up and smiled, gave a little wave. Time stopped. He'd heard people say that before but he never understood. Now he did. He could live the rest of his life in this moment.

He didn't know how long he stood there. Days? Hours? Minutes? If Molly hadn't left the window, he would have stayed there until the millennium.

Jessy met his eyes as he turned away. She didn't say a word. She didn't have to. Her smile said it all.

EIGHT

—⁂—

Before the first week was out, Molly decided that living with Jessy was a lot like living alone. Jessy worked long hours, sometimes not returning home until two or three in the morning, only to start over again at six. She was neat, quiet, self-sufficient. If she used the kitchen, she cleaned up after herself so completely that Molly was never quite sure she'd been there. One morning their paths crossed, and Molly took the opportunity to remind her that she had kitchen privileges. Jessy just nodded and said that she knew. She lived and breathed her work. Molly couldn't help wondering how it would feel to be so passionately involved in something beyond your own narrow life.

Spencer came to the house one evening to get Molly's signature on some papers. He was leaving just as Jessy pulled into the driveway. Molly watched from the living room window as the two of them chatted politely for a few moments, then Spencer climbed into his Porsche and drove away. If there was anything between them, it was invisible to Molly.

She wished Rafe had been there to see it. That would prove to him that he'd been wrong about Jessy's supposed infatuation with Spencer. Women could sense these things much better than men, and Molly definitely wasn't getting those vibrations about Jessy and Spencer—although she had to admit she was surprised when he suggested Jessy ride with them to the dinner-dance on Saturday. She wasn't sure if he was being polite to Jessy or reassuring Molly that he wouldn't take advantage of the situation between them.

He was attracted to her. That much she knew. And she certainly found him to be pleasant company and easy on the eyes. He listened when she spoke, respected her opinions, expressed the right amount of concern for the baby. It wasn't at all hard to imagine going through life with a man like that—he was exactly the man she thought she'd married. Life would be easy and comfortable, with no surprises and no upheavals.

And no passion. Don't forget about passion.

The thought brought her up short. She could live without passion. She'd lived without it through most of her marriage and never stopped loving Robert. Just because she'd entertained a few vivid fantasies about Rafe Garrick was no reason to think she'd suddenly lost her grip on what was really important.

Loneliness.

She was lonely. Deeply, unutterably lonely. She'd been lonely her entire life, even if this was the first time she'd ever come face-to-face with the depth and darkness of her loneliness. Her childhood had been spent in a sort of limbo, trapped between warring parents and new spouses and a sense of isolation that had shaped her character more than any other factor. She'd looked toward Robert and their marriage to end her loneliness, and when it didn't, when her heart still ached with longing, she told herself that these things took time. When Robert was finished with school, once he was established in a law firm, when their first child was born— that was when everything would change. That was when the loneliness would vanish.

Sometimes she thought about the baby, looking toward that tiny soul as a means to end her loneliness, but she knew that was a trap. It wasn't fair to put all of her hopes and dreams on such tiny shoulders. The baby deserved so much better.

So, for that matter, did she.

She found a note from Rafe on the kitchen counter. He had left early, something about another job over in New Hope. He was almost finished with the deck. He worked from first light to last, stopping only for his solitary lunch in the backyard. She went outside once and asked him if he wanted to join her for a bowl of minestrone, but he shook his head. She waited for him to say something, offer an explanation, but he turned his back and returned to work. She considered turning on the charm and trying to convince him to join her inside, but she knew it would be a waste of effort.

Besides, she wasn't sure she really wanted to share a meal with him. He unsettled her, that's what he did. Being around him made her aware of every movement she made, the shape of her breasts, the sound of her own voice. The last time she'd felt so painfully self-conscious was when she was thirteen and her mother sent her out to buy her first bra. She wasn't used to quiet men. Her father was a talker. So were Robert and Spencer. They understood small talk and used it well. Molly was good at small talk herself. Sometimes she thought her entire life had been composed of one meaningless conversation after another, all of them linked together until they formed the approximation of a life.

Rafe wasn't a talker. She watched him move through his wordless day and wondered how it would feel to hold your emotions so close to you that nobody knew they were there. Not that it mattered. His emotions were none of her business. In a few more weeks he'd be finished with the deck and the baby's room. He'd say goodbye and walk out the door, and she'd never know how he tasted. That struck her as a terrible shame, although she didn't know why it should since she hadn't the slightest idea how any man tasted.

"You're home early," Molly said when Jessy finally strolled into the kitchen.

"Just passin' through." She sounded almost giddy, as if she'd been drinking champagne. "I have to be back at eight."

"I was about to start dinner, if you're interested." She smiled at Jessy. "Supper, if that sounds better."

"I noticed you put sugar in the iced tea yesterday," Jessy said as she looped her purse over the back of a kitchen chair. "Thanks."

"I'm always open to new ideas."

Jessy watched her as she opened the fridge and removed a head of lettuce, two tomatoes, and an oblong Tupperware container filled with tuna salad. "Can I help?"

Molly's first instinct was to say thanks but no thanks, but she caught herself. If they were going to live together in some semblance of harmony, she'd have to learn to work in tandem with Jessy. At least now and then.

"I left a manuscript and a huge stack of papers on the kitchen table," she said. "If you'd gather up everything and put it in the dining room, I can set the table."

"I'll set the table, too," Jessy said.

"Be careful," Molly said, "I might get used to this."

"Don't," Jessy said with a quick smile. "I don't really live here. I live at the hospital."

To Molly's surprise, they worked well together. Jessy worked quickly and carefully. She had the kitchen table cleared and set before Molly got the lid off the Tupperware container.

"I don't think they taught you that at med school," she observed with a shake of her head.

"They taught me that at the Pancake Cottage," Jessy said, pouring them each a glass of iced tea. "I worked there during school."

"I waitressed once, right after Robert and I first got married," Molly said, scooping tuna salad onto their salad plates. "I was a disaster."

"It takes some organization," Jessy said, "but it's not brain surgery."

"It might as well have been," Molly said. "I screwed up orders, broke plates, and had a bad attitude."

"They probably blamed it on your red hair, right?"

"They blame everything on my red hair," Molly said, smiling naturally for the first time. "They might be right."

"I dyed my hair red once," Jessy said as she plucked a slice of tomato from one of the plates. "It was like putting a dress on a monkey."

Molly stopped what she was doing and took a good look at the woman. "I don't see you as a redhead," she said.

"There's a surprise for you," Jessy said. She sounded both defensive and self-deprecating, as if she'd had enormous practice with each. "I'm not exactly the glamorous type."

"Actually I see you with some blond highlights and maybe some wispy bangs. You have a blonde's complexion."

Jessy frowned. "I do?"

"You have beautiful skin." The last thing she'd expected to share with Jessy Wyatt was girl talk. "You should do something to show it off."

"Maybe I should switch specialties to dermatology," Jessy said with a swift grin. "Be my own best advertisement."

"Well, there you go," Molly said as she carried their salad plates to the table. "Who needs obstetrics, right?"

"I saw you coming out of Dr. Rosenberg's office day before yesterday," Jessy said as they both sat down. "Regular appointment?"

Molly nodded and unfolded her napkin. "He did a sonogram, but we couldn't tell the baby's sex. I'm kind of glad, in a way."

"And you're doing well?"

"Very." She seemed genuinely concerned, but Molly assumed it was as much professional curiosity as anything else. "I'd had a few problems last month, but they've resolved themselves."

"Stress, no doubt," Jessy said.

"No doubt," Molly said dryly. "This isn't the way I'd planned my pregnancy."

Molly's words were innocent enough. She was talking about her marriage, about the husband who'd walked away from a miracle. She couldn't possibly have known those words would find their mark in the hidden part of Jessy's heart.

"I didn't plan my pregnancy at all." Jessy heard the words tumble from her lips, but she couldn't quite believe them. What on earth had possessed her?

Molly's eyes almost popped out of her head. "Your pregnancy?"

"It was a long time ago," Jessy said, tapping her fingernails against the side of her iced tea glass. Why couldn't it be a glass of hemlock? "I don't know why I even mentioned it to you."

"Me neither," said Molly. "You don't even like me."

"I never said that."

"You didn't have to. It's right there on your face."

"That's ridiculous. I don't even know you."

"You don't like what you do know."

Good Lord, thought Jessy. Molly sounded like Granny Wyatt, who read your mind by reading your tea leaves.

"You're too much like everyone at the hospital," Jessy said bluntly. "You make me feel as if I'm the last one at the table."

"You make me feel as if you'd rather be at any table but mine."

"You're right."

Molly's face turned bright red, and she looked down at her salad plate.

Jessy was instantly overcome with remorse. "I'm sorry," she said. "I didn't mean to say that."

"Don't apologize," Molly said. "You'll only make

things worse. You said what you meant. Stick with it.''

Jessy wanted to crawl under the card table and stay there. Just three weeks up north, and already she'd forgotten everything she ever knew about good manners. "Look," she said, "it's my problem, not yours. It's not your fault if I'm pea-green with envy.''

"Now you've lost me," Molly said. "I thought we were talking about why you didn't like me.''

"We are," said Jessy. "I don't like you because you have everything.''

Molly started to laugh, that same full-bodied laugh that seemed so out of keeping with her delicate beauty. That laugh probably brought men to their knees. "Oh, yes," said Molly, "I have absolutely everything a woman could want. I can understand why you'd be pea-green. My husband left me for a judge's daughter, I can't afford this house so I'm taking in boarders, and—here's the best part—I'm pregnant.''

"You forgot the most important thing," Jessy said. "You get to keep your baby.''

Molly pushed away her plate and leaned across the table. There was nothing comforting about the expression in her big blue eyes, nothing warm and fuzzy. "If you want to tell your story, tell it," she said. "I'd like to listen. But if you're looking for a punching bag, you'll have to look elsewhere.''

"You're a lot tougher than you look," Jessy said after a moment.

"I'd better be." Her expression softened just the slightest bit. "So tell me what you want to tell me, or let's change the subject.''

Molly had her dead to rights. She'd dropped two enormous tidbits of information already. She'd look like a fool if she didn't tell the rest of the story. "I think you've figured it out already," she said, careful to keep emotion from her voice. "I made a mistake, got pregnant, and gave the baby up for adoption." She didn't flinch when she said the words. Some things really did get easier with time.

"How long ago?" Molly asked.

"Twelve years," she said casually, as if she didn't know the answer to the minute, day, and hour. "I wasn't supposed to hold her, but the nurse-midwife made a mistake and gave her to me."

They fell silent. What was there to say anyway? Those three minutes with her baby cradled in her arms had defined her life. Nothing that had happened before or since could compete with it. "I don't think about her very often," she said, looking to fill the silence. "I know she has a good life. I know that."

"I'm sure she has," Molly said. "It took a lot of courage to give your baby a better life."

"I gave myself a better life." The last of her ugly secrets rolled across the table and fell into Molly's lap. "I was about to start college, premed. A baby would have slowed me down." *Think of your future, Jessy darlin',* her mama had said to her. *There's time enough for you to have a family.*

"You were a baby yourself," Molly said. There was nothing patronizing about her tone, nothing insincere. She almost wished there was. "How would you have supported a child?"

"Other women manage."

"You wouldn't have been able to manage med school."

"I know," she said. Her mama's dreams would have

come crashing down around her own seventeen-year-old
shoulders. ''Sorry for droppin' this on you. I don't know
why I did it.''

''Maybe you needed to talk to someone.''

She shrugged. ''I don't usually talk to strangers.''

Molly looked away, and Jessy felt immediately con-
trite.

''I didn't mean that the way it sounded,'' she said.
''I'm just not much of a talker.''

''Don't worry,'' said Molly. ''It takes more than that
to hurt my feelings.''

But she was lying. Jessy could see it in her eyes, and
she felt terrible. All she'd meant— Oh, hell. She didn't
have any idea what she'd meant. Seeing Spencer had
completely unhinged her defenses, loosened her tongue,
turned her into a bundle of unruly emotion.

She poked her fork into the tuna salad. She'd heard
about awkward silences, but this had to be the world's
longest and most awkward. It sat on the table between
them like an overwrought centerpiece of gladioli and
lilies that you had to stand up to see over. She'd talked
to Molly Chamberlain as though she were a friend or
something, as if they'd grown up together or been college roommates. She'd talked to Molly the way she'd
never talked to anyone in her life.

Well, there was no hope for it. Now she'd just have
to kill herself.

You'd make one swell therapist, Molly thought as she
choked down her tuna salad. *The woman opens up to
you, and now she looks like she wants to bungee jump
without a cord.* The last time she'd seen someone that

unhappy had been in the IRS waiting room when she and Robert were being audited.

If somebody didn't break the silence soon, they could apply for membership in a monastery.

"Ten days until the dinner-dance," she said, adding a tad more sugar to her iced tea. "Have you decided what to wear?"

The stricken look on Jessy's face grew more tortured.

"Oh, come on," Molly said, starting to smile. "We're talking clothes, not nuclear disarmament."

"I'd rather talk nuclear disarmament."

"Uh-oh," said Molly. "Nothing to wear?"

"Not unless sequined scrubs are the going thing."

Molly wrinkled her nose. "I think you can do better than that."

"Maybe you can do better than that," Jessy said. "For me that's high style."

"You must have something," Molly persisted. "Doctors must go to a lot of cocktail parties."

"Lowly interns don't go anywhere," Jessy said, "and so far neither do residents."

"Well, we have ten days to find you something."

"I'm also broke."

"These days I specialize in broke." She motioned toward Jessy. "Stand up. Let me get a good look at you."

Jessy hesitated, then pushed back her chair and did as Molly ordered. "Not much to work with."

"You're tiny," Molly said. "What—maybe a size two on a good day?"

Jessy nodded. "When I dress up, I look like a little girl in her mama's clothes."

"I have a slew of things in my closet but I don't think

we could make them down for you." She was almost a foot taller than Jessy and three cup sizes bigger. Alterations on that scale would ruin the line of the garments. "There's a designer consignment shop in Rocky Hill," she said. "That's a possibility."

"Rocky Hill?"

"One town north of here, right on Route 206. I'd be glad to show you."

Jessy's spine stiffened visibly. "I don't want to put you out."

"You're not putting me out. It's my idea, remember?"

"We'd better be careful," Jessy said. "We might become friends."

"Anything's possible," Molly said, but she didn't really believe it.

"Spencer." The woman's voice held the sharp edge of annoyance. "You haven't heard a word I've said."

Spencer opened his eyes. He was still in that drowsy, postcoital state that rendered him monosyllabic. "I heard you, Court."

Courtney Wainwright, of the Boston Wainwrights, propped herself up on her left elbow and considered him. Except for the fact that she was naked, you'd never have known she'd spent the last hour making love with him in various exotic positions. She looked as sleek and composed in his bed as she did in the courtroom. He wasn't sure how he felt about that. He wasn't sure if he felt anything at all.

"I can have the cottage the weekend after next. So, if you're available . . ." She trailed one perfectly manicured fingertip through his chest hair. He resisted the urge to capture her hand and put it back on her side of the bed. Not a good sign.

"Can't make it," he said, aiming for the right level of sincerity. "I'm really sorry."

"I thought we'd blocked out the weekend of the seventeenth quite a while ago," Courtney said, her tone losing some of its practiced appeal. "I'm very disappointed."

Jesus, he thought. *Let's not go there.*

"I'm disappointed, too," he said, "but I have something else on the calendar."

"You could change your calendar."

"Afraid not."

She gathered the top sheet around her breasts and rolled away from him. "Not exactly the attitude I was hoping for, Spencer."

"Not exactly the understanding I was expecting from you, Court."

"Who is she?" Courtney's voice was flat. You wouldn't catch her emotions bubbling to the surface. She'd whipped them into submission a long time ago. He used to think that was one of the things he liked about her. "You're not as practiced a liar as you might think."

He started to protest, to tell her that there wasn't anyone else—at least not at the moment—when he realized this was the opportunity he'd been waiting for. "I didn't mean to hurt you." He liked to think of himself as a good guy. He never fooled a woman into believing there could be a future with him. He usually looked for women who were unavailable in some very basic way.

"Don't worry about that," Courtney said, reaching

for a cigarette on the nightstand. "I never let you close enough to hurt me."

She was right. He did the same thing. It wasn't that hard to hide behind a facade of charm. He'd been doing it now for thirty-five years, and it suited him down to the ground.

"So who is she?" Courtney went on between drags.

"What makes you think there's someone else?"

"Experience, darling. Nobody says good-bye unless there's someone waiting in the wings."

"Nothing serious," he said, thinking of Molly Chamberlain. "The lady isn't free yet."

Courtney leaned back against the headboard and laughed softly. "Then that should make her just about perfect for you."

You would think so. Molly understood his world. She'd lived in it. She knew what was expected. She was beautiful, warm, and sexy. Not even her pregnancy changed the effect she had on his libido. No normal man could look at her and not want to take her to bed. She seemed to enjoy his company, too. Their lunches always ran overtime, and she prolonged their good-byes with questions he'd answered hours before. Not that he minded. She was easy to be with, undemanding.

There was just one problem.

The lady didn't want him.

Heavy autumn rains swept in the next day. Rafe called Molly and told her he'd be working another job until the weather shifted again. She sounded vaguely annoyed but not terribly disappointed. He would have liked it better the other way around.

The job was a simple enough one. He was part of a

kitchen renovation crew, replacing cabinets and counters, installing a new double sink and dishwasher. There were four of them on the crew, and with luck they could finish up within the week. At first he'd resented the rain for keeping him away from Molly, but as the days passed, he began to think maybe it wasn't such a bad thing.

Maybe the rain would act like a cold shower.

Nothing else had worked. Not exhaustion, sublimation, aversion therapy. He'd tried everything he could think of to banish Molly Chamberlain from his mind but he'd failed every single time. If he hadn't known better, he'd have thought he was in love with her. That was ridiculous, of course. Not even he was that big a fool. If he was going to fall in love with a woman, he'd make sure that this time around he fell in love with one who liked him. She didn't have to like him a lot—he wasn't demanding—but it would be nice if she could manage to stay in the same room with him for more than three minutes without running away.

Molly couldn't seem to manage that. They'd barely exchanged more than a handful of sentences since the day she gave him the extra ticket to the charity dinner. He could still see the regret in her eyes when he stuck it in the pocket of his work shirt.

He was glad he wouldn't be around to see the relief in her eyes when he didn't show up.

NINE

❦

On Thursday morning, two days before the dinner-dance, the rains finally stopped. Molly was finishing her first cup of decaf tea when the telephone rang.

"It stopped raining," Jessy said in her deceptively soft Southern drawl.

"About time," Molly said, popping two slices of whole wheat into the toaster. "I was about to ask Rafe to build us an ark."

"I have a few hours free this afternoon," Jessy said, sailing right over Molly's joking remark. "I thought maybe we could visit that store you told me about, the one with the used clothes?"

Molly leaned back in her chair and suppressed the urge to stare at the telephone in amazement. "I didn't think you were interested," she said. "When you didn't follow up on it, I just assumed—"

"I've been real busy," Jessy said. Her tone was both apologetic and defensive. "If you can't, I'll—"

"No, no!" Molly pushed aside the stack of papers

next to her teacup. "I'd love to show you the consignment shop. How about I pick you up in front of the hospital around twelve?"

She'd been working nonstop, it seemed, for weeks now. The assignments were coming steadily, and the way to keep them coming in was by being reliable and accurate. She read thrillers, romances, Westerns, mysteries, and literary novels and offered up her opinions for pay. She'd also done a fair bit of copyediting and a few back-cover blurbs for some series mysteries her publisher put out. Her work engaged her mind but didn't engage her heart, which was exactly the way she liked it. Right now her heart belonged to her baby.

When she and Jessy had that surprising conversation about the baby Jessy gave up for adoption years ago, Molly had wondered if that would open the floodgates for more talks like that. She was hungry to share confidences about her pregnancy, the kinds of things she would have shared with Robert if he had only stayed around.

Who was she kidding? It wouldn't have mattered if Robert had stayed around. Not one damn bit. The baby was of no interest to him and never had been. No matter how hard she tried, she couldn't imagine him placing his lips against her swollen belly or laughing as the baby kicked against him when they made love. Maybe no man would. Maybe that was just a common female fantasy, right up there with Prince Charming and the knight on the white charger. Maybe pregnant women all over the world fell asleep to fantasies of men who wanted them more as the months passed.

She finished breakfast then went upstairs to shower and dress. She stripped off her nightgown and tossed it in the hamper, then caught a glimpse of herself in the enormous mirror over the vanity. Her hair was pinned loosely on top of her head. Stray tendrils curled down around her face and shoulders. But it wasn't her hair that surprised her: it was the way her body looked. Her breasts were high and round and very full. Her nipples had darkened to deep rose, a stark contrast to her pale skin. She still had a waist, not as narrow as it had been a few months ago, but it was still there. Her hips seemed rounder, more womanly, a more secure cradle for her blossoming belly. And there was no doubt her belly was blossoming. She could see the faintest network of veins beneath her taut skin and traced one with the tip of her finger.

The touch sent shock waves through her body. She drew her finger across her belly once again, aware of a tightening sensation deep inside that had nothing to do with the baby sleeping peacefully within her womb. She placed her hand flat against the swell, letting her palm absorb the softness of her skin and the heat, and her eyes widened as she watched herself in the mirror. She trailed her fingers lower until they slipped into the cushion of auburn curls between her legs.

She'd never touched herself like this before. Not deliberately. Three times in the last few weeks she'd awakened from a dream to find her hand trailing between her legs, her fingers damp and sticky. Her pubic hair was soft and springy both, like coiled silk. She'd read that once in a manuscript. A man had likened his lover's mons to a fragrant pillow beneath his cheek. Ridiculous, she'd thought at the time. The image was too poetic to be believed.

She cupped herself gently. She felt warm and lush to

the touch, dampening against her fingertips as she stroked lightly along the swollen lips. She lingered there, plying the supple flesh, discovering what felt good and what felt even better. Robert hadn't believed in foreplay. He'd rushed to the main event as if he was afraid she'd change her mind. There'd been no soft words whispered in the darkness, no poetry, no hot wet mouth pressed against her—

Her breath caught as she dipped one finger into her body. A voluptuous shiver rippled outward from her core as she watched her nipples tighten into rosebuds.

Rafe would do this, she thought as her body molded itself to the shape of her fingers. He would stroke her until she was wet and ready, then he would bury his face against her and drink her juices as if they were champagne. And when she was helpless with pleasure and desire, he would trail his mouth up over the swell of her belly to the valley between her breasts and the column of her throat until he found her mouth with his and she tasted herself, tasted him—

It came from nowhere. A quicksilver unfurling of sensation that spiraled up from her center then vanished, leaving her flushed and embarrassed and filled with even greater yearning than before. A shimmer of what was possible. A hint of what she'd been missing.

She'd asked the doctor about these feelings, and he'd handled it with the same practical honesty with which he handled everything else. Her body was performing the function for which it was designed, he told her. She was a woman in the prime of her life, brimming with good health and powerful hormones and basic needs. Her feelings were perfectly natural and to be expected.

In a more perfect world, the man she loved would be there to share the bounty.

But it wasn't a perfect world. She was alone, except in her dreams, and the only hand that touched her was her own.

Jessy grabbed a bagel and cup of coffee from the shop next to the consignment store then went outside to wait for Molly. She leaned against the side of her car and ate slowly, trying to imagine how it would feel to actually belong there. A steady stream of women marched in and out of the store—tall, elegant women who looked as if they stepped down from the cover of *Vogue*. They drove Saabs and BMWs and an occasional Mercedes, understated cars that didn't shout "money," but whispered it in tones more honeyed than Grandma Wyatt's biscuits.

She made a point of noticing things like that. Back home you wanted to make sure everyone knew just how much money you had in the bank. Why wear one diamond ring if you had three more at home feeling all lonely and neglected? Rich folk piled on the jewelry and darn near wore their fancy clothes with the price tags still attached. And they'd never drive one of those ugly foreign cars, no sirree. Not while there were still Caddies in this world.

It was harder to tell the rich people from the regular folks around here, but she was beginning to catch on. Not that she much cared who was who. As her mama used to say, "It didn't make no nevermind" to Jessy if her patients were rolling in money or on Medicaid. What did matter to her was that she looked as if she were part of the former, not the latter.

She told herself that was the only reason she was

there, so she could find herself a few fine outfits to help
her blend in with the rest of the Princeton gentry, but it
was only part of the truth.

Twenty minutes went by. She finished her bagel and
coffee and strolled around the parking lot. Maybe Molly
had forgotten about her. She was sure she wasn't number
one on the woman's *To Do* list. It wasn't hard to imagine
that something better had come along. Like Spencer. Her
heart twisted. He was always calling Molly, asking her
to lunch or stopping by the house under the pretense of
having papers for her to sign. You'd have to be blind
not to see that he was interested in her. Jessy couldn't
even blame him. What man wouldn't be dazzled by
Molly Chamberlain? Rafe was. There was no reason
why Spencer Mackenzie should be any different.

She wanted him to be different, though. She wanted
him to see her.

Molly whipped her car into the parking space next to
Jessy's then jumped out. "You were supposed to wait
for me at the hospital," she said, feeling more than a
little put out. "I sat there for twenty minutes."

"I'm sorry." The doctor's face reddened visibly. "I
totally forgot." *Ah totally fuhgot.*

"It happens," Molly said. They started across the
parking lot to the secondhand shop. "So what are you
doing out here? You should be inside, trying on
clothes."

"I was waiting for you," Jessy said, tossing a cup
and crumpled napkin into the trash can near the curb.

"And eating lunch," Molly observed.

"That, too."

Molly was sure that was only part of the truth. The

good doctor's nerves were practically vibrating. Molly didn't get that nervous going to the dentist, and she *hated* the dentist. She swung open the door and motioned Jessy inside. "Now, there's no guarantee we're going to find anything for you," she said. "The stock changes all the time. Sometimes you're lucky, sometimes you aren't."

Jessy nodded. She looked like a poorly dressed twelve-year-old. They had their work cut out for them and not much time.

Jessy had never seen anything like the way Molly shopped. She moved up and down the aisles with great deliberation, touching some items, ignoring others, evaluating the different outfits according to some mysterious criteria that Jessy was sure she'd never understand.

A soft pink swirl of fabric caught her eye. "This is pretty," she said to Molly. "I love pink."

Molly's scowl was forbidding. "You've been spending too much time in the nursery," she said. "Forget pink. I was thinking bronze or copper or maybe a beautiful burnished gold."

Jessy had been thinking pink or blue. "I always thought pink was my best color."

"Over my dead body."

Jessy laughed. "You take this very seriously."

"Darn right I do." She grabbed Jessy by the wrist. "Now, come over here. I think I've found exactly what you need."

It was a short, shimmery, nothing of a dress. Skinny straps, a straight column of golden brown fabric that stopped well above the knees.

"I look like a flapper," Jessy said as she stepped cautiously from the dressing room.

"You look wonderful." Molly motioned for her to turn around. "Lucky you. You have no hips. This dress is perfect for you."

"I hate it."

"Doesn't matter," said Molly. "I'm telling you this is the dress for you."

"But I hate it," Jessy repeated. That should count for something.

"You should hate your hair," Molly said. "That's what's wrong with the picture. You need a sleek, Louise Brooks type of bob . . . maybe a few highlights."

"Louise Brooks?"

"She was a movie star."

"I never heard of her."

Molly grinned. "She was a little bit before your time. She made silent movies."

"How do you know about her?"

"I copyedited a biography about her."

"And you think I should wear my hair like her?"

"Absolutely. The second you came out of that dressing room, I knew exactly what you should do."

"I'm not cutting my hair." Her hair was her only vanity. If she cut her hair, she might as well go in for a sex-change operation. Nobody would be able to tell she was a girl without a DNA test.

"Just think about it," Molly said. "It could change your life."

Molly knew there wasn't a snowball's chance that Jessy would cut her hair. It was a real shame because a short,

sassy cut and a few sparkling highlights would do wonders for her, especially in that dress.

That was one triumph, at least. Jessy bought the
flapper-style dress. Now all she had to do was find the
right shoes and she'd be set.

Which was more than Molly could say.

She came home from shopping in a fashion frenzy.
She flew upstairs to the bedroom, yanked off her clothes,
and began rummaging through her closet in search of
the perfect outfit. The sapphire blue slip dress looked
like a sausage casing over her pregnancy poundage.
Who would think twelve pounds could make such a difference? Naked it was barely noticeable, but try to fit
those same twelve pounds into a sleek dress and you
had a blueprint for disaster. Or at least a spot on Mr.
Blackwell's list. The rust-colored taffeta looked like a
clown suit. She couldn't zip up the skirt to the winter-
white dinner suit and couldn't afford a trip back to the
consignment shop for herself. There had to be something
in this closet that she could wear, some outfit that
wouldn't make people laugh and point at her over their
fruit cups.

Finally she hit on a hug of black silk, cut on the bias,
made to hug curves but not embarrass them. And her
curves were easily embarrassed these days. She slipped
the dress over her head and held her breath. Inch by inch
it slid down over her considerable breasts, her widening
waist, her baby-maker hips, and then it settled into place.
She approached the mirror with deliberation and caution.
If this didn't work, she was out of options.

It worked. She almost let out a cheer. Maybe it
worked a little bit too well. She looked like one of those
girls on *Baywatch* with the enormous breasts that defied

both age and gravity. Still, she could zip what needed to be zipped and she could breathe without worrying about splitting a side seam.

The doorbell rang as she was rummaging around at the bottom of her closet for the perfect shoes. She was expecting a box of manuscripts via FedEx, and they required a signature. They also never waited very long for her to get to the front door. She flew barefoot down the stairs. "I'm almost there!" she called out. "One more second and—"

She flung open the door and found herself face to face with Rafe Garrick.

TEN

⤜⟨◦⟩⤛

She was barefoot. Her cheeks were flushed, her hair tou-
seled around her face and shoulders.

Those shoulders.

Creamy. Fragile. Bare.

His eyes trailed across those bare shoulders and
dropped lower. If he'd ever wondered about the existence of magic in this world, he stopped wondering at
that moment. Her magnificent breasts, barely restrained
by the silky black dress, were all the proof he needed.

"Rafe!" She looked rattled, flustered. She wrapped
her arms across her chest in a protective gesture that
only deepened her cleavage. A man could lose himself
in there. "What are you doing here?"

"I tried to call you," he said, looking past her into
the hall. She looked lush and beautiful, like a woman
who'd just been loved. "Your machine's not working."

"There's nothing wrong with my machine," she said,
stepping aside and motioning him into the house. "It
was working this morning."

"I called five times," he said, trying not to notice the scent of Shalimar wafting up from her warm, bare skin. "It just rang through."

"I don't understand," she said, gliding toward the kitchen. The soft swirl of skirt molded her hips and hinted at the swell of her buttocks. A few fiercely vivid fantasies presented themselves to him, but he counted to ten and thought about nuclear disarmament instead. He didn't see any sign of company. No man's coat tossed casually over a chair. No tie on the stair railing. He already knew there wasn't a Porsche in the driveway. That was the first thing he'd looked for.

"The machine's on," she said, pointing toward the steady red light near the top.

"Yeah," he said, "but the tape's out." He pointed toward a microcassette on the counter.

"Damnation," she said, "The tape broke, and I forgot to put a new one back in."

"Mystery's solved," he said, tossing her the cassette.

She popped it in place, closed the lid, then turned back to him. She looked deliciously rumpled, the way she'd look after a night in his arms. The way she looked every time he made love to her in his dreams. What would she do if she knew he was making love to her right now, stroking her with his thumbs, piercing her with his tongue—

"Rafe." Her cheeks flushed even brighter red. "Why are you looking at me like that?"

Because I'm rock hard just from looking at you, he thought. *Because breathing the same air makes me want to take you right now, standing up, no preliminaries, no sweet talk.* He didn't say it, though. He angled himself behind the work counter and moved right on past the question.

"The weather broke," he said, as if that was all he'd been thinking about. "I could finish off the deck this afternoon."

"Oh." She looked at him as if she didn't quite believe him. "It's after two o'clock. Isn't that kind of late to get started?"

"I can put in a good five hours before it gets dark. That might be enough to knock it off."

"It's up to you," she said, glancing down at her slender bare feet. Her toenails were painted a vivid red. He would do that for her. The two of them in bed, her foot against his belly while he applied the polish slowly and carefully. "You're doing it again."

"Doing what?"

"Looking at me as if you've never seen me before."

"I haven't," he said. "I mean, not dressed like that."

She lifted her chin a fraction. "I was trying on clothes for Saturday night's dance. I'm showing more than I realized. This was the best I could come up with."

"You're beautiful." He hadn't meant to say it, but the words had a will of their own. "I mean, the dress is beautiful."

"Thank you." That was all she said. He waited for a smile, some flicker of recognition in those beautiful blue eyes, but there was nothing. Those two words stopped him cold.

"I'd better get to work," he said.

"I'd better change," she said.

Why? he wondered. Why would she want to change when she was already perfect?

•   •   •

Rafe finished the deck on Friday afternoon. Molly was on the telephone with Spencer, confirming their plans for tomorrow night when she heard the rumble of an engine in her driveway. "Hold on one second," she said to Spencer and ran to the front door in time to see Rafe's truck disappear around the corner.

She stepped out onto the porch to see if he'd left a note for her. She checked the garage and the back door. Nothing. He'd left without even saying good-bye.

"Is something wrong?" Spencer asked when she came back on the line. "You sound upset."

"I'm fine," she lied. Rafe didn't owe her a good-bye. He didn't even owe her the deck he'd just rebuilt. "You were saying . . ."

He picked up the conversation where they'd left off, some bit of office gossip that, if she were being totally honest, meant nothing to her. His small talk was comforting, and she had deluded herself that they were becoming close friends. He was so good at it that it had taken her weeks to realize that they talked about nothing at all that mattered. She knew he'd lost a brother some years back and that family dynamics had changed in some way, but he never opened up to her and shared the particulars. She wasn't sure he would know how. Spencer's defenses were securely in place, and Molly doubted he'd lower them any time soon.

She enjoyed his friendship, felt comfortable with him, but she never stopped feeling lonely in his company. She knew even less about Rafe than she did about Spencer, yet she never felt lonely when he was around.

Jessy was at the hospital all day Friday. Molly thought she heard her come in after midnight, but when she woke up Saturday morning, Jessy was nowhere in sight.

Molly made breakfast then settled down to the wonderful rituals that surrounded a night out. She couldn't remember the last time she'd indulged herself this way—manicure, pedicure, hair, perfume, makeup—even a garter belt and stockings, although nobody else on earth would know she had them on. She supposed it was ridiculous, a lonely pregnant woman indulging her sensual side, but lately she found she couldn't ignore her body. For the first time in her life it wouldn't let her.

She was blooming. Her breasts, her belly, her outlook, her needs. She wanted to share this miracle with someone who loved her, someone who would touch her and caress her and help her explore this miracle that was her body.

Another of life's little jokes, she supposed. She finally awoke from her sensual slumber, only to find herself alone.

She wished she'd asked Rafe if he was going to the dance. Not that she expected he would. She couldn't imagine him enjoying anything so staid and dull. Besides, who said he was alone? A man who looked like that probably had more women than he could handle. He probably juggled lovers like circus performers juggled apples and knives and red rubber balls.

You know that's not true. You know he's as lonely as you are.

She pushed the idea aside. That kind of thinking led women to make terrible mistakes. She didn't know anything about him, not really. He was from Montana. He was divorced. He lived up near Stockton by the river. That was the sum total of her knowledge of Rafe Garrick.

He's alone, Molly. Nobody has to tell you that. You've known it right from the start.

It didn't matter. Their lives weren't connected in any way beyond the obvious. Once he finished repaying his debt he'd be gone, and she'd never see him again.

It's your own fault. Why didn't you ask him to the charity dinner?

She gave him a ticket. What more did she have to do?

You know there's a difference between giving him a ticket and asking him to join you.

"Oh, shut up," she muttered as she turned on the water for her shower. None of this mattered a damn. He had his life, and she had hers. It would take more than a ticket to a dinner-dance to bring the two of them together.

It would take a miracle.

"I know she's home," Molly said to Spencer a few hours later. "Her car's in the garage, and I heard the shower running."

"I don't hear a shower running now." Spencer glanced at his watch. He didn't need to. He already knew they were running late. "Maybe she lost track of time."

"I'll go upstairs and see what's what."

Heat gathered low in his belly as he watched her go. You'd have to be dead not to react to the sight of her lush body in motion. She looked so magnificent that she scared him. Where she'd been beautiful before, she was otherworldly now. Woman to the infinite power.

Powerful. That was the word to describe her these days. She radiated sensual power. He'd always thought of pregnant women as having an asexual, Madonna-like appeal, but Molly blew that thesis to bits. He felt sorry for Jessy, having to compete with a goddess. No wonder she was still upstairs. If he almost felt like bolting, Jessy must be damn near suicidal.

He paced the foyer, considered lighting a cigarette, then thought better of it. He heard voices, the staccato tap of high heels, laughter. He turned toward the staircase.

"I found her," Molly said. She had a funny smile on her face, as if she couldn't quite believe what she was saying.

"Are you sure?" he muttered, looking at the woman gliding down the steps behind her. Jessy Wyatt was a small, forgettable little brown-haired bit of attitude who thought a clean pair of scrubs was haute couture.

"You'd better smile or somethin'," Jessy said, "because the way you're lookin' at me is makin' me real nervous."

"Wow," he said. "You look incredible." He wasn't lying. Her tiny body looked amazing in that flapper-style dress, delicate and heart-stopping. He looked at her more closely. "Did you do something to your hair?"

Jessy and Molly laughed out loud.

"If you consider cutting off two feet of hair doing something," Molly said.

"It's more than that," he said, admiring the sleek geometric bob. "The color—"

"Highlights," Jessy said, giving her head a little toss. "It was Molly's idea."

"Good idea," he said. He couldn't take his eyes off her. "You really do look incredible."

"You said that already."

"And I'll probably say it a dozen more times before the night's over, so get used to it." He grabbed his car

keys from the small table beneath the hall mirror.
"Come on, ladies. We don't want to miss the first
dance."

Jessy had wondered how they were all going to fit into
Spencer's Porsche. He must have wondered that, too,
because he left the little sports car home and brought a
roomier Jaguar instead. She didn't wonder who was going to sit in the back, however. There'd never been any
doubt about that. She dutifully slipped into the backseat,
while the radiantly pregnant Molly claimed the spot next
to Spencer.

In a way she was glad she was in the back. She could
stare at Spencer all she wanted, memorize the way his
hair kissed his collar, the way his elegant hands held the
steering wheel, maybe even catch his eye in the rearview
mirror and see him smile. She didn't even have to go to
the dance. The look on his face when he saw her come
down the stairs was everything she'd ever dreamed
about. She could hold that one moment close for the rest
of her life and die happy. He'd seen her, really seen her.
He'd looked past Molly and into Jessy's eyes, and the
only reflection she saw in his eyes was her own face.

She'd lived her mama's dreams for so long that she'd
almost forgotten they weren't her own. Nothing she'd
ever accomplished, no scholarship or honor, had ever
come close to making her feel the way she felt tonight.
It didn't matter that she'd spend the evening watching
him dance and laugh with Molly. She'd known that was
the price of admission, and it was worth it.

Molly and Spencer were chatting about the traffic,
making idle, friendly conversation. There were no sparks
flying between the two of them, at least none that Jessy

could see. They sounded like two old friends, which their body language didn't dispute. Jessy was looking for a way to join in when her beeper sounded. She glanced at it, saw the hospital code, and nearly cried in disappointment.

"We need to stop," she said. "I have to phone the hospital."

"Use mine," said Spencer. He handed her a small cell phone in a leather case.

Her heart dropped. She was probably the only adult in captivity who'd never used a cell phone. She slipped it out of the case and stared at it. What on earth was she supposed to do now?

He met her eyes in the rearview mirror. She was glad it was too dark in the car for him to see her blush. *Good going, Dr. Wyatt. You can deliver twins but you can't dial the hospital.*

"Just flip it open, press the Power button, dial your number, then hit Send. The phones are all different."

He knew she was stuck and he offered her a lifeline without making her ask for one. If she hadn't already loved him, that would have been enough to make her tumble. They fell silent in the front seat while she talked with the hospital.

"False alarm," she said, handing the phone back to Spencer. She wondered if they could hear the relief in her voice. She felt like throwing back her head and shouting hooray to the world. "They forgot I'm not on duty tonight."

Molly half turned in her seat. "I'm so glad," she said. "You're way too glamorous to deliver babies tonight."

Jessy found herself grinning like a fool. "I am," she agreed, feeling positively giddy. "If they think I'm turning in this dress for scrubs tonight, they don't know Jo Ellen's baby girl.''

"Jo Ellen," said Molly. "Is that your mother?"

"None other," said Jessy. "Jo Ellen Grady Wyatt. If it wasn't for her, I'd still be back in Mississippi."

They started peppering her with questions, first Molly, then Spencer, and before she knew it she was telling them all about Jo Ellen and her daddy, Jim, about barefoot summers and hardscrabble winters, about how one woman's dreams can change a young girl's life.

She didn't talk about the baby, though, and she prayed Molly wouldn't bring her up. She danced around it and held her breath until Molly said something about college and leaving home that let Jessy know she was safe. The last thing she wanted to do was think about her baby. She'd waited all her life for her Cinderella moment and she wasn't going to let anything ruin it.

It felt so natural to Molly, sitting next to Spencer while they drove to the hotel. She felt as if she'd been sitting next to him for years. If she hadn't known better, she'd have thought she was sitting next to Robert. There was no sexual tingle, no jolt of sensual awareness. This time last year, that lack wouldn't have bothered her. She probably wouldn't even have noticed. She felt comfortable, relaxed, and vaguely bored. That last one embarrassed her. He was witty and quite entertaining, and, judging from the sound of her laughter, Jessy was anything but bored.

It struck Molly that maybe there was something to what Rafe had said. Jessy seemed more vibrant than Molly had ever seen her before, almost flirtatious if you got down to it. Molly had attributed the change of attitude to the wonders of a new dress and hairstyle, but there could be more to it than that. Spencer had been duly complimentary, but Molly hadn't sensed anything out of the ordinary about his interest in Jessy. She'd been wrong once tonight. Maybe she was wrong again.

A line of cars curved around the driveway that led up to the hotel entrance. Valets galloped past at breakneck speed, claiming as many cars as they could for their own. A freckle-faced red-haired girl opened the driver's door for Spencer then raced around to the passenger side to help Molly before Spencer had the chance to round the hood. She didn't notice Jessy sitting quietly in the backseat. Molly was about to say something when Spencer extended his hand to Jessy. She swung her slender legs from the car and climbed out.

Jessy had a certain grace to her that Molly had never noticed before, and she cast a sharp eye at Spencer to see if he'd missed it. His expression was blandly appreciative, but then again it always was—no matter how he really felt about the person. It was part of his upbringing and part of his training as a lawyer. Robert had been the same way. He'd actually smiled pleasantly when he told her he was leaving. She wished she'd had the guts to slap that smile off his face, but all she'd wanted was to crawl into his arms and stay there forever. Now she couldn't quite remember why.

Spencer escorted the two of them into the lobby, where they were directed to the Yankee Ballroom. He kept a proprietary hand under Molly's left elbow and one under Jessy's right. A knot of anxiety suddenly formed in Molly's throat, and it was all she could do to keep from bolting for the door. What if Robert was there? She knew the odds were slim that he and the beauteous Diana/

Dianne/Diandra/whatever-her-name-was would make the trek from the canyons of Manhattan to central New Jersey for the charity dinner, but stranger things had happened. If there was one thing Molly had learned since the day Robert said he was leaving, it was that anything was possible.

"Molly Chamberlain!" Celeste Colwin, whose flashing brown eyes missed nothing, met them at the door. "Dick and I have been hoping you wouldn't disappoint us." Celeste had chaired the committee that put together the charity event. She also was the biggest gossip in town.

"Good to see you, Celeste," Molly said. "I'm sure you know Spencer Mackenzie. I'd like you to meet Dr. Jessy Wyatt. She's an OB-GYN at the Med Center."

They all exchanged pleasantries. This would have been her life if Robert hadn't left her: day after day, month after month, year after interminable year of small talk, social chitchat, soul-numbing boredom. She would have found herself lunching with the likes of Celeste, trading tidbits about other people's lives, withholding as much of her own as she could.

They engaged in a few moments of empty conversation while Celeste tried to pretend she wasn't calculating Molly's state of mind by the state of her wardrobe and grooming. *Take a good look, Celeste. The abandoned wife, her lawyer, and her boarder. You may never see our like again.*

She wondered why she'd ever thought coming here was such a brilliant idea. This wasn't her life any longer. She wasn't part of this world and never would be. She was a pregnant wife who would soon be a single mother with limited prospects. Not exactly the kind of woman who hobnobbed with the Princeton elite.

She glanced toward Jessy. The woman was aglow with excitement. She looked positively radiant as they stood in the doorway to the ballroom. Molly's heart went out to her. She didn't want to say or do anything to dim Jessy's excitement. Few dreams in life held up to the light of day. Jessy might as well enjoy it while it lasted. Maybe Molly could sneak away after the appetizer, call for a cab to take her home. Maybe she'd bump into a nice couple who was heading back to Princeton Manor and she could hitch a ride with them. All she wanted was to be home in her favorite nightgown, snuggled up in her own bed with a cup of tea and a good book.

"I wouldn't have figured him for the charity dinner type." Spencer's voice penetrated her thoughts.

She turned to him. "Who isn't the charity dinner type?"

He pointed toward a table in the corner. "Your handyman."

A buzzing started inside her head. Not in a million years. It was impossible. Couldn't happen. She couldn't bring the image of Rafe Garrick, stripped to the waist and glistening in the sunshine, into line with this starched and pressed crowd. That would defy the order of the universe. She would step out of her old life, and there'd be no turning back.

ELEVEN

Rafe stood up and walked toward her, and Molly's old life scattered like birds before a storm. He was the only thing she saw, his voice was the only one she heard.

"You're late," he said to her, with a nod toward Jessy and Spencer. "I thought you'd changed your mind."

He wore a dinner jacket instead of his usual denim work shirt. His shiny black hair was neatly combed. But it didn't fool her. She'd have been surprised if it fooled anyone. He radiated danger. Pure shimmering sexual danger. He was every mother's nightmare, the erotic dream come to life.

Her dream.

"Don't be silly," she said, all light and breezy and insincere. "I've been looking forward to this for weeks."

"She has," said Spencer. "That's all she's talked about."

Rafe turned away from them and said something to Jessy that turned the woman's cheeks bright red. She hadn't considered Jessy in that light before. Both Rafe and Jessy were unattached. They could walk out that door and head straight for a motel on Route 1, and it wouldn't be anybody's business but their own.

She linked her arm through Spencer's. "They're playing my song," she said, even though she hadn't the foggiest notion what song it was. "Care to dance?"

"He never shuts up," Rafe said to Jessy as they watched Molly and Spencer out on the dance floor. "Look at him. That mouth is always moving."

"He's a wonderful conversationalist," Jessy said, without taking her eyes off the lawyer. "You should be half as good."

"He's a talker," Rafe said, glowering as the lawyer danced Molly in the general vicinity of the patio. "I don't trust talkers."

"Wearing your heart on your sleeve tonight, are you?" Jessy's Mississippi drawl softened the sting of her words.

"Look who's talking. I know what you're thinking, but you're not in his league, kid. Not even in your pretty new clothes."

Jessy turned to him, her brown eyes wide with hurt. "You're not number one on her dance card either, in case you haven't noticed."

"You're right," he said, leaning back in his seat until he was balanced on the two rear legs of the chair. "We've got that much in common."

Molly's laughter drifted toward them over the music and conversation.

"I hate that sound," Jessy said.

"I'm not crazy about it myself."

"Back home, a gentleman would have asked me to dance by now."

"Yeah," said Rafe. "The lawyer's got a lot to learn."

"I'm not talking about Spencer," she said. "I'm talking about you."

"You don't want to dance with me."

"That's right," she said, "and you don't want to dance with me." She inclined her head in the general direction of Molly and Spencer. "But we both want to dance with them."

Why hadn't he thought of that? He stood up and held out his hand to Jessy. "Come on, Doc. Let's give them a run for their money."

He and Jessy must have looked like father and daughter out there on the floor. They were comically mismatched in size and dancing ability.

"This isn't a waltz," Jessy said to him.

"It isn't?"

"It's a fox-trot. Didn't you know that?"

"No," he said. "Where did you learn so much about dancing?"

"My mama, Jo Ellen, teaches ballroom on Tuesday nights at the senior center."

"So what now?" he asked. "Should we bump into them?"

Jessy sighed loudly. "Do I have to spell everything out? We'll just dance up to them and casually suggest changing partners."

"What if they say no?"

"They won't say no. They're too polite for that."

Maybe that snake Mackenzie was too polite to say no, but Molly wasn't. He'd seen flashes of her temper on more than one occasion. She wouldn't hesitate to leave him standing there in the middle of the dance floor.

"You've got it all planned, haven't you?" The little doctor was more complicated than he'd figured.

"I'm goal-oriented," she said as he steered them across the dance floor. It was clear Spencer was her goal.

She reminded him a bit of Karen toward the end of their marriage. Karen had had that same single-minded quality, and it had paid off for her. She'd managed to catch her man. Too bad the man she caught wasn't her husband. He'd never regretted letting Karen go without a fight, but lately he found himself wishing he'd fought for his daughter.

The sense of loss would grab him by the throat when he least expected it. He'd be working on Molly's deck and happen to catch sight of her profiled in the window, her graceful hands resting on her round belly. He'd find himself wishing those were his hands on her belly, his child growing within her body, their future she dreamed about. He could ease her loneliness. He knew how.

He knew she could ease his pain.

They danced alongside Molly and the lawyer, and Jessy sprang into action.

Spencer was charming and personable and a wonderful dancer. He held her close but not too close. That wasn't her choice. She wanted to be held close, pressed up against his body. She wanted Spencer to kiss the side of her throat, to nuzzle her ear, to make her forget Rafe even existed. She leaned closer to him, and the baby chose that second to kick hard against her belly. He pulled away, looking startled.

"Don't worry," she said. "The baby's not a black belt yet."

"You're sure?" He laughed, but she caught a note of uncertainty in the sound.

"Positive." She leaned closer to him again, and although he didn't pull away, she could feel his discomfort, which made her feel lonelier than she ever had when she was alone.

This is who I am, Spencer, she thought as he guided her around the floor. *Like it or not, the baby is part of me.*

He guided her around the floor with skill and flair. Lush music, romantic atmosphere, a handsome partner, a child growing inside her womb—Molly had everything she could possibly want, and it wasn't close to enough. There was a deep, yearning emptiness inside her heart that not even the baby could fill. Maybe nothing ever could.

"You haven't said a word," Spencer remarked as they danced closer to the patio doors at the far end of the dance floor.

"I'm enjoying the music," she said, then caught herself. "And the conversation, of course." Light and bright. Glib and facile. As insubstantial as cotton candy. Silence would resonate more deeply than this.

"Is it the handyman?" Spencer asked. "I'm as surprised as you are that he showed up."

"Of course it's not Rafe," she said. *Amazing, Molly. You lie like that, and your nose didn't grow a millimeter longer. Somebody up there must like you.* "He's welcome to be here with us. I did give him the ticket, didn't I?"

"You were hard-pressed to do anything else, given the situation. Four people in the room, four tickets in

your hand. Most men would have realized you were being polite and refused.''

"He did refuse." She heard the snappish note in her
voice and did nothing to soften it. "I wouldn't let him
give back the ticket."

If that surprised Spencer, he didn't let on. "Fine," he
said, "but that didn't mean he had to show up."

"Oh, for heaven's sake, Spencer, will you stop going
on and on about this? From what I can see, he's Jessy's
problem now, so why don't we just shut up and dance?"

She didn't want to think about Rafe. She especially
didn't want to think about him dancing with Jessy. Jessy
looked doll-like in his arms, fragile and lovely. Molly
looked anything but fragile these days. She was too
ripely pregnant, all hips and breasts and hungers. The
sight of them dancing together caused her physical pain.

"Fancy meeting the two of you here." Jessy sounded
almost giddy with delight as the two couples danced
next to each other.

"Small world," Spencer said, looking down at Jessy.
"You'd think we shared a dinner table or something."

The remark didn't warrant Jessy's gales of laughter.
Jessy made another remark that didn't register on Molly.
It was spoken too low for her to understand anything
more than the slightly flirtatious tone of the words. Spencer said something back. Jessy laughed again and, a second later, Spencer and Jessy danced off together, leaving
Molly and Rafe standing in the middle of the dance
floor, looking at each other. As always, his expression
was unknowable. It made her angry. She didn't want
unknowable. She wanted passion and warmth and tenderness and everything else the human heart had to offer.
Unknowable wasn't on the list.

The urge to turn and run was almost overwhelming.

"Looks like they served dinner," Molly said. "Maybe we should—"

"Later."

He didn't ask. He pulled her into his arms, and she didn't resist. She could have but she didn't. There was a moment when the decision was hers, when she could have pulled away and he would have let her go, but she let that moment pass.

"Relax," he said as they started to sway to the music. "I won't hurt you."

You might, she thought. If she gave him that power over her, he might even break her heart.

She angled her body so that there was space between them. She didn't want to give him the chance to pull back the way Spencer had. She wasn't sure she could handle a second rejection. Especially not from Rafe.

He moved forward slightly. She drew back. He increased the pressure of his hand against her back, just enough to urge her closer to his body. To her surprise, her eyes filled with tears, and she looked down, desperate to regain control of herself and the situation. But it was too late for that.

"You don't want to dance with me," he said, looking down at her.

"I don't know what I want," she said honestly. She only knew what she didn't want. She didn't want him to turn away from her.

"I'm a lousy dancer," he said, "but I do better if I can feel my partner."

She moved closer on a sigh. Her belly pressed against his intimately, and he grinned. "That wasn't so hard, was it?"

She shook her head. The baby shifted position then kicked hard. Rafe's eyes widened comically.

"The baby kicked me," he said.

Her breath caught as she realized he hadn't moved away from her. Their bodies were still locked in a dancers' embrace.

"I know," she said cautiously. "Imagine how it feels from the inside."

He chuckled. The sound warmed her heart.

"What does it feel like from the inside?"

She thought about it for a moment. "Normal," she said. "Isn't that strange? Another person is kicking me from the inside, and it feels utterly natural."

The baby launched a series of jabs that made both of them laugh.

"Boy or girl?" Rafe asked.

"I don't know. The angle was wrong on the sonogram."

"What are you hoping for?"

"A girl," she said. "I've always wanted a daughter."

"I hope you get your little girl."

"Me, too," she said. It was such a nothing of a conversation. Why on earth was it having such an astonishing effect on her? "Don't tell anyone, but I'm knitting a pink-and-white sweater."

"Pretty risky proposition," he said. "You have a fifty percent chance of being wrong."

"And a fifty percent chance of being right," she said. "I'm the optimistic sort." She hadn't been for a very long time, but tonight, for the first time, she remembered how it had felt to be hopeful and happy. "Besides, I'll be just as happy if it's a little boy. The way I see it, if the baby's healthy I can't lose."

His touch changed. He didn't pull her closer but he pulled her deeper. She couldn't explain it any other way. She rested her forehead against his shoulder and shut her eyes, letting the music wash over her like a benediction. He smelled wonderful—clean and male, with the slightest hint of something fresh and outdoorsy. Did he always smell like that? She could easily get high on that smell. It made her feel light-headed and loopy with pleasure. She wondered if you could fall in love with the smell of a man's skin. She'd never heard of such a thing but she was sure it was possible.

Rafe wondered what she would do if he put his hand on her belly. She was so lush, so womanly, so ripe, that he wanted to feel the swelling of her body beneath his palm. Once with Karen he had tried to kiss her belly, touch her in a way that conveyed the wonder he felt, but she had pushed him away as if he were a stray dog bent on slobbery, desperate affection. He never tried again. They'd moved through her pregnancy in angry lockstep, growing apart while the baby grew bigger. They'd never really had a chance. Everyone else knew it. Only Rafe had been foolish enough to think the gods of destruction would look away. He and Karen had been a mistake from that first night in the back of his pickup truck with only the stars overhead for company, only the pounding of their hearts for music.

The baby kicked again, fluttery staccato movements that beat against him like an insistent woodpecker.

"She's not always this feisty," Molly said, looking apologetic.

"I think she's a redhead like her mother."

"Don't say that!"

"What's wrong with being a redhead?"

"What isn't?" she said, then laughed. "When I was little, I used to beg my mom to dye my hair."

"Your hair is beautiful." He'd spent nights dreaming about her hair, how it would feel against his skin.

"I want a happy, serene baby brunette," she said. "Nobody teases brunettes." She looked up at him, and if he didn't know better, he would have thought she was flirting with him. "Can you imagine terrible twos with a redhead?"

He couldn't. He hadn't been there for the terrible twos. Some other man had been playing daddy to Sarah by then. "I've always wondered what's so terrible about being two," he said. "They're short, and I can outrun them."

"They're unionized." Her blue eyes danced with mischief. He'd never seen her more alive, more beautiful. More irresistible. "Didn't you know that the one who wears the diapers rules the house?"

He liked seeing her this way, lighthearted and funny, the way he imagined she'd been before her husband took a hike.

The way he imagined she would be if she belonged to him.

When Jessy was a little girl, Jo Ellen would sit by her bed every night and read to her. "That's what the rich people do," she said to her daughter. Rich people read to their babies before they were even born, filling those little heads with stories about love and happiness and success. Jo Ellen read from Dickens and Shakespeare. She brought home huge coffee-table volumes of great art from the library then opened them on Jessy's lap as

if they were children's picture books. Jo Ellen didn't
know any more than Jessy did about art and history, but
if it meant helping her baby girl, she'd learn.

Daddy Jim thought Jo Ellen was crazy. "Quit filling
her head with dead men!" he'd bellowed more than
once. "Teach her something she can use." Like how to
fix her hair real pretty and put on makeup and maybe
learn how to dress like a girl instead of some scrawny
little tomboy.

But Jo Ellen wouldn't listen. She didn't want that for
Jessy. She wanted her daughter to do more than marry
into a better life. She wanted Jessy to build that better
life with her own two hands. Jessy wanted to read about
Cinderella and Sleeping Beauty and daydream about
reading those stories to her own little girl one day. When
Jo Ellen found a book of fairy tales under Jessy's pillow,
she'd burned it in the fireplace then put the ashes on her
daughter's pillow.

"No man can make you as happy as you can make
yourself," Jo Ellen told her the day Jessy started high
school. "You remember that, or I'll know the reason
why."

You're wrong, Mama, Jessy thought as Spencer Mackenzie spun her around the dance floor. *I've found a man
who can make me happier than I ever imagined.*

Spencer didn't know it yet, but that was all right. It
was enough that he showered her with compliments
while they danced. It was enough that he held her in his
arms as if she was something delicate and lovely. She'd
engineered the whole thing, yet he didn't seem to mind
one bit. He danced with her as if it had been his idea,
as if he couldn't imagine anything he'd rather do.

He's being polite, Jessy. Don't go reading anything into it or you'll only end up hurt.

Of course he was being polite. Rich people were always polite and kind. Noblesse oblige they called it. Jessy didn't care. All that mattered was that she was in his arms, and he showed no signs of letting her go.

He introduced her to a half dozen of his colleagues, tall and handsome men with pedigrees like his own. Yesterday's Jessy would have felt cowed and uncomfortable; she would have retreated behind a screen of diffidence. Today's Jessy kept up her end of the conversation and darn near preened over the way those handsome young men hung on her every word. New hair, new dress, new attitude—that was all it took. Anything was possible now.

Spencer, though, was harder to figure. They danced a fox-trot, two waltzes, and a spirited salsa; then he suggested they sit out the next set. Molly and Rafe were at the table. The wait staff was starting to serve the main course. Rafe had the slightly glazed look of a man who'd had too much champagne, although his glass hadn't been touched. Molly was downright radiant.

A stab of envy pierced Jessy from breastbone to spine. There wasn't enough makeup and hair color in the world to turn her into Molly Chamberlain, no fancy dress that could provide the magic. God must have been feeling awfully generous the day Molly was born, and had decided to bestow all of his gifts on that one little baby girl. She could have been mean-spirited and coarse; her beauty would have compensated. She could have been colorless and plain; her sweet nature would have supplied the radiance. But she wasn't any of those things. She was genuinely good-hearted and beautiful from head to foot. Jessy was jealous as hell, but no matter how hard she tried, she couldn't hate Molly.

That didn't mean she was going to sit there and watch Spencer fall under her spell. Most women would come up short in a side-by-side comparison with Molly Chamberlain. Jessy knew she couldn't compete when it came to beauty, but there was one area where she could level the playing field and tip the odds in her favor.

TWELVE

Dinner was lost on Molly. She had no idea if she'd eaten filet mignon, roast duck, or fried shoelaces. She was vaguely aware of conversation going on around her but she couldn't tell if they were talking about nuclear fusion or the New York Jets. At one point Spencer asked her a question, and she stared at him as if he were speaking in tongues.

Poor man. She felt sorry for any man who had to stand in Rafe's shadow.

Somewhere between the entrée and the dessert, Molly rallied from her fog long enough to realize Jessy had left the table.

Rafe was sitting across from her. The coffee cup looked absurdly fragile, cradled in his hand. She had a sudden image of that enormous hand against the bare flesh of her belly and she shuddered.

"Are you okay?" he asked.

"Fine," she said.

He slipped out of his jacket, then got up and walked

around to her side of the table. "Put this on," he said. "There's an air-conditioning vent right above this table."

"I'm not cold," she said. "I—" *What are you going to tell him, Molly? That you shivered because you could feel his hands on you?* "I don't want to steal your jacket."

"No arguments," he said, draping the jacket over her bare shoulders. "You don't want to catch cold, do you?"

"You don't catch cold from being cold," she said. "You can catch cold only from someone who has a cold."

"That's not what my grandmother said."

"That's not what my grandmother said either." The jacket was still warm from his body. The satiny lining felt like a caress. She wanted to bury her face in the fabric and breathe deeply. She wanted to burrow deep inside the folds and pretend she was in his arms.

She wanted.

"What did your grandmother say?" He sat down next to her. His knees brushed against hers. Neither one moved away.

"I don't remember," she said, looking into his eyes. "Something about chicken soup, I think."

"Chicken soup is good," he said.

"I hate chicken soup." But she loved the way the candlelight made his dark blue eyes glitter like stars in a night sky.

"My grandma made potions." He traced a design along the side of her wrist. Who would have figured the wrist bone was an erogenous zone?

"Potions?" *Love potions. Make my grandson irresistible to women . . .*

"She was an Ojibwa medicine woman. She knew all the herbs and flowers and how to heal with them."

"I didn't know you were Native American." That explained the glossy black hair and strong features. But those blue eyes—where did they come from?

"Half Ojibwa, half Scots. Ojibwa doesn't mean much around here."

"Did it mean much in Wyoming?"

"Montana," he said. "Yeah, it meant a hell of a lot."

His expression closed in on itself again, and she wished she could pull back her words. "I'm Jewish and Irish," she said. "More guilt than you can shake a rosary at."

He laughed out loud.

"So you can laugh," she said, tilting her head slightly as she looked at him. "I wasn't sure."

He slid his index finger over her wrist bone, along the side of her hand. Her breath caught in her throat. She prayed he hadn't heard the sound but she knew he must have. Everyone in the ballroom must have heard it. He turned her hand over, and instinctively her fingers closed over her palm. If he touched his mouth to her palm, she would be lost forever.

She pulled back her hand, and the ballroom swam back into focus. "I wonder where Jessy went."

He met her eyes, and she knew that he understood the meaning behind her words. "She was here a minute ago."

"She'd better hurry back, or I might steal her chocolate soufflé." The truth was she wouldn't know a souf-

flé from sawdust right now. The only thing she knew
was how much she wanted him.

Rafe pushed his dessert toward Molly. "Here," he
said. "I'm not big on desserts."

"This isn't dessert," she said. "This is chocolate.
One of the four basic food groups."

"My tastes run toward other things."

It was a simple statement, said with no particular degree of emphasis or innuendo. Still, her whole body re-
acted to his words as if they were a quote from the Kama
Sutra.

"And where's Spencer?" she asked, dipping her
spoon into the center of the soufflé. It sighed then settled
into more earthbound dimensions. "His dessert might
be in danger, too."

"He's standing to the left of the orchestra," Rafe said,
"talking to some guys who look just like him. I'm not
surprised you can't find him. Every guy in this place
looks like his clone."

"I'll admit there's a certain style among Princeton
men, but they're not cloned."

"They should wear name tags." The hint of a smile
curved the left corner of his way-too-sensual mouth.
"How do their wives find them at the end of the night?"

"Maybe they don't want to be found."

"Maybe they're not worth finding," he said.

"Some of them aren't," she said. She clicked her
spoon against the side of her plate. "It took me a while
to figure that out."

"And you've got it figured out now?"

She nodded. "Now I miss what could have been, instead of what was. What was isn't worth the tears."

"It takes some people years to reach the same conclusion."

She placed her hands on her belly and moved them in small, comforting circles. "Nothing like a baby to give you a new perspective."

The orchestra returned from break, and lush music once again filled the ballroom.

Rafe stood up. "Dancing's not chocolate," he said and held out his hand.

"I know," said Molly, placing her hand in his. "It's better."

"Oh!" The dark-haired matron placed a beautifully manicured hand over her heart. "I didn't know anyone was in here."

"No problem," said Jessy, hitting the Off button on the cell phone. "It was too noisy out there for me." She was curled up in the far corner of the pink brocade sofa in the ladies' room lobby.

The woman frowned as she patted her steel helmet of a hairstyle. "The orchestra has been on break since the entrée."

Jessy tilted her head. "I hear Gershwin."

"I mean they're only just now back." The woman looked at Jessy as if she couldn't understand her without a translator. "If you don't like noise, you're going to be terribly unhappy."

"I just needed a break," Jessy said, wondering why so much explanation was necessary. "I'm fine."

The woman murmured something Jessy was sure she'd hate if she could understand it, then exited stage right.

Jessy forgot all about her before the door slammed

shut behind the woman. She'd placed a call to a colleague at the hospital. Risa worked in pathology and had
weekends off. It would take at least twenty minutes to
get a call back, which was just perfect. With any luck
at all she'd be dancing with Spencer when her beeper
sounded and she put the rest of her plan in motion.

She stood up and let her dress settle around her thighs.
She half-expected someone to take her aside and tell her
to go home and finish getting dressed. *Look at you, sister,* her daddy would say. *Ain't you too old to be playin'
dress-up?*

This isn't dress-up, she thought. This is the way
grown women are supposed to look if they want to at-
tract a man. The old Jessy Wyatt with her plain face and
braided hair would never have stood a chance with a
man like Spencer. If she wanted to make her dreams
come true, she'd have to make sure some of his dreams
did as well.

Which was what tonight was all about.

"The song is over," Molly murmured.

"Don't worry." Rafe's lips brushed against her hair.
"They'll play another one."

"People are looking at us."

"Do you care?"

She swayed closer to him. "No," she said. "Not one
bit."

"Good."

The magic would end with the music. It always did.
He'd have given everything he owned to make sure the
music never stopped.

After a while they stopped dancing entirely and just
held each other. Her breasts pillowed against his chest.

He wanted to lower his head and draw his tongue along her cleavage and taste her skin. Her belly was pressed against his groin, a warm insistent presence. Everything about her was warm—her hair, her laugh, her voluptuous body. He was drunk on the feel and smell of her.

But it wasn't a perfect world. The lights went up. The orchestra said good night. People milled around, gathering up coats and car keys and anecdotes to tell at work on Monday morning.

He and Molly stood together at their table and waited.

"I think you've been stood up," he said as the ballroom quickly emptied. "I don't see the lawyer anywhere."

"That's impossible." Molly scanned the room for easily the tenth time. "I can't believe they'd leave me stranded."

"You're not stranded," he said quietly. "I won't leave you."

Those words were her undoing.

I won't leave you.

"I can call a cab," she said. "I'll be fine."

"Where I come from, men don't leave women alone in the middle of the night."

"Where I come from, it's called business as usual."

"We're playing by my rules tonight, Molly. I'll take care of you."

He slipped off his jacket once again and settled it around her shoulders. It felt familiar to her now, both comforting and wildly exciting. The push-pull of emotion made her feel dizzy. His hand enveloped hers, and she was instantly anchored.

"I parked myself," he said as they exited the hotel.

"The lot's on the other side of that footbridge. Stay near the doorman. I'll be right back."

"I'll come with you," she said.

"You're tired, and it's cold. I'll be back before you know it."

She wrapped his jacket close around her body. The doorman smiled at her, and she smiled back.

"Your boyfriend's a park-it-yourself type," he said. "Don't see many of them around here."

She was about to say that Rafe wasn't her boyfriend, but something in the doorman's tone got under her skin. She nodded her head instead and kept silent. Robert and the doorman had a lot in common. Both men judged people by the externals, as if parking your own car made you a lesser human being. Robert always used valet parking, and he'd walked out on his pregnant wife. She wondered what the doorman would think of that.

"You should tell him people notice these things," the doorman went on. "Little things make a difference. A classy woman like you deserves only the best."

"I already have the best," she said as Rafe parked his battered red truck at the curb.

Let the doorman think about that for a while.

It was only half a lie.

Spencer's Porsche rolled to a stop at the far end of the parking lot near the lake. Jessy watched as he shifted into neutral, let out the clutch, then set the parking brake. He turned to her, his face shadowy in the dark interior of the car. She wished she could see his eyes. Maybe that would make this easier.

"Is this where you wanted me to park?" He sounded curious, a little puzzled, definitely intrigued.

She nodded. She felt more like herself there than anywhere else in Princeton, surrounded by trees that had withstood the Revolution, land that echoed with stories.

"I thought you needed to get to the hospital as soon as possible."

"I lied to you," she said in as clear and steady a voice as she could manage. "They don't need me at the hospital."

"They paged you," he said. "I was there when the call came through."

"It was a setup, Spencer." That was the first time she'd called him by name. Just saying it excited her. "I arranged for a colleague to ring me."

He drummed the steering wheel with the fingers of his right hand. "Why did you do that, Jessy?" His tone was still neutral. Back home people let their feelings flow like tap water.

She sucked in a deep breath then blurted out, "Because I love you."

His head shot back as if he'd been struck a blow.

"No," she said, raising her hand. "Don't say anything. I know you don't love me but I can change that."

"Jesus, Jessy, I—"

"Hush," she said, slipping back into her old speech pattern. "I'm not tryin' to hurt you, Spencer. I love you is all."

"You can't love me, Jessy," he said, dragging a hand through his hair. "You don't even know me."

"Doesn't much matter," she said, inching her skirt higher up her thighs. "I love you."

His gaze dropped to the expanse of bare leg she was exposing. "This is a mistake, Jess. You don't know what you're doing."

"You're right," she said. "I'm crazy. Out of my mind. I can't be held accountable for my actions." She slid her panties down over her hips and skimmed them off.

She could hear the sound of his breathing in the quiet car. Yes, she thought. This was the right thing to do. No matter what happened, she would always have this.

"I'll do anything for you," she said simply. "Whatever you want."

"Put your panties back on, Jessy. This is crazy."

She took his hand and placed it between her thighs. "I'm wet," she said. "That's what you do to me, Spencer. Without even touching me, that's what you do." She'd never talked that way before. Not even in her dreams. She'd never said those forbidden words to anyone.

His fingers curved around her mons. She shuddered and closed her eyes. She was afraid to breathe, afraid that the slightest sound or movement would shatter the magic spell. She heard him slide closer to her. His fingers threaded through the nest of curls then slipped down to explore her body. She settled back against the seat and moved her legs slightly apart.

He groaned. Or maybe she did. The sound seemed to galvanize both of them. He slipped two fingers inside her body, and she clutched him with muscles she didn't know she had. She turned toward him and pulled the skimpy dress up over her head then tossed it into the backseat.

The sound he made almost brought her to climax. He wanted her. There was no doubt about that, no doubt at all. She fondled his erection through the fabric of his trousers. Rock hard, she thought. And she was respon-

sible for it. Not Molly Chamberlain. Not some fantasy
figure.

Just her.

She came hard against his hand, her body convulsing
around his fingers, her head thrown back against the
seat. That beautiful leather upholstery would be marked
with her juices, and he didn't seem to care. That thought
alone made her come again, more violently this time,
her body bucking wildly against him until she cried out.

She felt bereft when he withdrew from her, as if she'd
lost part of herself. He reached into the backseat and
retrieved her dress.

"Put this on," he said. He didn't sound like himself.
There was an edge to his voice, an urgency she'd never
heard before.

She cupped his erection. "But what about you?"

He met her gaze, and she saw the unmistakable fire
in his cool gray eyes. "We have all night."

THIRTEEN

I won't leave you.

The words resonated inside Molly's heart as Rafe drove her home.

I won't leave you.

Had Robert ever said that to her? She couldn't remember. He'd pledged to love and honor her. He'd vowed to be there in sickness and in health. But had he ever said he wouldn't leave her?

She didn't think so. She didn't think anyone had ever said that to her in her entire life. Certainly nobody had ever meant it.

She'd grown up with the sound of her mother's tears for a lullaby. Her parents' marriage had been a passionate and dramatic one, brief periods of calm followed by long stretches of rage. She'd cowered under the covers as a little girl with her hands clapped over her ears to keep the ugly words away. "Your daddy and I love each other very much," her mother used to tell her after the storm had passed. "It has nothing to do with you."

And that was the trouble. None of it had anything to do with her. When her parents finally split up, they moved on to other relationships, other marriages, other battles, and left eleven-year-old Molly to fend for herself. She bounced from parent to parent, school to school, friend to friend, searching for something or someone she could count on.

Robert was supposed to be that someone. Although he never said it in so many words, she'd known he was as solid as the ground under her feet, as dependable as the air she breathed. They were a team, he said. They knew how to work together toward a common goal: his law degree. She'd admired his single-minded dedication to the task at hand, even when that dedication got in the way of their marriage. There would be plenty of time for their marriage once he was established. Once he had their future locked in, it would be her turn. She could quit her job, or at least scale down her hours, get pregnant, create the family she'd always wanted.

I won't leave you.

Last Christmas she and Robert went up to Bridgewater Commons to do their gift shopping. The mall swarmed with people. You couldn't reach into your pocket without bumping into someone else's hand. They settled on some little electronic gadget for Robert's older brother, and Molly got on the endless line to pay for it. "Where are you going?" she'd asked Robert as he moved away from her. "Don't go far! I'll never find you in this crowd."

"Don't worry," he said. "I'll be right outside the door."

He wasn't. She stood there in front of the entrance to Sharper Image and scanned the crowd for Robert as a knot of anxiety formed in her throat. She told herself not to be a fool, that it wasn't as if she were stranded in Tibet or something with no guide, no money, and no way home. She was at the mall. He knew where she was. All she had to do was stand there, and sooner or later Robert would wander back again and join her.

There was no reason for the stomach pains that started up as the minutes passed, no reason for the tears that burned behind her eyelids. She was a grown woman. She wasn't about to burst into tears in the middle of Bridgewater Commons just because her husband was off window-shopping.

The minutes passed, and her imagination kicked into overdrive. Maybe something had happened to him. Maybe he'd gone out to the car for a minute and a carjacker had kidnapped him. Maybe he'd been hit over the head by a mugger trying to grab his wallet. Maybe he forgot Molly was with him and was halfway home.

They had one of their rare fights that night. He couldn't understand why she was so upset, and she couldn't explain it to him.

I won't leave you.

She'd waited all her life to hear those words.

He pulled into her driveway a little after midnight. Her heart was pounding so hard she wondered how the baby was able to sleep. You'd think the sound would echo inside her womb like a trip-hammer.

"Stay put," Rafe said as he unbuckled his seat belt. "I'll help you out."

He jumped from the truck and walked around the hood to open her door.

"Thank you, but I can manage." She unbuckled her own seat belt and reached for his hand.

Instead of taking her hand, he swept her into his arms and swung her to the ground.

She laughed in surprise. "You must be very strong," she said. "Nobody's done that to me since I was ten years old."

"Easiest way to get the job done," he said.

"You're still holding me."

"I wanted to make sure you had your sea legs."

"Of course," she said, still smiling. "We drove here. That makes perfect sense."

"I thought so, too."

I won't leave you.

She pulled slightly away, and their eyes locked.

"I wonder if Jessy's home," she said, for lack of anything better.

"I'll wait until you check the house."

Her breath caught. She hadn't breathed normally since the day they met. "Why don't you come in for coffee?" she asked in as casual a tone as she could manage. "You have a long drive home. The coffee will help wake you up." *Stop babbling, Molly. You're making a fool of yourself. He knows what you're really saying.*

He hesitated, and instantly she regretted making the offer. He was looking for a graceful way out, and now she'd thrown a roadblock in his way.

"Please," she said. "You don't have to stay. I make lousy coffee anyway."

"I'd like a cup."

"You would?" She coughed to cover up her embarrassment. "I mean, of course you would. If you need caffeine, you've come to the right place."

She had no idea what she meant. She had no idea if she were speaking English. She felt as if she were having an out-of-body experience. *It's just coffee,* she told herself as she let the two of them into the house. Awkward conversation followed in the kitchen while she found the beans and the filter and the water and the heat required to make magic. He'd take a sip or two, try not to grimace, then say good night.

Nothing had changed between them, after all. They'd shared a few dances, the edges of a meal. Nothing life-altering or memorable for anyone but her.

Remember that, Molly. Don't make that mistake.

"Make yourself comfortable," she said, gesturing toward the living room. "The furniture's yours. You might as well enjoy it." Two weeks ago he'd found her an oversized chintz-covered sofa that dominated the room. How many hours had she spent dreaming about him on that sofa?

"I'll help you with the coffee."

"Oh, you don't have to do that," she said, aware that she was babbling. "There's nothing hard about making coffee."

"I'll keep you company."

"You don't have to—" She stopped. "Tell me to shut up."

He rested his right hand on her shoulder. "Shut up, Molly." He said it softly, with more sweetness than she'd ever heard the words *I love you* spoken.

She started to melt.

He turned her around to face him.

"Shut up, Molly." His voice was low, intimate. He cupped her face between his hands. His fingertips traced the contour of her cheekbones. Her eyelids fluttered closed for a second.

I'm dreaming. This isn't really happening . . .

She'd imagined his hands on her, his fingers warm against her skin, but nothing had prepared her for this.

His eyes never left hers. He didn't say another word. He didn't have to. What he wanted, what she needed—it was all there in the heartbeat between them. The kitchen was dark. A faint splash of moonlight washed across the floor. The edge of the counter pressed against the back of her thighs. Could you smell desire? She thought she could, but maybe it was her imagination. Desire was foreign to her. *Terra incognita.*

What she did know was this: She wanted to press her face against his chest and breathe deeply. That would be enough. She would drink in his smell, his touch, the sound of his heartbeat, burn the sensations into her memory because nothing lasted. This least of all.

His thumbs found the corners of her mouth, and she began to tremble. He traced the place where her lips met, easing his thumb between, and her mouth opened on a sigh of pleasure. She placed her hands flat against the wall of his chest and felt the power of her touch. He groaned and dipped his head down, brought his mouth to hers in a kiss of such stunning sweetness that she thought she must be dreaming.

Wet. Hot. Irresistible. Everything a kiss should be. She could live off that kiss forever. She wanted to memorize every detail, every degree of sensation. If this was all she would ever have of him, then she would make it part of her skin, part of her soul.

He cradled her face as if she were precious to him, as if he could be satisfied by that touch alone.

She wanted his hands to slide down the column of her throat, to slide over the curve of her shoulders, to discover the weight and contour of her breasts. She wanted to feel his warm, wet mouth on her nipple. She wanted to gather as much of him as she possibly could before she woke up and found that it had all been a dream.

It had to be a dream. She imagined his hands along her throat, and they were there. He slid the skinny straps of her dress from her shoulders and kissed the marks they left behind. He drew his tongue along one of the depressions, and her legs went weak as a baby's. He caught her up against him and held her close. He was gloriously, undeniably hard. His erection fit against the swell of her belly. It pressed against her; she pillowed around it.

He lifted her from her feet and sat her on the counter. Her skirt slid halfway up her thighs, and he parted her knees and settled himself between her legs.

The fabric of his trousers scratched deliciously against the thin nylon of her stockings.

The frilly edge of her garter belt showed beneath the hemline, and she reached to tug at her dress, but he captured her hand with his.

"Let me," he said—part question, part statement.

She nodded. *Anything,* she thought. *Anything you want.*

He slid his hand under her hemline, and found the bare flesh above the top of her stocking. How could she have lived so long and understood so little about the nature of touch? She'd touched herself. She knew the firmness of her thighs, the softness of the curls. She knew these things but she knew nothing at all about the depth of pleasure possible.

It all felt like the first time.

She wore silky bikini panties to accommodate her

blossoming belly. He cupped her through the delicate fabric and she could feel herself as she must feel to him—the heat and the damp and the unfurling. He found the center of pleasure with the pad of his thumb, and she bit her lip to keep from crying out.

He moved with a rhythm that matched her own, a rhythm he had no way of knowing, since she hadn't known it herself until that moment. He pleasured her with subtle, increasing pressure, using both thumbs, building, building toward the unknowable. The unimaginable.

Then, just as she was climbing into the stars, he dropped to his knees in front of her and buried his face between her thighs. She heard the hushed rip of fabric as he tore the panties from her body. She heard the sound of her heart thundering in the quiet room. He nipped the soft skin above the top of her stocking, toyed with her garter. He lifted her dress higher, above her waist, and tears formed in her eyes as he exposed her belly to his view. She wanted to cover herself, to shield her new body from him, but she couldn't move.

"I don't always look this way," she whispered as he traced the faint blue veins with his tongue. "I—"

He said something. She felt the words against her skin. She didn't need to know what they were to understand them. His kiss told her everything she needed to hear.

The baby shifted, a gentle stretch in its sleep. Rafe laid his cheek against the rippling surface of her belly and closed his eyes. She placed her hand on his head. His hair was silky and cool. She'd waited all her life for this moment, to feel this sense of connection. You could know someone's heart without knowing their history. You could tell that and more in a touch.

I won't leave you.

She saw Robert's face, hard and unyielding, when she told him she was pregnant.

Are you sure? Could there be a mistake?

She saw him throw back the covers and climb from bed. She saw him pull on his clothes. She saw him walk out the door.

I won't leave you.

She knew better than to believe that. They always left. Her father had. So had her husband. Why would Rafe be any different? Why would there be a connection between them that existed nowhere else?

She couldn't answer that with logic or reason. She could answer it only with her heart. The connection between them was real and it was powerful, and that connection was ripping down the fences that she'd put up to keep her heart safe. She was naked in every way that mattered, in ways that she'd never been naked before.

The first few months of her pregnancy had been filled with so much heartache and anger and stress that she hadn't had time to appreciate the fact that her dreams of motherhood were going to come true. When she finally had a moment to catch her breath, she was in her second trimester, ripe and fertile and so deeply lonely for someone to share this wonder with that there were times she thought her heart would break.

"You can say no," he told her. "You don't have to be afraid."

She nodded. She didn't trust herself to speak.

His hands were large and beautifully made. He splayed his fingers across her belly, and the sight of his tanned hands against her pale skin struck her as almost unbearably erotic. The baby fluttered again, and she saw the look of wonder and delight in Rafe's dark blue eyes.

"How does it feel?" he asked her, moving his hands in large circles, meant to soothe and gentle.

She didn't have to ask what he meant because she knew. "It feels wonderful," she said, "as if this is how it's meant to be."

"It doesn't hurt?"

"Not at all. Sometimes he gets a little rambunctious, but it's all pretty wonderful."

"You know it's a boy?"

"Just guessing," she said. "He's such a good kicker, I figure he must be a future soccer player."

"It's a girl," he said, brushing his lips against the spot where her skin rippled.

"You're an expert in these things?"

"A girl," he repeated. He reached for her hand and placed it over her navel. "Feel the way she moves under your hand. A girl. No doubt about it."

Molly laughed softly. "And why should I believe you?"

"My Ojibwa grandmother could tell the sex of a baby by laying her hands on the mother's belly."

"And you've inherited that ability?"

"I'll tell you after you deliver."

He covered her hand with his, and another set of defenses crumbled at her feet.

She rested her forehead against his shoulder and closed her eyes. The baby fluttered once more then settled down. *You know, don't you? This feels as right to you as it does to me,* she said silently to her baby.

She leaned into his touch, willing her doubts and fears

to lie quiet for just a little while. It seemed absurdly natural to sit there on the kitchen counter with her dress hiked up over her hips and her panties curled at her feet while a man who was practically a stranger rubbed her pregnant belly. The feelings he brought to life were a powerful blend of the sensual, the sexual, and the spiritual—and they transcended explanation.

You couldn't explain magic, and that's surely what this was.

They spoke without language. They heard without words. He gripped her by the waist and urged her to scoot forward, to wrap her legs around his hips. She'd never done anything like that, never felt so wildly passionate and hungry. She held him tight with her thighs then looped her arms around his neck as he lifted her from the counter and carried her toward the staircase.

"No," she said. "Not upstairs." She wanted a place that belonged only to them. She wanted to stay one step ahead of reality.

He carried her into the living room, to the big old sofa he'd found for her. It was wide and deep, and they lay together with their arms wrapped tightly around each other. She'd imagined them there a hundred times but she'd never once believed her fantasy would come true.

She unbuttoned his shirt. He pulled her dress over her head. She unfastened his trousers. He stripped off the rest of his clothes then covered her body with his. They were a perfect match. Their bodies fit together as if they'd been fashioned for that purpose. His powerful erection throbbed against her belly, and she wondered how it would feel to take him in her mouth and hold him until he came. She'd never done that, never taken a man in her mouth before, never wanted to taste a man the way she wanted to taste him.

How do you tell a man that you wanted to do that to him? Her one experience with expressing a preference had ended badly, with Robert feeling shocked and Molly humiliated. What if Rafe turned her away or, even worse, laughed at her? She didn't know the first thing about making love, not really. Sometimes it was hard to believe she'd gotten pregnant. She and Robert had rarely made love, much less experimented with anything inventive or even mildly exciting. Her fantasy life had been nonexistent until very recently.

He kissed the way she'd imagined he would kiss. He engaged every sense. She didn't know the first thing about kissing the way he kissed. Suddenly she felt clumsy and stupid and she wished she were anywhere on earth but where she was.

She pulled away from him and grabbed for her dress.

"I'm sorry," she said, struggling to hold back her tears. "I can't. I just—" She stopped. What was there to say anyway? This was all a terrible mistake. Surely he could see that now.

His expression closed in on itself. She actually saw the moment when the joy drained away, and it came close to breaking her heart.

"I wasn't thinking." Why had she said that? She was only making things worse. He looked so hurt, so lonely.

"The coffee," she said as she stood up. "You haven't had your coffee."

"It's late," he said. His tone betrayed nothing at all. "I'd better get going."

"But I promised you a cup of coffee to help you stay awake."

"Don't worry," he said. "I'll stay awake."

"I'm sorry," she whispered. "I didn't plan any of this."

"Neither did I, Molly."

"I know that." The baby kicked her hard, and she placed her hands on her belly. A tiny hand or foot beat against her right palm. "I wish I—"

"Don't."

"But I—"

"There's no point, is there?"

"No," she said. She felt utterly defeated. "There's no point."

She walked him through the foyer to the front door.

"The deck is finished," he said as she unlocked the bolt. "You'd said something about the baby's room."

Make a clean break of it, Molly. Make it easy on both of you. There's no way you can undo this.

"I don't think so." She started to offer a convoluted explanation about north light and infant sleeping patterns and maybe putting the house up for sale, but in the end, what difference did it make? All that mattered was that they put an end to all the things that never were.

His eyes were dark, and once again the expression in them was unreadable. "Take care, Molly."

"You, too."

He stood in the doorway, a silhouette in the moonlight spilling through the trees. "You'd better have that chimney checked before you light any fires," he said. "And watch out for this porch step. You need to replace it."

They both knew this was good-bye, although neither one of them said the word.

"I'll remember about the step."

His eyes were dark and fathomless. "Take care, Molly," he said again.

"You, too," she said, wrapping her arms around her chest as a chill wind blew. "You take good care of yourself."

He turned and walked down the porch steps.

I won't leave you.

Of course you will, she thought. *You just did.*

FOURTEEN

The thing to do was put as much distance between himself and Molly as possible, but Rafe wasn't sure the universe was big enough for that.

Her scent lingered on his skin, a combination of sweetness and something darker, more intensely female. He'd wanted to brand himself with her smell and he would have if she hadn't stopped him. He would have worshipped her.

You did the right thing, Molly. You recognized a loser when you saw one.

He could feel her hands on his shoulders as she pushed him away. He'd never forget the frantic, guilty look in her eyes.

What the hell had he been thinking? You didn't get more off limits than Molly. She was a pregnant Madonna with a husband still out there somewhere, even if he was campaigning to be her ex-husband. Rafe knew how that particular story usually played out. In every marriage one partner loved, and the other was loved.

Molly loved. He understood that. He knew it took more than divorce papers to break the chain.

Maybe she thought there was still a chance for her and Chamberlain. Maybe she believed he'd come around before it was too late and check back into their old life. For the first few months after Karen left him, he'd actually believed she would come back, that one day he'd open the front door and she and little Sarah would be standing there and he wouldn't say a word. He'd just step aside, they'd walk into the house, and it would be like nothing ever happened.

Molly probably believed the same thing, and maybe she'd be the one who got the happy ending.

He stopped at a 7-Eleven near Route 206 and bought a giant cup of black coffee then hit the road again. He drove past Stockton and Fallen Rock, driving north with the Delaware River. He had no destination in mind and almost laughed at the way that paralleled his own life. No destination. No course neatly mapped out. He'd drive until he ran out of road and then he'd turn around and drive some more.

Sunrise found him at the foot of the Poconos. A Sunday-morning stillness shimmered against the fiery reds and golds and yellows of the autumn landscape. He drove up and down little residential streets tucked into the woods, past postage-stamp ranch houses with tiny plots of well-tended land. Here and there a light burned behind the window, and he slowed to a crawl, trying to see into the heart of a family. Any family.

What went on inside a family anyway?

It was all mysterious to him. He didn't know how it worked. There had to be some secret handshake involved, a password maybe that opened up your heart to happiness. His parents hadn't known about it. He remembered an endless coil of dark nights that echoed with the sound of tears and anger. He remembered the day the principal called him out of class—sixth-grade geography—to tell him that his mother was dead.

A suicide.

The town buzzed about that for years. It marked him, her suicide did, marked him more indelibly than anything he might have done himself ever could. Depression, the doctor called it. The long lonely Montana winters finally wore her out. Rafe knew better. Her long lonely marriage was what had worn her out. Her spirit died long before her body, and he wished he'd been old enough, smart enough, to have made a difference.

But he was just a little boy then, looking for the unconditional love the other kids took for granted. Kids needed more than food in their bellies and a roof over their heads. He was proof of that.

He'd thought he could have a family with Karen. Those first few months after the baby arrived were the happiest of his life. They were the happiest of Karen's life, too, but for a different reason. She was in the process of planning her escape into a more successful, more profitable marriage.

The front door of a white Cape swung open, and a middle-aged woman in a pink terry bathrobe stepped outside to fetch the Sunday newspaper from her porch. She noticed Rafe and stood very still, watching him, as he drove past. *Don't you have someplace to go?* her look said. *Isn't there somewhere you belong?*

No, he thought. Not one goddamn place on earth.

He found a small pancake restaurant just outside East Stroudsburg. The hostess, a plump matron in a blue

dress and Ping-Pong–ball pearls, smiled up at him.
"How many?" she asked.

"One," he said.

She plucked one menu from the stack. "Don't get too
many singles on Sunday morning," she said as she led
him to a tiny booth near the rear of the restaurant. "Usually family time for us."

There was nothing he could say except, "Thanks for
the menu."

The server popped up a few moments later to take his
order and fill his coffee cup. He gulped down the caffeine then looked around at the other customers. The
hostess was right. Families were everywhere. Young
parents with newborns and toddlers. A couple well into
middle age with an infant in a car seat. A multigenera-
tional group with grandparents, parents, surly teenager,
and gangly adolescents. He was the only one there alone.

A couple sat down across the aisle from him. The man
was young and well scrubbed. The woman was very
pregnant. Her belly bulged against her too-tight sweater.
He could easily see her navel popping through the fabric.
They both wore that slightly embarrassed look of pride
that he remembered seeing in the bathroom mirror for
the entire nine months of Karen's pregnancy.

Karen had tried to hold the experience at an arm's
length from her emotions. She went through all three
trimesters with an almost stoic air of acceptance. Little
did he know she was already planning her escape.

He'd wanted to share every second of Karen's pregnancy, while she'd wanted to pretend it wasn't happening. It wasn't like that with Molly. She'd cried when he
caressed her belly. He'd seen tears shimmering on her
cheeks when he kissed the tautly stretched skin. She

craved all the things his ex-wife had pushed away with both hands, but she didn't crave them from him.

That about said it all.

She wanted him, but not enough to risk taking the whole imperfect package. Half-Ojibwa handymen didn't register too long on her radar screen. He'd been painfully out of place at the dinner dance. He was surprised they hadn't sent him to the kitchen to sit with the help. He only knew which fork to use because he followed her lead. He worked with his hands. Sometimes they even got dirty. He went to work in jeans and T-shirts, not thousand-dollar Italian suits.

Mackenzie was the obvious choice for her. They both knew how to use finger bowls and understood why sorbet was served in the middle of dinner and not at the end like any normal dessert back in northern Montana.

You had to go with your own kind, the people who understood your world and your place in it. The kind who wouldn't embarrass you in public or want you too much in private.

Wasn't that what Karen had taught him during their brief time together? Somewhere along the way he'd forgotten that valuable lesson, the one that had cost him his baby daughter. He'd forgotten it in the glow of Molly's smile.

As far as Spencer was concerned, sex was sex and nothing more.

There was nothing transforming about it. Nothing transcendent. Physical exertion didn't translate into spiritual fulfillment. He worked up a sweat but he didn't see God.

It was the most intriguing activity two reasonably

healthy humans could engage in and, in most ways, the
least satisfying. Nothing left him feeling less connected
to the human race than the afterglow of love. Mostly
because there was no afterglow.

He had just spent the last three hours making passionately unexpected love to Jessy Wyatt, and now all
he could think about was how to get her out of his bed
and back to her own. She was sprawled diagonally
across the mattress. Her face was buried in his pillow,
her tiny feet angled toward the opposite side. Before
tonight he'd thought of her as skinny and plain. Now he
could see the delicate bone structure, the perfect skin,
appreciate the supple limbs and laudable flexibility.

I love you, she'd said to him, and he'd pretended not
to hear. She'd said it once more before she fell asleep,
and whatever remained of desire died with those words.

People said things during sex they wouldn't say over
dinner. He'd said things himself, things he later wished
he could erase from that universal tape that captured all
human folly. That's the kind of thing you learn how to
control as the years roll on and the disappointments pile
up on the pillow next to you. He could always see the
ending implicit in the beginning. It was always out there
in the middle distance pointing out the futility of it all.

Or maybe that was his father.

*Can you see me, Dad? I'm the second son . . . the one
you're stuck with.*

That's what he got for ducking his old man's call the
other afternoon. No matter which side of the guilt fence
he came down on, he felt like a bastard. Hell, being
Owen Mackenzie's bastard son would be easier than being the one who'd lived. What was the headline when
Owen, Jr. died? *Mackenzie Dynasty Hopes Shattered in*

Crash. Owen, Jr. and Spencer had been tooling up from Virginia in Owen, Jr.'s flame red Austin-Healy. Owen had just asked Glory Mathers to marry him, and Owen, Sr. had been over the moon.

"I'm on the fast track now," Owen, Jr. was saying just before the crash. A seat in the State House of Representatives was opening up, and he was the golden boy. The heir apparent. "Dad's talking to Glen Alcott tomorrow about . . ."

Spencer had been listening to this since they passed Timonium, Maryland, but he'd quit actually hearing the words near Dover, Delaware. That was at least an hour ago. The good thing about his brother was that he didn't particularly give a damn if Spencer listened to him or not. All Owen, Jr. wanted was center stage. Spencer had been drifting, daydreaming, when he looked out the window in time to see an eighteen-wheeler spinning across six lanes of Jersey Turnpike traffic, heading straight for them.

When he woke up two days later, his brother was dead, and so were his father's dreams. Spencer had a broken right leg, a concussion, three broken ribs, and damage to his spleen. That was the good news. The bad news was that he was the brother who'd lived.

Next to him Dr. Jessica Wyatt murmured something in her sleep then slid closer to him. She pressed her small straight nose against his side and sighed. Spencer reached for a cigarette on his nightstand and settled back to wait for dawn.

All along Jessy had told herself that one night with Spencer was all she wanted. One night in his arms would be enough. She would live off that for the rest of her life.

She'd believed that. With her entire heart and soul, she'd believed it. Right up until the second he took her in his arms and she found out how wrong she'd been. One night wasn't near enough. She wanted a week, a month, a year. She wanted forever. He made her feel beautiful and desirable. He made her feel womanly and soft.

And he didn't want her.

He was too much of a gentleman to say so, but she knew just the same. She'd dozed after they made love, and when she woke up he was sitting with his back against the headboard. He was smoking a cigarette, and somehow she knew exactly what he was thinking. She pushed her face deeper into the pillow and pretended to be asleep, because the second he knew she was awake he'd be pushing her toward the door.

"Sorry about breakfast," he said later as he turned onto Lilac Hill. "I have to be up in Greenwich by noon."

"You don't have to apologize for anything, Spencer." She aimed a big bright smile in his direction. "I appreciate the ride home."

He looked vaguely uncomfortable, and she found herself torn between sympathy and glee.

"Do you work today?" he asked.

"Does it matter?" she asked him.

His face reddened. She almost regretted her remark. Almost. She knew she'd never see him again, not this way. She could say anything. She could tell the truth. It didn't matter.

He pulled up in front of Molly's house, then came

around the front of the car to open her door. Good manners, even at the end. There was the difference between the boys she'd grown up with in Mississippi and a real live Yankee rich boy. Good manners. One of her hometown boys would have gunned the engine impatiently while she fiddled with the door handle. Not Spencer. Spencer made her feel wanted even when the only thing he really wanted was to get rid of her.

That took talent, she thought as she climbed out of the car. That took class.

This time she was being dumped by a pro.

Spencer sat behind the wheel of his Porsche and watched Jessy walk up the pathway to the front door. He felt guilty, driving her home early on Sunday morning without even taking her for breakfast. Hit-and-run wasn't exactly his style, but she hadn't given him a choice. At least not a choice he could have made. When a woman strips down to her skin in the front seat of your car, the matter has pretty much been decided for you.

Once a year the Mackenzie clan gathered to commemorate the life and times of Owen, Jr., the son who hadn't lived long enough to disappoint anyone. This was the day of the command performance. Attendance was mandatory. No exceptions, not even if it meant you had to turn a woman out of your bed.

He drummed his fingers on the steering wheel. It seemed to be taking her a hell of a long time to get to the front door. If he didn't hit the parkway soon, he wouldn't make it to Greenwich in time for the church service at noon.

She turned once when she reached the porch and

waved, then she opened the door and disappeared into
the house.

The relief he felt embarrassed him even though there
was nobody there to see it.

Twenty minutes later, he was on the turnpike headed
north.

Greenwich and Princeton had a lot in common. The
similarities struck Spencer every time he made the trek
up to the family home for one of his infrequent command performances. Both towns were verdant, both in
landscape and in affluence. Both towns fancied themselves highbrow bastions of respectability. He could see
only one discernible difference, other than the obvious
geographical one: Princeton was built around intellectual
pursuits; Greenwich revolved around financial ones.

He'd always thought he'd live his life right there in
the town where he'd grown up. The rest of his family
had. Owen, Jr. would have set up shop there. Everyone
knew it would have been a short and easy jump from
partner in a local law firm to a run for the House.
Owen's death had changed everything. His parents became keepers of the shrine. His sisters dedicated themselves to raising perfect children who would follow in
Owen, Jr.'s giant footsteps. Their husbands were both
ambitious men who understood the way the Mackenzie
name opened doors that would remain locked before
mere mortals.

They were holding a memorial this afternoon to
Owen, Jr. One in a never-ending series of elaborate
homages designed to remind the rest of them that they
could never live up to the things Owen, Jr. might have
accomplished if he'd lived long enough. How the hell
did you compete with smoke and mirrors and broken

dreams? Damned if Spencer knew. But there he was, rolling toward the Greenwich exit, the second son on his way home for a command performance.

Sometimes Spencer felt like the kid in that old story, the one who shouted, "The emperor has no clothes." His whole damn family was so blinded by the past, so mired in what could have been, that they couldn't see what they had. He'd tried to fill Owen's shoes, but his father made it clear that nobody could do that. Especially not his second son.

So Spencer quit the family firm, packed up his condo, and moved south to Princeton, where the winters were a little milder and expectations were lower. Nobody at Steinberg, Corelli, and Winterbourne expected more from him than billable hours. He didn't have to save the world. He didn't have to defend freedom of speech, women's rights, or the environment. All he had to do was sniff out couples in trouble and be there to catch the wife before she found another lawyer to defend her interests against her big bad husband.

That was how he had met Molly. One dance at a party somewhere and he had a client. He might have had a woman if he'd pursued her, but something had held him back from taking the next step.

One half mile to the Greenwich exit. He eased into the right-hand lane and reduced speed. Not that the Greenwich cops would give him a speeding ticket. The Mackenzies had a pass on things like that. A Mackenzie could do ninety in a thirty-miles-per-hour zone, and nobody would notice.

He knew one thing a Mackenzie couldn't do. He couldn't bring home a pregnant, married, underemployed Irish-Jewish woman and call her his date. Two centuries of judgmental Mackenzies would rise up from their graves and beat him senseless. He'd thought about it. Any red-blooded man with the requisite percentage of testosterone would have thought about it. Most of them would have given it a shot.

Not Spencer. The weight of disapproval easily spanned the distance between Greenwich and Princeton, and so he'd angled his interest from the personal back to the social. The professional always took care of itself.

He doubted if Molly even noticed.

I love you, Spencer.

Jessy's words curled themselves around his ear as he made the left onto Water's Edge Road, which led to the Mackenzies' private drive.

She'd said she loved him, and he'd said that he had to make it up to Greenwich by noon and would she like a ride back to Molly's place. She'd looked so damn vulnerable, with the sheet held against her breasts and her new shorter hair tumbling into those big sad eyes, that he'd considered making love to her again, but that would only have complicated things.

She loved him, and he didn't love her back.

Jessy would get used to it. Everybody did sooner or later.

It was called real life.

Molly was sitting at the kitchen table, nursing her second cup of decaf tea with milk, when she heard Jessy come in. She'd been sitting at that table ever since Rafe left, replaying everything that had happened that night and regretting most of it—the things she didn't do as much as the things she did.

Twice she'd grabbed her car keys and started for the

door, determined to throw caution aside and herself at his feet, and twice she'd talked herself out of it. She didn't know the first thing about having an affair. She didn't know the first thing about sex, and she was glad she'd stopped things before he found out what a pathetic excuse for a woman she was. The women he knew were probably limber and inventive. She had the feeling they weren't pregnant with another man's child. She was quickly moving past voluptuous into cumbersome. Sometimes she didn't even recognize her own body in the mirror—the swollen breasts, the fecund belly, the naked and vulnerable look in her eyes.

She'd always looked confident and in control. Whatever she was feeling deep inside stayed there, hidden away where it belonged. Those days were gone. Her emotions were right there at the surface for everyone to see. Emotions she hadn't known she had.

She wanted Rafe. She wanted to explore every beautiful muscle and hollow of his body. She wanted to curl up somewhere inside his brain and absorb his secrets. She wanted to learn the contour of his heart from the outside in.

You had your chance last night, Molly. He would have worshipped you, and you pushed him away.

Of course she'd pushed him away. What would he have thought of her when he saw how awkward and unsure she was when it came to making love? When he realized how little she'd learned during ten years of marriage to a man who didn't love her?

Do you really think that would matter to him, Molly? Do you think he's looking for an acrobat or a lover?

She buried her face in her hands. *I don't know,* she thought. Maybe he was looking for both. Maybe he'd found both with a thousand other women along the way. The thought of being measured and found wanting made her physically ill. Pushing him away was the smartest thing she could have done. Let him think it was because she was ashamed of her pregnant body. Let him think she was still in love with her husband. It didn't matter what he thought as long as he didn't know the truth: that she was afraid she'd disappoint him.

"Molly?" Jessy's voice drifted toward her from the foyer.

"I'm back here." She brushed her hair off her face and fixed a pleasant smile on her face. She was very good at creating a pleasing facade. She'd had many years of practice, starting when she was a little girl.

"So tell me," she said when Jessy, still in her fancy dress, walked into the room. "Was it a boy or a girl?"

Jessy looked at her, a puzzled expression on her face. "What?"

"A boy or girl," Molly said. "You just spent the night at the hospital delivering a baby, didn't you? What was it?"

Jessy's cheeks reddened, and her small face took on the classic deer-in-the-headlights look.

"Oh, Jess," Molly whispered. She tried to dim the vivid images that came instantly to mind.

The look on Jessy's face suddenly shifted into utter radiance. Molly thought her heart would break as she saw the glow in Jessy's dark eyes. Sometimes life made no sense at all.

"You and Spencer?" she asked tentatively.

Jessy didn't answer, but then again she didn't need to. The truth was written all over her face.

Molly looked down at her cup of tea. *That could be you, Molly. You could have been lying in Rafe's arms right about now, glowing even brighter than the good doctor.*

"Well," she said, "how long has this been going on?" She tried to sound cheerful and nonjudgmental but was afraid she'd failed miserably.

"Since last night," Jessy said. "Not that it's any of your business." Some of the glow faded with her words.

"He's my lawyer," Molly said, feeling an unexpected burst of sympathy for the contentious young woman. She was going to get hurt. That was the one sure thing in this whole business. "You're my boarder. I feel responsible."

"Don't," Jessy said. "You had nothing to do with this."

"I brought you together."

"No," Jessy said carefully, "you introduced us, but I'm the one who brought us together."

Molly locked eyes with her across the table. "You made the first move?"

"Somebody had to." Jessy considered her. "Spencer wasn't about to, not with you in the same room." The words carried a sting that brought Molly up short.

"There's nothing between us," she said. "We share some points of reference is all."

"Right," said Jessy with a sigh, "and he never noticed the way you look."

"I have no idea what he has or hasn't noticed about me, Jessy. I'm telling you the truth from my perspective."

"I guess you wouldn't know," Jessy said, as much

to herself as to Molly. "You probably wouldn't notice one more man falling at your feet."

"Like my husband?"

Jessy's cheeks reddened. "I'm sorry. I didn't mean it that way."

"I think you did," Molly said, "and that's okay. We might as well put our cards on the table."

"Cards?" Jessy sat down opposite her. "I don't care if your husband walked out on you. You're still the one who was dealt the winning hand."

"You're amazing. Do you think that because I look a certain way I don't have feelings?"

"I didn't say that."

"No, you didn't, but you imply it every single time you talk to me."

"I think you're reading too much into this, Molly."

"And I don't think you're half as smart as you think you are, Jessy. Getting dumped hurts. Having your husband walk out on you hurts like hell. Being alone and pregnant—" She stopped, and once again the two women locked eyes. "I'm sorry. This time I'm the one who wasn't thinking."

"There's a lot of that going around." Jessy fiddled with the top of the sugar bowl. "You're right about what you said before. I'd pretty much decided you'd been given a pass in life."

"Some pass." Molly resisted the urge to pull the sugar bowl away. "I wouldn't wish my predicament on—" She started to laugh. "I wouldn't wish it on my husband."

Jessy's serious expression began to lighten. "Who better than your husband?" she tossed back. "I'd say he deserves it."

"You're right," said Molly. "He does deserve it. That and nine months of morning sickness."

"I never had morning sickness," Jessy said. "Not once. I was healthy as a horse."

It was hard to imagine the slender woman great with child. Molly's imagination couldn't quite bring the image to life. "Is that how you ended up an OB?"

"That and Jo Ellen."

"Jo Ellen?"

"My mama. She had plans for me."

"What about your own plans? Didn't they matter?"

"If you knew Jo Ellen you wouldn't ask that."

"It must be nice to have a mother who cared enough about you to plan your future," Molly said. "Mine only cared where her next husband was coming from."

"That's not how I pictured you." Jessy rested her elbows on the table and settled her chin in her hands. "I imagined you as the princess with doting parents."

"Not quite," Molly said, feeling the pinch of old hurts. "My parents loved each other and hated each other, and I was the go-between for all of it. Sometimes they'd look at me as if they couldn't quite remember if I was their daughter or the kid from next door."

"My mama made all my decisions from the time I took my first breath," Jessy said. "The only decision I ever made on my own was to get pregnant."

"You mean it wasn't a mistake?"

"No," Jessy said in a soft voice. "The only mistake was giving her up."

Molly glanced down at her own belly. "I can't even imagine that."

"Me neither," Jessy said, "but Jo Ellen had plans for me, and a baby wasn't one of them."

Molly tried to imagine how it felt to be young and poor and pregnant, with a mother who was determined to make your decisions for you.

"At least you had someone who cared what happened to you."

"All I wanted was the space to make my own mistakes."

Molly stifled a sigh. All she'd ever wanted was someone to hold her when she did make mistakes.

They were quiet while Jessy made herself a cup of tea then sat down again.

"So you're telling me that you made the first move with Spencer," Molly said after Jessy added sugar and milk to her cup.

"Yes," Jessy said, peering at her over the lip. "Why is it I have the feeling you never made the first move in your life?"

The baby kicked hard, and Molly absently rubbed her belly with her left hand. "You're right," she said. "I never have made the first move." Even if she had the guts, she wouldn't know where to start.

"Beautiful women never do," Jessy said without bitterness. "That's for the rest of us."

"I was brought up to believe the man made the first move."

"So was I, darlin'," Jessy said, "and I'd still be waiting for my first date if I hadn't decided to chart my own course."

"I don't want to hurt you," Molly said, "but I don't think Spencer's the marrying kind."

"This was sex," Jessy said, "not love. I know the difference."

Do you? Molly wondered.

Did anybody?

FIFTEEN

⟞⟞⟞

The candles were burning in the windows of the main house when Rafe got home early Sunday evening. The candles only appeared in the windows when Miriam was home and, last he heard, Miriam was still in Florida. She was the closest thing to family he had, and he missed her company. She'd come into his life at its lowest ebb and given him both shelter and friendship. That was more than anyone had ever done for him, and he loved her for it.

He parked the truck then let himself in the back door of the main house. He wasn't exactly looking for trouble, but his senses were on alert.

"Miriam?" he called out as he walked through the empty kitchen. "Are you here?"

"Good Lord!" Ginny, the occasional housekeeper, appeared in the back hallway. "Least you could do is ring the bell before you come barging in."

He and Ginny had, at best, an adversarial relationship, which grew more adversarial the longer Miriam stayed away. Ginny had made it clear she considered Rafe a threat to her livelihood, and nothing he could say or do had changed her mind.

"I saw the lights," he said. "Since when are you here on Sunday nights?"

"Miss Miriam is coming home. She called me this morning when she couldn't get you on the phone."

"When?" he asked. Something didn't feel right about this. Miriam had claimed she was settled now in Florida and would only return north in an emergency.

"I didn't ask."

"Where was she calling from?"

"If you've got so many questions, why don't you stay home and answer your phone?"

Arguing with Ginny was a lost cause. She'd seen him as a threat from the beginning, and that wasn't about to change. He whistled for Jinx then headed across the backyard to the carriage house. Ginny must have gotten it wrong. Miriam wouldn't come back north in October.

The first thing he did when he got inside was reach for the phone. He punched the speed dial number then waited as the phone in Florida began to ring.

"Cantwell residence. Leila speaking."

"Leila, it's Rafe. Let me speak to Miriam, please."

"I believe Ms. Miriam is asleep," the nurse said. "May I take a message?"

"I need to talk with her."

"I can't go waking her up. Doctor's orders. She's resting for the trip north."

"That's what I'm calling about, Leila. What's with that trip anyway?"

He could hear Leila breathing on the other end of the line, but she didn't say a word.

"Leila?"

"I'm here."

"You're not going to answer me, are you?"

"Good thinking. Anything you want to know, you'll have to ask Ms. Miriam."

"Is something wrong?"

"It's not for me to say."

"She's doing fine, isn't she?"

"She's ninety years old," Leila said. "There's a limit on how fine she can be."

He managed to get a little bit of travel information out of the woman and was about to hang up when a familiar "hello" broke into their conversation.

"Hang up, you silly woman," Miriam said. "I'm not dead yet."

He laughed despite himself. That statement was pure Miriam Cantwell. "So what's with the trip to New Jersey?" he asked.

"A woman can't come home without everyone asking questions?"

"A Florida woman doesn't come home to New Jersey this time of year, Mir. We both know it. What gives?"

"I'm coming home," she said simply. "That's all you need to know."

The hairs on the back of his neck stood up and saluted. His mother used to say it meant someone was walking over his grave. "Why don't I fly down and we'll talk about it?"

"By the time you got a flight, son, I'd be on my way."

"I can't change your mind?"

"Not even you, Rafael."

"Nobody calls me Rafael but you."

"It's your name, isn't it?" she demanded.

"Even I forget that sometimes."

"Then it's a good thing I'm coming home to remind you."

The next sound he heard was the dial tone in his ear. Once again, Miriam Cantwell managed to get the last word. He'd have to wait until she arrived to find out why she was coming there in the first place.

Jinx settled herself on one of the kitchen chairs while he opened a can of cat food and upended it in her bowl. He yawned, thought about opening a can of something for himself, then decided to hell with it. He'd been awake thirty-six hours, and fatigue was finally catching up with him.

He stripped off his shirt as he made his way toward the bathroom. He was surprised to see he was still in the tux from the night before. That would explain some of the looks he'd been given in McDonald's on the way home. He threw the wrinkled shirt on top of a chair. It slipped and fell across the cradle near the hall and caught on a rough edge of pine. The cradle looked crude to him now, large curves of wood with no subtlety of design or execution.

She wouldn't have liked the cradle, he thought as he moved past the unfinished piece. It was too much like him.

Molly spent much of the day trying to nap. Feeling like Goldilocks, she wandered from room to room, searching for the right place to settle down, but sleep still eluded her. Too much autumn sun streaming through the bedroom window. The chair in the sewing room was too hard and uncomfortable. She tried to curl up on the living room sofa, but every time she closed her eyes she saw Rafe and felt his hands, smelled his skin, tasted his—

She'd made a mistake, that's what she'd done. It was so clear to her now that she wanted to laugh. She should have pushed reality away, as any other sane woman would have done, and followed her heart.

Jessy had followed her heart. She'd had the guts to put her heart out there on the firing line and take her chances. That was more than Molly had ever done in her entire life. Maybe it was because she'd grown up in the midst of chaos, but she'd gone out of her way to avoid turmoil ever since. She chose the safe road, the sure thing, the path of least disappointment.

That's why you chose Robert, isn't it, and see where that got you.

"I know," she said out loud. She'd been thinking about that ever since he walked out. Robert had been the safe choice, the sure thing, and he'd left her and hadn't looked back. For weeks now she'd taken that as proof of her own inadequacy. She'd chosen the right man; she simply hadn't figured out a way to be the right woman for him. It never occurred to her that she'd chosen Robert with her head instead of her heart, that she'd been willing to overlook the lack of passion between them as long as she got security in return—which was a good way to end up with nothing at all.

This time it was her heart that was telling her what to do, to take a chance for once in her life, even though the odds were stacked against her.

She had nothing to lose. Her husband was in love with another woman. She was pregnant and about to be divorced, living in a house she couldn't afford, reduced to renting out a room to a boarder who wasn't afraid to take a chance with her life. Why not risk a broken heart?

It couldn't hurt more than being alone.

Rafe couldn't sleep. Every time he closed his eyes, he saw Molly's sad eyes and distant smile.

A fool, that's what he was. A goddamn fool of the worst kind. When he had the chance to tell her what was in his heart, he'd told her to have her chimney inspected instead. She knew he wanted her but she had no idea he worshipped her.

He'd never had that trouble with Karen. For a time, when things were good between them, the words had come easily to him. Saying what was in his heart had been as natural as breathing.

He should have done that with Molly. He should have told her with words what he'd tried to tell her with his body. The sight of her naked had obliterated everything but the call of the blood. When she pushed him away from her, there had been a moment when instinct came close to overpowering civilized behavior. It took a superhuman effort to reclaim his self-control.

But there was no reason he couldn't have loved her with words.

He'd tried to call her a little while ago, but she wasn't answering her phone. He'd listened to her voice on the machine then hung up without leaving a message. What he needed to say to her could only be said face-to-face, breath to breath.

Heart to heart.

He needed to say it now before it was too late.

• • •

Molly pulled into a 7-Eleven just south of Stockton to ask for directions. The roads were narrow and unlighted. The street signs were almost impossible to read. She'd been circling around for almost an hour, trying to find Fallen Rock Road with no luck. She wished she had a house number or a cross street, something to make her believe she wasn't here on a wild-goose chase.

He might not even be home, Molly. Did you ever think of that?

No, she hadn't thought of that and she wasn't going to think of it now. It was ten o'clock at night, and she was in the middle of nowhere. He had to be home. She refused to consider any other possibility. She couldn't imagine mustering up her courage to do this a second time.

The clerk, a tall young woman with waist-length chestnut hair, wrinkled her nose. "Fallen Rock Road? I don't think I've ever heard of it." She began to ring up Molly's purchases. Molly prayed the condoms would be camouflaged by the tissues, newspaper, and toothbrush. "Why don't you call for directions?"

"No!" Molly's cheeks flamed. "I mean, I don't know the phone number."

"I know Fallen Rock Road," said the man on line behind Molly. "It's a private road up past the schoolhouse on the right."

"A private road?" Molly said. "You must be mistaken." A handyman who lived on a private road? Not very likely.

"I'm sure it's a private road," the man went on. "When the old lady was around, they had a guard posted."

Old lady? Guards? She must have the street name

wrong. None of this sounded like Rafe. "Thank you," she said. "I might have made a mistake."

"No price code," the clerk murmured, flipping over the package. She turned toward the back of the store. "Sal, I need a price on Trojans lubricated." She looked again at the package. "The three-pack."

A hush fell across the 7-Eleven. Molly wanted to dig a hole through the linoleum with her bare hands and throw herself headlong into it.

"I'm sure these aren't for you," the clerk said after Sal called back a price. "You're way past needing these now, aren't you, honey?" She leaned over and patted Molly's belly as if it were a particularly friendly puppy.

Molly couldn't manage more than a nod of her head. Everyone around her was chuckling at the thought of an obviously pregnant woman needing condoms. She gave the clerk a ten-dollar bill then ran from the store without waiting for the change. She could live without that extra $2.37.

"Okay, that's it," she said as she slipped behind the wheel. If she'd been looking for a sign that she and Rafe were meant to be, this was it. They weren't. She couldn't find his street. She'd been humiliated at the local 7-Eleven. Even the most bright-eyed optimist would have to admit those were undeniable signs that she was headed down the wrong path.

She turned the key and flipped on her headlights. Her tires crunched over the gravel as she turned right out of the parking lot and headed for Stockton.

She told herself she was just looking for Fallen Rock Road to satisfy her curiosity. She'd find the schoolhouse, locate the road, then turn around and drive home again. Simply an intellectual exercise in navigation, that's all it was. She just wanted to prove to herself that she could do it.

The schoolhouse loomed in the darkness. It dated back to the early nineteenth century and was built almost flush with the road. You could open your car door and step inside the classroom without ever touching the street. Fallen Rock Road was right behind it.

Okay, you've found it. Now turn around and go home.

She signaled right then turned onto Fallen Rock Road. Her headlights reflected off some water in the drainage ditches on either side of the road. She couldn't make a U-turn without dropping a wheel into one of them, so she continued driving up the hill. What else could she do? Fallen Rock was a narrow, one-lane road with corkscrew turns that only made sense if the street was closed to regular traffic. She couldn't see beyond the reach of her headlights. The heavy woods on either side of the road soaked up all the moonlight and wouldn't relinquish a ray.

She drove past a turnaround located just beyond a small wooden bridge. She could have easily made her U-turn there. Her Jeep had a small turn radius, and she was a good driver, but she kept driving up the hill. Her heart beat so fast and loud that again she was amazed the baby could sleep through it.

What if he lived with someone? For all she knew he might have a lover and six kids. And who was the old lady that man had mentioned? What on earth was that all about? Maybe he lived with his mother. Maybe he lived with his grandmother.

Hello, Mrs. Garrick. Is your grandson home? I'm here to have sex with him.

A huge stone house appeared at the end of the drive.

She gripped the wheel so tightly it would have taken the Jaws of Life to pry it out of her hands. Electric candles, the kind people used at Christmas, burned at each of the first-story windows. Somehow Rafe didn't strike her as an electric candle kind of guy. A knot formed in the pit of her stomach.

She dimmed her lights and slowed to a crawl so she wouldn't draw any attention to herself.

Burglars do that, too, Molly.

That was too bad. She was faced with a limited number of options. Stealth seemed the lesser of the two evils. She had to remember to tell the cops that, when they came shrieking up the driveway after her. All she wanted now was to turn around and get out of there before Rafe knew what she'd done.

Another structure caught her eye. It looked like a carriage house set toward the back of the property. A single light burned in a second-story window. She slowed to a stop and stared across the wide expanse of yard toward that light. The window was bare. She could see the edge of a plain white lamp shade to the right of the window and the vague outline of a dresser. The walls were painted a very pale sandalwood color.

Rafe's bedroom. She didn't know how she knew but she knew.

This is why you came here, Molly. Are you going to turn away from him a second time?

She turned off the engine. Deep silence surrounded her. She stared up at that window as if it held all the answers she needed.

You can't sit here all night, Molly. Put one foot in front of the other and walk up to the front door.

She climbed out of the car, clutching her purse and

the 7-Eleven bag. She could almost hear her knees knocking together. She could definitely hear the sound her heart made as it slammed over and over against her rib cage. She tried to move lightly across the gravel, but each step sounded like a team of horses. He had to know she was out there. People in Philadelphia probably knew she was out there.

Don't think about it, Molly. Just do it. For once just follow your heart.

What if her heart told her to get back in the Jeep and drive home? What if her heart told her this was the absolutely craziest idea she'd had in her entire life and that she should get out of there before she embarrassed herself so badly she'd never be able to look in the mirror again as long as she lived?

What if her heart was playing tricks on her, making her think she saw Rafe standing not ten feet away from her, watching her with those midnight-sky eyes?

Her breath left her body on the wings of a sigh as he covered the distance between them in a few long strides. He stopped in front of her. She was dizzy from the smell of pine and wet earth and his skin. God, the smell of his skin . . .

"I'm dreaming," she said, reaching out to place the palm of her hand flat against his chest. "I don't want to wake up."

He placed his hand against her left breast, curving his palm around the fullness. Her breath caught, and he smiled.

"It's not a dream," he said, then caught her up in his arms.

She pressed her face against the side of his neck. Of course it was a dream. A beautiful, impossible dream.

He kicked open the front door and carried her inside. The smell of pine filled her head. She saw exposed beams, oatmeal-colored walls hung with vibrant woven blankets and wood carvings, but mostly she saw him. He had a small cleft in his chin. Why hadn't she noticed that before? His face was smooth. There wasn't the hint of stubble anywhere. She wanted to lick his cheek, his chin, his lips.

She rubbed her cheek against his. "You shaved." Robert had been a morning shaver. He'd never particularly cared what happened after dark.

"I didn't want to scratch you."

She touched the tip of her index finger to the cleft in his chin. "You didn't know I was coming here tonight."

"I was on my way to see you."

Whatever resistance remained, whatever tiny hold she still had on good sense, melted like a quick-burning candle.

SIXTEEN

They reached the landing at the top of the stairs.

"You can put me down," Molly said in her lush contralto. "I'm tall and I'm pregnant. That's asking a lot of a man."

"Quiet," he said and then he kissed her. He would have carried her to the ends of the earth and beyond if it meant she wouldn't leave him.

It was a gentle kiss, sweet as spun sugar, sweeter than he thought a kiss could be. She had this way of sighing when he kissed her, a sweet soft rush of breath as their lips met that spun his head around.

He placed her gently on top of his bed.

"A feather bed!"

"You sound surprised."

"This isn't at all what I expected."

"You are," he said. "You're all that I expected and more."

Her eyes glittered with tears, and she looked down at her hands but not before he saw her lips curve into a

smile. He wanted to take credit for each one of those
tears and for that smile, but he knew that pregnancy
heightened a woman's emotions. What she felt tonight
she might not feel tomorrow morning.

This was all they had, all they might ever have. He
knew it, and so did she.

Her beauty stunned him. She leaned back against his
pillows, and her body curved naturally into a pose of
such grace that he was torn between desire and worship.

He bent down over her and reached for the buttons
on her blouse. He heard the sound of her breath as it
caught in her throat. Her eyes locked with his, and she
didn't move or react as he unbuttoned the creamy silk
blouse. She leaned forward slightly to help him slip it
from her body then lay back against the pillow once
again. She wore a lacy bra the color of the palest champagne. He worked the front clasp with two fingers, and
she sighed as he freed her breasts.

The urgency of the night before had been replaced
with slow exploration. He bent low over her, tracing the
contours of her beautiful breasts first with his fingers and
then with his tongue, circling each nipple in turn until
they glistened wet and deep rose.

"The light," she whispered as he eased her jeans over
her belly and hips, and he extinguished it before she
drew her next breath. He could still see her in the faint
glow of moonlight that filtered through his bedroom
window. She had removed her panties and lay before
him, naked and lovelier than any dream of paradise he'd
ever dreamed.

"I don't want to disappoint you," she said as he took
off his own clothes and tossed them in a corner of the
room.

He struggled again to find words to give meaning to all that he was feeling, all that he'd felt for her for so long. "You're beautiful," he said, then kicked himself for the inadequacy of those simple words. "You couldn't disappoint me."

She ducked her head for an instant then once again met his eyes. She gestured toward the bed with a graceful arc of her hand. "I might," she said simply.

He touched her lips with the tip of his index finger. "You couldn't."

She took his hand and kissed it, then held it fast. "Please listen," she said. "I've only been with my husband, and we weren't—" Her face flooded with embarrassment. "We weren't very passionate."

The words he'd struggled to find came to him in that instant, and he started to talk. She was the most sensual, beautiful woman he'd ever known. Her sensuality was deep and true, a result of who she was and not what she'd done along the way. And he wanted her. He would swim an ocean to be with her, scale the highest mountain, walk through fire if that was what it took. He didn't care where she'd been, what she'd done or hadn't done along the way. This moment, who they were together, what they did—that was all that mattered.

She listened to him, her body silhouetted in the moonlight as she sat at the edge of the bed, and then she held out her arms to him.

He approached the bed. Magic was everywhere. She slid her hands around the backs of his thighs and rested her cheek against his belly. His erection leaped at the brush of her hair against him. He saw the way her eyes widened in surprise and he held his breath as she lightly drew her tongue down from his navel to the base of his

penis. She was trembling. So was he. The touch of her
delicate tongue was enough to take him where he needed
to go, but he willed himself to hold back, to make the
moment last.

Forever, if possible.

He'd settle for forever.

He was hard and soft and hot and wet and every shat-
teringly wonderful sensation in between. Her hands
trembled, and he took the condom from her and quickly
put it on. She drew her tongue from tip to base, laughing
softly as he danced to her tune. She'd never known
power like this before. She was in charge of every magnificent inch of his erection. It was hers. She knew it
instinctively. She was ripe with child. Her breasts were
round and full and exquisitely sensitive to his touch. She
felt powerful and generous and more female, more womanly, than she had ever felt in her life.

Life flowed from her fingertips to his. From her lips
to the tip of his erection. From her belly to the universe.
The secrets and mysteries that had eluded her all her life
came clear to her now, and she could only laugh at the
years she'd wasted living only half a life. When it was
right, when the magic held a man and woman in its
thrall, you just had to follow your heart.

She circled him with her tongue then wet her lips.
Somewhere in the distance she heard a low moan but
she couldn't say which one of them had made the sound.
She felt connected to him in every way possible. Tomorrow there would be time enough to worry about
what she'd done and how—tonight there was only soft
skin over hot steel and dreams of heaven.

She explored him with her tongue. She licked every

inch. She worried him gently with her teeth and lips. She stroked him with curious fingers, smiling each time she found a hidden spot of profound pleasure. She pulled him down on the bed and straddled him, running her hands over his broad chest, delighting in the tickle of thick curly hair beneath her palms. She loved everything about his body—the way it looked, the smell of his skin, the rough sound of his breathing when she sucked him deeply into her mouth and slid her tongue along the ridge of his shaft. She had no road map to guide her, no experience to draw upon, only sweet hunger and the overpowering desire to make him happy.

His hand slid down his thigh and came to rest between her legs. His fingers slid through the nest of curls and stroked her gently. She touched his leg and drew back, surprised to find that he was wet where she'd straddled him. Heat filled her, a blend of fierce longing and embarrassment. He knew what she was thinking—somehow he knew—and he took her hand and brought it to his mouth. He licked each finger slowly until she cried out for something she couldn't define but had looked for all her life.

He brought his hand, wet with her juices, to her lips, tracing the seam between top and bottom, urging her to open and taste herself for the first time. Unimaginable. Forbidden. She tasted sweet and salty. She tasted like a woman, like herself, like someone who had only now come to be. She closed her lips around his fingers and sucked them deeply. His guttural moan was her reward. This was a place she'd never thought to go. This was a place she hadn't known existed, this world of pleasure. She wanted to sink into its dark embrace and vanish into ecstasy.

He rolled her gently onto her back, and she lay, thighs open, with her head on his pillow while he worshipped her breasts then kissed his way over the rise of her belly.

"I wish you'd seen me before," she whispered, wanting to please him with the beauty she'd taken for granted up until now. "When I wasn't pregnant and—"

"Juicy," he said. His words brushed soft against her skin, and she laughed. "Like a ripe peach." He liked what he saw, what he felt.

He shifted position as he drew his tongue along the crease of her inner thigh. She began to tremble uncontrollably. She had never wanted anything more than she wanted his mouth against her, and she'd never feared anything more as well.

He urged her to relax. He whispered things, words and thoughts and dreams that turned her into flame. He was extravagant with praise, this wordless man. He made love to her with words first, and then he made love to her with his beautiful lips and tongue.

She cried out at the first touch of his tongue. The shimmering line between pleasure and pain blurred for an instant and she teetered on the edge, not knowing which way she would fall, knowing the fall was inevitable. Somehow he cradled her back with his arms, urging her knees to fall open more completely. She knew how she must look to him, wanton and hungry, unable to do anything but arch her hips up to meet his mouth. He toyed with her, working her center of pleasure with his lips and teeth until she heard herself whimpering incoherent words of surrender and longing. And then he cupped her buttocks and plunged deep inside her and her body molded itself to his tongue, her muscles contracting around him, as shooting stars and comets and meteors flashed in front of her and she exploded into the night sky.

He was stroking her gently when she drifted back down to earth. Looking into his beautiful face was like looking into the face of the sun.

"That was your first time, wasn't it?" he asked.

"I didn't know," she whispered, pressing closer to his warmth. "My friends talked about it, but I thought they were lying."

He was rubbing her belly in slow, sensuous circles that made her shiver with pleasure. He made her glory in every abundant inch.

"I want to hold you in my mouth," she said. "I want to learn how to make you happy."

"You've already made me happy," he said, then claimed her mouth again with his. She tasted herself again, a sweet and smoky taste, and the images it evoked were almost enough to send her hurtling toward the sky.

She slid down his body and drew him into her mouth again, playing, experimenting, glorying in the taste and texture and heat of his passion for her. He cradled her head between his hands, his fingers massaging her scalp, smoothing back her hair when it fell across her face.

"I want to be inside you the first time," he said and again the powerful simplicity of his words sent shock waves through her body.

She went to roll over onto her back, but he stopped her.

"No," he said. "You set the pace."

"I can't," she whispered. "I've never—"

"I want you to be able to see us together," he said, holding her by the hips as he positioned her over him. "This will be easier for you and the baby."

His words charmed and excited her both. The fact that he could see through the fiery haze of passion and remember her comfort only proved the rightness of her choice. He was protecting her in ways even she hadn't thought of.

She felt exposed and vulnerable. Her breasts and belly must look huge from that angle, she thought, but he didn't seem to notice. He caressed her with more tenderness than she had ever known in her life, stroking her between the legs until she felt herself flow again with readiness. The baby filled her body. Wild emotions filled her heart. And yet somehow, in some primal way, she felt emptier, hungrier, more incomplete than she'd ever felt in her life. She needed him. She needed his physical self, to join with him, to bring their bodies together, to somehow become one.

She lifted her hips. He positioned himself. Slowly she lowered her body, unable to control the gasp of shock, as she felt him pressing against her labia for entry. He was so large, so hard, so powerful. Nothing had prepared her for his glorious self. Nothing in her past had even hinted at such wonder.

"Ride me slowly," he urged. "We have all night." She could take him an inch at a time, settle her body around him, let her muscles fit themselves to his size and splendor, until they were fully joined. His control was staggering. He balanced himself on one elbow, leaning forward to caress her nipples with his lips and tongue.

After awhile all the disparate sensations ran together in one warm run of free-flowing honey. He filled her as completely as a man could fill a woman, and when her muscles rippled around him, she thought she would die from the sweet pain of pure joy. She rocked against him then rose up on her knees, only to slide down again, welcoming him deep inside her body once more. She could do this forever, she thought. This was why she'd been put on earth, for this miraculous connection, this utter ecstasy.

Finally he couldn't hold back any longer and he rolled her onto her back and settled himself between her legs. He plunged deeply into her, straight to her soul.

And he never stopped looking at her, never once broke the connection between them. She saw herself the way he saw her, as a woman worth loving. A woman with the capacity to give and receive pleasure.

She saw herself as a woman for the very first time.

He was lost in the lush splendor of her body. Her body molded itself to his length with a silky, sinuous strength that brought him instantly to the edge.

You couldn't live a dream without courting madness. That was part of the gamble, the dangerous appeal of making fantasy come true. She loved him with a heart-wrenching combination of shyness and abandon. Coupled with her uncommon beauty and his good fortune, it was an experience matched only by the gods in the heavens.

His rhythm grew faster, more urgent, and she matched it with a rhythm all her own. Their rhythm, that's what it was. A rhythm that hadn't existed before they found each other. He felt the slightest rippling movement from the baby, and for a moment he wished he could turn back the clock and claim the baby as his own. He wanted to erase her husband's existence, banish all prior claim to her body. He could love this child. In a way he already did. He wondered if Molly knew that, if she had any idea.

He could love her the way she dreamed of being loved if she would give him the chance.

He wondered if she knew that he'd fallen in love with her the first moment he saw her—no, from the first moment he heard her cry of pain piercing the gentle suburban afternoon air. She'd touched his heart, the heart he thought had died the day Karen and Sarah walked out the door and left him behind. The moment he saw Molly in the foyer of her empty house his heart thundered back to life and fell at her feet.

It belonged to her now. Everything he was or would be, everything he would ever accomplish or dream of doing was hers.

She cried out his name as she climaxed, and that was all he needed to bring him home where he belonged.

He talked after making love. He talked and he held her close, held her as if the afterglow were every bit as important as all that had come before. She discovered that it was easy to let yourself sink deeply into contentment and never come up for air.

They lay together face-to-face. Her belly pushed up against his as if they'd slept together every night for years. Even the baby seemed happy and serene. She had never been that comfortable with Robert. After sex he'd always leaped from bed, eager to shower and get on with it. She'd come to dread making love with Robert because the loneliness she felt when it was over came close to breaking her heart. He hated the earthy messiness of sex. He never said as much, but she'd known by the way he recoiled at anything approximating body fluids.

She'd always thought she hated it, too, until tonight.

It was so different with Rafe. He didn't leave. He just held her close. She closed her eyes and let herself pretend, just for a moment, that this was real. That it meant as much to him as it did to her. That there could be a future.

It was nearly midnight when the baby woke her. She sat up, rubbing her belly, trying to place herself in time and space. The night came rushing back at her in vivid sensual detail and the urge to run was overwhelming. Quietly she swung her legs from the bed and gathered up her clothes from the floor where she'd tossed them hours ago when passion ruled. This was how it was done, wasn't it? You gathered up your things and disappeared before it all got awkward.

She didn't want to see his face the morning after, that look of apprehension and regret she knew would be there. And who could blame him? She'd been every bit as aggressive as Jessy had with Spencer, and with about as much of a chance for a happily-ever-after ending.

The best she could do was get out with her dignity still intact.

He slept deeply. His breathing was regular. He hadn't heard a thing.

She slipped out into the narrow hallway and quickly dressed. The house was chilly, and she shivered. It had been so warm in his arms. That bed had been a haven. For a little while she'd had the feeling that she'd finally found what she'd been searching for, that elusive place called home. How easy it would be to climb back into that warm bed and curl up next to him, pressing her nose against the warm spot under his arm, and pretend she belonged there, that she'd never belonged anywhere else, that sex and love were the same thing.

She had to leave while she still had the nerve.

She took the stairs on the inside, praying they wouldn't creak. She didn't want to have to explain herself to Rafe. She wasn't sure she could. The only thing she knew for sure was that she'd rather die than be sent home the way Jessy had been. Jessy had tried to put a good face on it, but Molly hadn't been fooled. Spencer had politely given her the boot, the Princeton equivalent of cab fare home.

For the life of her she couldn't remember anything about the setup of the main floor of the carriage house. She stood at the foot of the stairs, trying to get her bearings, then took a step to the right and cracked her toe against something hard.

"Damn!" she murmured, hopping about on one foot. Who would stick a road block in the middle of the traffic pattern? She bent down to inspect the culprit. A white shirt was draped across whatever it was. She picked it up and saw that it was the same dress shirt Rafe had worn to the dinner dance Saturday night. Without thinking she pressed it to her face and inhaled. His scent lingered in the fabric and mingled with the evocative smell of raw pine. A work in progress, she thought, running her hand along the rough curves and angles. So he wasn't just a handyman.

Curious, she knelt down to take a better look. The breath left her body in a sharp rush of emotion. A cradle. It was unfinished, more a promise of things to come than anywhere near the final article, but the sweet grace of it was unmistakable.

And so was its intent.

In the faint wash of waning moonlight she saw her

initials. They were etched very lightly near the arc of the runner, a graceful, looping MKC that looked wonderful all by itself.

She covered her face with his shirt and cried as if her heart were breaking.

Rafe woke up the second she left his bed. He lay still, listening. He heard her moving quietly about the room, then the sound of her footsteps as she walked down the hallway. The bathroom, he figured, and he settled back against his pillow to wait for her return. Except she didn't. He listened for sounds of running water or the toilet flushing, but everything was quiet.

He had a sudden, terrifying image of her unconscious on the bathroom floor, her hair red as blood against the white tiles. The image was so real to him that his palms began to sweat. The hallway was pitch black. She didn't know the first thing about the layout of the place. She could have stumbled and fallen, hit her head, hurt the baby somehow—

He was out of bed in a flash and into the hallway. No sign of her there or in the bathroom. He checked the small office at the opposite end, but the door was still closed. A sound caught his attention. Soft, almost inaudible, but somehow it reached him. He looked over the railing and saw Molly bent low over the cradle.

A moment later he was by her side. He noticed she was dressed. Her car keys lay at her feet.

She tried to push him away, but he wouldn't go.

"It's not finished yet," he said as she struggled to contain her tears. "I wasn't sure you'd want it." Or him, for that matter.

When she looked up and he saw the expression in her

eyes, he felt as if God had handed him a second chance at life.

"You did this for me." It was a statement of wonder, the way she said it.

He nodded. The cradle spoke for him.

She held his face between her hands and looked at him for the longest time.

He had the sense of being in a dream, that time and space no longer had any power over them.

"Come back to bed," he said, brushing her hair off her face. "You need your sleep."

There was a moment after he said that when he might have lost her. He could feel the chill whisper of wind between them as she considered walking out the door and back into her old life. He would never know what changed her mind and he would never ask. All he knew was that when she put her hand in his, he had everything in life he'd ever wanted and more.

SEVENTEEN

~❦~

The room was cold, and he gave her a T-shirt to sleep in, soft, well-washed cotton that clung to her breasts and belly like a second skin.

"I'm stretching it out of shape," she said with an embarrassed laugh.

He kissed her belly then each breast in turn. "It's never looked better."

He brought her a pot of hot tea and a platter of bagels with cream cheese, and they feasted in the middle of his big feather bed. She licked crumbs off his chest with the tip of her tongue. He kissed her while her mouth was still warm from tea.

He made her feel like a goddess. With every look, every touch, every word, her heart seemed to swell with emotions she'd never before experienced. Passionate, unruly emotions like love and desire and envy. Some woman had been his wife. She'd lain in his arms night after night, just like this.

You were a fool to leave, Molly thought as he drifted

off to sleep next to her. *How could you leave a man like this?*

She lay quietly, listening to the night sounds outside the open window and the steady metronome beat of his heart. She smelled the river, that earthy wet smell of life, and the sharp scent of pine. The air was crisp and just cool enough to warrant the down comforter Rafe had placed over them. It was a thick, luxurious comforter, but it couldn't compare to the warmth of his body close to hers.

Nothing was the way she'd expected it to be. She'd expected a shack somewhere near the river, with dirty dishes on the floor and a cot pushed up against the wall, but this was a real home—a man's home, sensual in a way that made her dizzy. The walls had texture to them, not just a layer of paint. Wooden surfaces gleamed. Nothing seemed planned, but everything was exactly the way it should be. As solid and real and masculine as he was.

It felt more like home than anyplace she'd ever been in her life.

She got up twice during the night to use the bathroom. Both times Rafe woke up and turned on the light so she could find her way through the unfamiliar darkness. When she woke up the third time, sunlight splashed through the windows, and Rafe was gone.

Her first instinct was to panic the way she used to in the mall when Robert disappeared, but she forced herself to keep her imagination under control.

Rafe's side of the bed was still warm. He was probably in the shower, she told herself as she swung her feet to the polished wooden floor. This was his house. He wouldn't walk out on her there.

Robert did. He walked out of his house and left you with the mortgage.

Rafe was nothing like her husband. If she'd had any doubts about that at all, last night had erased them. Still, her feelings of abandonment ran deep. She peered out the window and almost cried with relief when she saw his truck parked at the top of the drive, not far from where she'd left her Jeep.

He could leave the room without leaving her life. She had to remember that.

She took a quick shower and was surprised he didn't join her. A big pile of white oversized towels rested on a series of heavy pine shelves next to the bath. She wrapped herself in one, amazed by the level of comfort he obviously enjoyed. She didn't want to poke around in his linen closet looking for a hair dryer so she braided her hair instead, then finished getting dressed.

He'd said he owned his own place, and she'd assumed he meant a handyman's special. She was half right. This carriage house was certainly special. She couldn't help but wonder how he managed to pay for it. Nothing about him suggested great wealth. He drove a beat-up old truck. He wore jeans more often than not. He said he'd grown up on a failing Montana ranch where electricity was as capricious as the weather. He did yard work and deck repairs to repay his moral obligation when he couldn't repay Robert's deposit money.

Yet he lived on an estate, within shouting distance of the beautiful main house with the candles glowing in each and every ground-floor window. He couldn't possibly own the main house. The idea almost made her laugh out loud. No man who owned a house like that would push around a lawn mower at Princeton Manor once a week.

Her clothes were draped over the chair in the corner of the bedroom. The chair was a wonder of bent wood and intricately carved legs. She ran her hands along the elegant curves and instantly knew that it was Rafe's work. There was so much she wanted to learn about him, so much she wanted to know. For the first time in her life, she felt of one piece—body and soul and heart.

She hurried downstairs, eager to see him in the light of day. The first morning they'd spend together as lovers. She felt shy and wild and hopeful and terrified and everything in between. She wanted to see his magnificent face, the look in his deep blue eyes when he saw her, hear his voice.

He wasn't in the great room or the kitchen or the downstairs bath. She looked out the back window. He wasn't on the deck or in the yard. She let herself out the front door and scanned the area. Not a sign of him anywhere. Their vehicles were still parked side by side where they'd left them last night. She looked toward the main house. Two of the windows were open. So was the back door. A large, sleepy-looking cat sat on the top step, lapping milk from a white bowl.

Rafe, she thought, and started toward the main house.

"If you're going to look at me like that, sonny, you can hightail it back to your house and leave me alone. If I wanted crying, I could go back to Florida. That's all they do down there." Miriam leaned back against her pillows and closed her eyes.

"Gimme a break, will you, Miriam?" he said as he paced her bedroom. "You come home unexpectedly then drop a bomb on my head. What do you want me to do—tell jokes?"

"I'm ninety years old. You can't tell me you're surprised."

He was surprised, though. Somehow he never thought Miriam would die. She was mother, grandmother, conscience, and friend. She'd thrown him a lifeline when he was drowning, and now that she was in trouble, she told him to back off.

"Somehow I thought you'd find a way around this," he said.

"Poor boy," she said, her eyes still tightly closed. "You always did have trouble with endings, didn't you?"

He couldn't argue the observation. He'd hated endings since he was a little boy and his mother faked one suicide attempt after another, right up until the morning she sent him off to school then put a gun in her mouth and blew her brains out.

He heard the carriage house door swing open then closed. Miriam heard it, too. "What's going on?" she demanded. "Do you have someone in your house?"

"Yes," he said.

She opened one eye. "A woman?"

"Yes," he said again.

She opened the other eye. "Well, it's about time."

"You didn't come home from Florida to supervise my personal life."

"No," she said. "It's an unexpected dividend."

"Rafe?" Molly's voice floated up to them. "Are you in here?"

He thought of that old movie *When Worlds Collide*. "Upstairs," he called out. "First room on your right."

Miriam had closed her eyes again. She looked so frail and still that he found himself staring at her chest to see if she was breathing. He heard Molly's steps as she approached.

"You were gone when I woke up," Molly said as she appeared in the doorway. "I was afraid I'd—" She stopped abruptly as her gaze scanned the room.

"Miriam," he said, "there's someone I'd like you to meet."

Miriam didn't stir.

He leaned forward. "Miriam, I want you to meet Molly Chamberlain."

"Rafe," Molly said quietly, "please don't wake her up."

"She was awake a second ago," he said, peering closely at Miriam.

"She's sound asleep," Molly said. "Don't disturb her."

They stepped out into the hallway. "She came home from Florida a few hours ago," he said. "I think she's exhausted from the trip."

"I would imagine," Molly said as they moved toward the center staircase. "Who is she?"

"She owns the house and most of the land."

"You bought the carriage house from her?"

"And a few acres of land."

"That's an odd thing to do, splitting up property like this. She must be very fond of you."

"I helped out around the house."

"Chores? Yard work?"

"A little of everything." He put his arm around her shoulders. "Come on," he said. "Let's grab some breakfast before it gets any later."

Molly looked at him as if she didn't quite believe that was the whole story, and she was right. It wasn't even close.

They went back to the carriage house and made breakfast together. She was comfortable in the kitchen. For some reason that surprised him. She worked easily and seemed to know what he needed before he knew himself.

"How did you know I needed the milk?" he asked.

"Because I needed the milk," she said, punching him lightly on the arm. "I'm pregnant, remember?"

Sunshine spilled through the windows and seemed to find its focus on her beautiful face. Why should the sun be any different? That was where he found his focus, too.

"You don't have to leave," he said when she finally slid behind the wheel of her Jeep.

"I have a manuscript to read, phone calls to make," she said. "I really have to get home."

"I have a phone."

"You don't have a manuscript."

"I'll write one," he said. "Give me a year or two." He leaned in the window and kissed her. "You're coming back tonight."

"I am?"

"Yes." He kissed her again.

"Rafe, I—"

"We've wasted enough time apart, Molly. I don't want to waste any more of my life without you."

As the days passed, the two-story colonial in Princeton Manor ceased to exist for Molly. Piece by piece she moved her life to Rafe's carriage house by the river.

She worked at her house, made her phone calls, but

she didn't live there. It was nothing more than a glorified office.

Jessy was working round-the-clock hours. She looked pale and exhausted, which was probably the usual state for a first-year resident, but Molly knew it was more than that. She'd come home one Sunday evening after spending the weekend with Rafe to find Spencer's car next to Jessy's in the driveway. She'd hesitated, not wanting to intrude, then realized how foolish she was being. This was her house, after all. If they were having sex, they'd be smart enough to have it in Jessy's room where they wouldn't be interrupted. At least she hoped they would be.

She needn't have worried. Jessy stood by the window, choking back tears, while Spencer sat on the arm of the sofa. Jessy's shoulders were slumped with despair. His posture was downright military. Her heart went out to both of them. There were no easy answers in life. That fact became more clear to her with every day that passed.

If someone had told her a year ago that she would be pregnant with Robert's child but practically living with another man, she would have suggested serious therapy. But there she was.

Her path hadn't crossed again with Miriam Cantwell's. Not that she'd imagined it would. Rafe certainly didn't know her neighbors, and there was no reason why he'd even want to. Still, she found herself more curious about that relationship than the situation should have warranted. He seemed very concerned about the woman, almost familial when he talked about her. Actually he'd told her little about his life, and she hadn't pressed him for details. He was content with the bare-bones version of her own childhood and teenage years, and she was glad. The past had never had much of a hold on her. She would be very glad to let it go in favor of a future she could call her own.

Every now and again Rafe asked her about the progress of her divorce, and her answer was always the same: no progress at all. The strange thing was she didn't care. Robert and the divorce seemed part of somebody else's life. The only things that were real to her were the baby and Rafe. She increased her workload and found herself enjoying the process more than she had in a long time. She also enjoyed the marked increase in her income. Her focus was clearer, her concentration sharper.

Life was good, and she was intensely grateful.

She hoped it would last forever.

"Dr. Wyatt."

Jessy jumped at the sound of Dr. Cirone's voice behind her left shoulder. "I'm sorry," she said, struggling to bring her mind into focus. "You were saying?"

The assembled doctors and students stared at her as if she'd strolled into the room buck naked. Even the patient, a hugely pregnant woman in her mid-forties, was staring at her.

"We're waiting for you to say something, Doctor." Cirone's voice held a sharp tone of censure that she knew was only a harbinger of things to come. "Mrs. Hughes is complaining of swollen limbs and dizziness."

Her mind was utterly blank. Swollen limbs . . . dizziness . . . swollen limbs . . . what did any of this have to do with her? She couldn't find the connection. All she heard was the rush of air inside her head as everything went black.

"I'm so sorry," she said later on as Molly drove her home. "They shouldn't have called you. I could drive myself home."

"Have you looked in the mirror?" Molly asked, glancing at her when they came to a stoplight. "You look like you're ready to pass out again."

"I'm fine," Jessy said. She'd looked at herself in the bathroom mirror before they left the hospital, and the sight had put the fear of God into her.

"Sure you are," said Molly, "and I'm still a size six."

Jessy hunkered down lower in the passenger seat. She wished she could close her eyes and make everything go away. "I'm not much in the mood to talk."

"Neither am I, but I'm in the mood to ask a few questions. What's going on, Jess? What's wrong with you?"

"Nothing's wrong with me that a good night's sleep won't cure." She summoned up a smile. "That and a quart of Ben and Jerry's."

"Are you sick?"

"Sick?" She laughed. "Of course not. Where'd you get that idea?"

Molly leaned over and flipped down the sun visor so that Jessy was eyeball to eyeball with her own reflection. "Do you still have to ask that question?"

"I'm not sick," Jessy repeated. Talking seemed to take every ounce of energy she had.

"I don't believe you," Molly said as they were waved

through the gates into Princeton Meadow. "If you're not sick, then what are you?"

Jessy turned and looked straight at Molly Chamberlain. "I'm pregnant."

Molly stared at her as if she were speaking in tongues, but Jessy didn't care. It felt so good to say it finally, to let the terrible secret out into the light.

"I'm pregnant," she said again, beginning to laugh. "Can you imagine that? I spend half my life lecturing young girls about taking responsibility, and look what happened to me." Her voice shook on the last word, but she refused to cry.

Molly said nothing. She looked straight ahead as she made the turn onto Lilac Hill Road then pulled into her driveway.

"It's Spencer's, isn't it?" she said when they were alone in the house.

"Yes, it's Spencer's." She wasn't going to deny it. Truth was, she wanted to shout it from the rooftops.

"Does he know?"

She nodded. "I told him last week."

"The day I interrupted the two of you?"

She nodded again. "It wasn't our finest hour."

"He didn't take it very well?"

"He wants to marry me."

Molly sank onto the arm of the living room sofa. "Say that again."

"He wants to marry me."

"And what did you tell him?"

She wrapped her arms around her middle to keep from breaking apart. "I told him to go to hell."

"I thought you loved him."

"I do," she said. "But it's just not enough anymore."

Life had played a nasty little trick on her, and she didn't mean the pregnancy. She'd told herself she could be content with whatever little bit of him life threw her way, but she'd been wrong. She wanted everything. She didn't just want his body, she wanted his heart. She didn't want a wedding ring, she wanted a marriage.

She didn't just want a baby, she wanted a family.

She might as well wish for the stars, because she had a better chance of dancing on the rings of Saturn than finding any of those things with Spencer.

EIGHTEEN

❦

"I know what you're doing," Miriam Cantwell said to Rafe one morning a few weeks after she returned to New Jersey. "You're keeping her away from me."

"You're delusional," Rafe said as he repaired the window frame nearest to her bed. "I think the cold weather's rattling your brain."

"You have no respect for age," she said in the tart tone of voice that put fear in the hearts of hired help from one side of the state to the other. "Just wait until your old bones are feeling the cold. Then you'll know."

"There's nothing wrong with you that getting out of that bed wouldn't cure," Rafe said as he pried away a chunk of dried paint. "You're getting soft."

"I'm old," Miriam said. "I'm entitled."

"I don't want to hear it," Rafe said. "I've never known you to be a quitter."

"You've never known me to be dying before," Miriam shot back.

"You're not dying," he said as he pounded a nail

into the right side of the window frame. "I didn't hear the doctor say anything about dying."

"He said it, son. You just didn't want to hear it."

She was right. He didn't want to hear it. His life was perfect, or damn close to it. He wouldn't allow Miriam to die. It wasn't part of his plan.

"I suppose now you'll tell me you're not getting paranoid on me," he said, reaching for a chisel. "That stuff about keeping Molly away from you is a boatload of crap."

"I'm merely making an observation."

"You go to sleep earlier these days, Miriam. Your schedule doesn't cross with Molly's."

"I wasn't born yesterday," Miriam said.

He grinned at her. "That's for damn sure."

"I worry about you," Miriam said. "Here I spend my time praying you'll find someone to love, and you go and take up with a pregnant married woman."

"She's getting a divorce," Rafe said. It was old territory.

"She's still pregnant."

"I know," he said, "and it's not a problem." He found himself awed by the miracle happening inside Molly's beautiful body. He felt privileged that she allowed him to be a small part of it.

And he'd be lying if he said there weren't times when he wished they both belonged to him.

"She's going to hurt you," Miriam said in her most uppercrust tone of voice. "You mark my words, it isn't over with her husband yet."

"It's over," Rafe said, reaching for a screwdriver. "He's in love with someone else."

"And what about your Molly?" Miriam asked. "Who does she love?"

"That's none of your business," he said.

"Are you afraid of the answer, son?"

A man's voice rumbled up from the floorboards. Rafe had never been more grateful for an interruption. They'd crossed over into dangerous territory, a place he'd been avoiding from the day he met Molly.

"Dr. Van Lieuw is here," Miriam said.

"Nothing wrong with your ears," Rafe said, forcing himself to shift gears. "I'm telling you, you're healthier than I am."

"If I am, then you'd better write your will."

Rafe was still chuckling when he stepped out into the hallway to give Miriam and the doctor some privacy. Miriam had been born to money and privilege. She'd never known what it was like to wonder where her next meal was coming from. The Cantwells were one of New Jersey's founding families, with a proud history as long as his arm. Rafe had spent enough time working in rich people's houses to know how isolating wealth and lineage could be. It was a testament to Miriam's expansive heart that she'd never let her background separate her from the rest of the human race.

He was checking the sash on one of the hallway windows when Dr. Van Lieuw left her room.

"She's doing great, isn't she?" Rafe asked as the doctor approached him. "I mean, look at her. She's awake, alert, eating well."

Van Lieuw didn't rise to the bait. "Nothing has changed, Rafe. Her heart is very weak. I don't know what's keeping her with us."

Rafe did. Miriam wasn't ready to go yet. He'd seen

the endless stream of lawyers coming and going as she took care of the details that surrounded the end of a woman's life. One of those esteemed attorneys had pointed out to Miriam that she could have accomplished the same thing from her comfortable house in sunny Florida, but she was determined to die at home, in the place where she'd been born. She spent endless hours on the telephone, calling old friends and relatives, having her say, getting things off her chest, reassuring them that they'd be well taken care of after she was gone. She'd have him married off to a vestal virgin, if she had her way.

He hated the whole goddamn thing. He hated the fact that Miriam was right. He had been keeping the two women in his life apart. Molly was his future. Miriam knew all the secrets of his past. If he brought them together, he was afraid he might lose them both.

The November rains showed up right on schedule. It seemed to Molly that she hadn't seen the sun in weeks.

"I don't like you making the drive home in this weather," Rafe said one Monday morning as he walked her outside to her Jeep. "Why don't you stay?"

"You know why," she said, rising up on tiptoe to kiss him. "I'd never get my work done if I stayed here." She'd climb up into that feather bed and never climb back down.

He said he understood, but she wasn't entirely convinced. She wasn't sure she understood the dynamics herself, and they were her dynamics. She felt as if she and Rafe existed someplace apart from the real world: a place where Robert and the progress of her divorce meant nothing to her, where her big beautiful house on

Lilac Hill was only an assemblage of wood and stone and plasterboard, and where they'd elected a governor last week, and she hadn't even realized it was Election Day.

They kissed good-bye three times, and each time she promised she would drive carefully.

"I'm going to drive you from now on," he said as she started the engine.

"We'll talk about it."

"In the car," he said, "when I'm driving you back here."

She smiled all the way home. She was still smiling as she replayed the string of messages on her answering machine. One, in particular, caught her interest, and she returned the call immediately.

"This is Molly Chamberlain, Annie," she said to Spencer's assistant. "I'm returning Mr. Mackenzie's call."

"Good morning, Mrs. Chamberlain," Annie said. "Would you be available for a two o'clock meeting today with Mr. Mackenzie?"

In the past Spencer had made these phone calls himself. Molly felt mildly put out as she agreed to the time. Nothing had been the same since the night of the dinnerdance. The casual phone calls had stopped. No more chats about mutual friends and acquaintances. She wasn't sure if he avoided her in order to avoid Jessy or if he realized she was involved with Rafe. Either way, she missed their conversations.

Spencer ushered her into his office at the stroke of two.

"Thanks for coming by on such short notice, Molly."

He looked vaguely uncomfortable, and she noticed he had difficulty meeting her eyes.

Molly took her usual seat and crossed her legs. Another few weeks, and that simple gesture would be a thing of the past. "So what's this about?"

He winced. "You know, don't you?"

"That you and Jessy slept together or that she's pregnant?"

He let out a long, slow breath. "I asked her to marry me."

"She told me that, too."

"Then you know what her answer was."

"She's not a fool, Spencer. She knows you don't love her."

"She told you that?"

"She didn't have to. I saw her face."

Spencer dragged a hand through his perfectly barbered hair. "I wasn't cruel to her, Molly. That's what you're thinking, isn't it?"

"You have no idea what I'm thinking, Spencer."

"I don't want to hurt her."

"And I don't want to hear this," she said. "It's between you and Jessy." She stood up. "If this is all you wanted—"

"Sit down," he said.

She arched a brow. "Excuse me?"

"Please sit down," he amended. "This is business."

She didn't like his tone of voice, not one bit. "Let me guess," she said, sitting back down. "Robert's changed his mind about the divorce. He loves me madly and wants me back."

"You're half-right."

"What?" Her fingers curved around the arms of the chair.

"He doesn't want you back, but he does want the divorce."

"That's not exactly news, Spencer."

"He wants it *now*," Spencer said, fiddling with a Montblanc fountain pen. The shiny golden nib twinkled in the lamplight.

"Now?" She sounded like a pregnant parrot.

"As in *right now*."

"I'm not the one who's been incommunicado," she said, hearing her voice rise in distress. "Robert's the one who's been delaying things."

"Not anymore," Spencer said, watching her closely. "He suggested that the two of you fly down to Santo Domingo and get it over with in a weekend."

Her heart was pounding so fast that it frightened her. "Are you talking about one of those quickie divorces?"

"That's what I'm talking about." He leaned forward and gave her one of those serious-young-attorney looks that Robert had been born wearing. "He wants out right now, Molly, and he's willing to pay for the privilege."

She flinched. "He'll pay for the privilege of getting rid of me faster?"

"If that's the way you want to put it, yes."

The information buzzed around in her skull like a wayward housefly. She waited for a thought, a fragment of a thought, to form, but there was only that damned buzzing fly.

Spencer went on, spitting out information like one of those old ticker-tape machines: Robert was sorry for putting her through such misery. He wanted to make amends. She could keep the house. He would support the baby in every way, share joint custody—

Joint custody.

There it was, the knife hidden inside those sweet promises.

"No," she said, rousing from her stupor. "I won't share custody with him."

Spencer looked shocked. "This is a very generous offer, Molly. He's giving you everything you could possibly want, including a quick divorce. Why won't you share custody?"

"Because he doesn't deserve to be part of the baby's life, that's why. He walked out on us. He made the decision, now he has to live with it."

"He's the child's father, isn't he?"

"That's an accident of biology, nothing more."

Spencer flinched. "That's all you think fatherhood is?"

"That's all I think fatherhood is to him."

"Go home and think about it," Spencer advised in one of those phony soothing voices television announcers used. "I'm sure you'll see that this is the deal we've been waiting for."

"I don't want the house either," she said, her temper rising. "I don't even care about the divorce. I can wait for the State of New Jersey to get around to it."

"You're being irrational."

"You're crossing the line, Spencer," she warned.

"Listen to me," he said. "He's the baby's father. You can't cut him out of the child's life."

She was so angry her right lower eyelid began to twitch. "He cut us out of his life. I can return the favor. He's the one who wanted out, not me. He's the one who hasn't so much as asked how my pregnancy is progressing.''

"You sound as if you don't want the divorce," Spencer said, "as if you want him back."

"That's not what I said."

"These are dream terms, Molly. Normally I'm wary of taking divorce cases out of the country, but it seems to me you'd benefit greatly from accepting his terms."

She stood up. Adrenaline made it impossible to stay seated. She felt turbocharged. "Yes, I want the divorce, but I'm not going to barter away my child to get it."

"I think you're making a mistake, Molly. This would solve all of your problems."

"Right," she snapped, almost trembling with anger, "and what would it do for my baby? Do you really think I'm going to give joint custody to a man who walked out on me right after I told him I was pregnant with his child? Think again, Spencer. That's not about to happen."

She slammed the door so hard that Annie came in to make sure Spencer was okay.

"I'm fine," he said. "Mrs. Chamberlain was a bit upset."

"A bit?" Annie lingered in the doorway.

"No details," he said, "so you might as well go back to your desk."

Annie mumbled something and closed the door softly behind her.

You really blew it this time, Mackenzie. She hates you right now almost as much as she hates her husband.

He swiveled his chair around and watched as she made her way across the street to the parking lot. Pregnant, and she still walked like a dancer. He'd never seen a woman with a more graceful, provocative walk than Molly Chamberlain's. There'd been a time when he'd spent many hours replaying that walk in his mind.

When had he stopped doing that? He couldn't remember. It seemed as though one morning he woke up and Molly Chamberlain was a client and friend, nothing more. He could finally admit she had never offered more.

Jessy's serious little face popped into his mind. He tried to turn her away, but she had this habit of pushing past his defenses.

Marry me, he'd said to her that day in Molly's living room. *We're not a pair of starry-eyed kids. We don't believe in rose-covered cottages and happily-ever-after endings.* He'd seen what happened when lovers turned into husbands and wives, and it wasn't pretty. The ones who took it hardest were invariably the ones who'd brought the most to the table, the ones who believed they were special, that they could beat the odds.

Marriage was a business. He'd tried to explain that to Jessy when he proposed. They were two rational, clear-headed professionals. It should be easy for them. The thing to do was approach this whole baby situation with all of the problem-solving techniques at their disposal and make the right choice for the three of them.

Jessy threw a sofa cushion at him when he suggested that.

This isn't 1957! she'd shouted at him. *I don't need your help, your name, or your money. I need you.*

He'd spent his life coming in second to his brother. Even in death, Owen, Jr.'s star shone brighter than Spencer's ever would.

Except to Jessy.

She loved him. He didn't know why or how, but she did. She'd said it to him the night they made love, and she'd said it to him twice since then, both times in anger, as if she'd change it if she could.

He didn't love her back. He wasn't sure he even knew how to start. Still, there was something about her that touched his heart. The sex had been pretty damn incendiary, but great sex wasn't all that hard to find. It was more than that, something more elusive. She challenged him. He'd never been with a woman who was so unafraid of her own emotions. Jessy stated her case in no uncertain terms. *I love you.* She said it plainly, with no flirtation, no guile. *I love you.* She wasn't looking past him for someone better. To Jessy, he was the best.

There was something pretty damn appealing about that.

He'd felt a momentary sense of relief when she threw that cushion at him. He'd done the right thing and been rejected. What more could a man in his position ask for?

He knew the answer to that. Maybe he'd always known it.

Love, he thought, as he watched Molly Chamberlain drive away. *You could ask for love.*

NINETEEN

༄~♧~

Jessy hesitated in front of the door to Room 627. It sounded easy enough: Go in, say hello, take the patient's history, say good-bye, then leave. She'd done it a thousand times since she started med school and never batted an eye.

"Something wrong, Doctor?" Mrs. Haynes, the head nurse on day shift, appeared at her elbow.

Jessy shook her head. "Just gathering my thoughts."

"Don't forget to stop for supper. You look like you've lost a few pounds."

Mrs. Haynes was right. She'd lost three pounds since finding out she was pregnant. Her mama used to say she was so skinny she could slip between the raindrops. Jo Ellen would have a conniption if she saw her daughter now.

The first time Jessy was pregnant she gained only fifteen pounds, most of it right up front. She hadn't begun to show until late in her sixth month, which was when

her mama and daddy shipped her out to Aunt Lula's
until after the baby was born.

"You just put it all out of your mind, honey," her
mama had said as Jessy tried to settle back into her old
routines. "You have a whole big bright future ahead of
you. You're going to be someone special."

"Dr. Wyatt." Mrs. Haynes placed a hand on her right
forearm. "You don't look well."

"I'm fine," Jessy said, forcing out a smile. "You're
right about supper, though. I'll make sure to stop for a
sandwich."

Mrs. Haynes nodded then moved off down the hallway.

*You can't keep it a secret forever, Jessy. Sooner or
later you're going to have to tell them you're pregnant.*

She'd deal with that when her belly was too big to fit
into scrubs. Right now she was going to concentrate on
her patient's problems and put her own aside for a while.

The girl was sleeping. She was so little and skinny
she barely formed a bump under the pale blue blanket.
Jessy stepped over to the computer terminal next to the
bed and pressed in her code and password. The girl's
chart came up a second later.

Her name was Lorraine Mills. She was fifteen years
old, unmarried, and four months along. She had had un-
diagnosed stomach pains that finally led her parents to
take her to the emergency room late last night. The doctor on call ran the usual battery of tests. They turned up
nothing significant, but he still recommended she stay
overnight for observation. *Patient won't talk,* read one
notation. *Mother answered all questions.*

Jessy moved closer to the side of the bed. "Lorraine?"

The girl didn't stir.

Jessy projected her voice a bit more forcefully. "Lorraine, I'm Dr. Wyatt. I'd like to ask you a few questions. I know you're tired. I promise I won't keep you awake more than five minutes."

The girl's eyelids twitched, but she didn't say a word. *So you're awake,* Jessy thought as an odd tug of sensation settled inside her heart. Awake and scared and wishing she were back home in her little-girl room with the stuffed dogs lined up across the skinny single bed, where she'd dreamed so many dreams that would never come true because they weren't her mama's dreams.

She smoothed the blanket over the child's shoulders.

"I'm not in any rush," she said softly. "I'll be right here if you want to talk."

The girl shifted position the tiniest bit, just enough so Jessy would notice.

"I saw some orange juice in the lounge fridge," Jessy said in a conversational tone. "Think you'd like some?"

No answer.

"I could go for some tea myself or maybe one of those packets of hot chocolate—"

One eye opened. "I like hot chocolate."

"Terrific," Jessy said. "We'll have some hot chocolate while we talk."

"Roses," Spencer said to the clerk. "About a dozen of those red ones and maybe a dozen of those white ones, too."

"Cream," the clerk corrected him. "A wonderful choice."

"I'd like you to put them in one of those long shiny boxes," he said, "and tie it with a big red ribbon."

"Of course," the clerk said, looking slightly aggrieved. "That's the way we always present our roses."

He knew that. He'd bought enough roses in his life to decorate a Rose Bowl float. What the hell was he getting so agitated about anyway? Jessy wasn't one of his Ivy League girlfriends. She wouldn't judge him by the size of the satin ribbon on the box or the pedigree of the florist. She'd judge him by tougher standards. She'd judge him by what she believed was in his heart.

Hell, he wasn't sure himself what was going on inside his heart. He'd paced his office after Molly left. He tried to work on a brief, but the words spiraled up and out of reach. Funny how he'd never thought all that much about divorce before. He worked in the rubble of broken marriages every day and he hadn't given it a thought until he watched Molly walk alone across the parking lot. She was determined to keep Robert away from their baby and she just might get her wish. Chamberlain was eager to marry his paramour, and if Molly applied any kind of pressure, he'd probably drop the quest for custody in return for his quickie divorce. Chamberlain would have his freedom and his new bride, while Molly would have her house and her new baby.

And Spencer would get his fee no matter which way the broken hearts crumbled.

That was the thing about being a divorce lawyer. Fairness didn't matter. Neither did those broken hearts. His job was to push through the divorce with minimal bloodletting and move on to the next one. He made his living promoting the idea that families were basically transient, that playing musical chairs with spouses and children was as American as baseball and apple pie.

He told himself that he didn't cause the divorces any

more than he'd caused the marriages that preceded them. Molly and Robert Chamberlain were a bad match, and no amount of counseling or good intentions would ever change that.

Maybe he and Jessy Wyatt were a bad match, too. Maybe they didn't stand a chance in hell of making a go of marriage, but he was willing to take that chance. She made him feel things he'd never felt before, question things that had been absolutes before she came into his life.

And there was the small fact that she was carrying his child. He'd never thought of himself as a traditionalist. He'd seen enough marriages fall apart to have little faith in the institution and even less in the sanctity of the family. His own family had fallen apart with the death of Owen, Jr., and not even ties of blood and bone had been enough to help him claim a place in his father's heart.

He'd never planned on having kids. He'd seen it done well and seen it done badly, and he wasn't convinced which side he'd come down on. None of that mattered now. God . . . fate . . . destiny—whatever you want to call it, life had other plans for him.

And what about Jessy? You think she had this in mind when she seduced you?

She'd been at the Med Center for two months. This was going to blow her position there all to holy hell. No wonder she was angry and defensive and pushing him away with both hands.

When she'd first told him she was pregnant, he hadn't known what to say. A brief surge of primitive elation had been instantly replaced with wariness and dismay. She'd stared at him, almost challenging him to say the wrong thing, and damned if he hadn't obliged. *What are you going to do?* he'd asked. *Are you going to have the baby?*

It was an honest question. Not every woman these days was happy to be pregnant. Not every pregnancy resulted in a happy, healthy baby. There were options available out there. Decisions a woman could make with the law, if not all of society, on her side.

Not Jessy. She was taking the hard way and she was willing to go it alone. There were few people on earth he respected, and Jessy was now on the top of a very short list.

But he didn't love her. He wasn't even sure he knew how.

"You'll come back and talk to me," Lorraine said to Jessy. "You promised, right?"

"Right," said Jessy. "I'll stop in before I leave for the night."

"And you'll call my mom and tell her?"

"I promised, didn't I?"

"Yeah," said Lorraine, "but lots of people promise things. That doesn't mean much."

The girl was right. Promises were cheaper than canned peas on sale at Shoprite. "I'll speak to your mama," Jessy said. "You don't have to worry about that anymore."

She stepped outside into the hallway and leaned against the wall. "Damn," she whispered as the tears spilled down her cheeks. "Damn, damn, damn." This was all she needed, to be pulled into the problems of some pregnant teenager. She'd made a vow her first day in med school that she'd never get personally involved

with any of her patients and, for the most part, she'd
found it easy to keep that vow. But this was cutting too
close to the bone.

A trio of orderlies walked by. They cast curious looks
in her direction. The tallest of the three whispered something to his two coworkers, and she knew they were
talking about her by the way they suddenly tried hard
not to look at her again.

Doctors weren't supposed to cry. She knew the rules.
Death, dismemberment—it didn't matter. You subli-
mated your emotions and got on with your work. She'd
never found that particularly hard to do until now. That
skinny little thing huddling under the blue hospital blanket was the girl she'd been not all that long ago. She
felt as if she'd stepped back through a time portal and
was confronting herself, all of her fears and longings and
insecurities. *Let me keep my baby, Mama . . . I can still
go to medical school with a baby . . .*

But Jo Ellen had had other ideas and the will to go
with them. *You're just a girl,* she told Jessy, *you don't
know how a baby changes everything. All those dreams
of glory disappearing under a mountain of diapers and
disappointment. I want better for you, Jessy,* her mama
said. *I want you to be what I never could.*

Of course Jo Ellen hadn't said that last bit, but Jessy
could hear her mama's voice saying it just the same as
if she had.

The same thing was happening to Lorraine. She was
being bombarded with expectations, buried under the
weight of guilt. She needed someone to talk to, prefer-
ably someone who had wanted to keep her baby but
hadn't—and would regret it every single day of her life.

A pair of doctors strolled by, and she ducked her head

over her notebook and pretended she was scribbling something so they wouldn't notice her tear-streaked face. She had to get out of there. The head nurse was right. She had forgotten to eat today. Maybe she'd go down to the cafeteria and grab a tuna on rye and some milk. She started down the hallway, rounded the corner, and walked straight into a faceful of roses.

"Oh!" She stepped back, laughing apologetically. "I'm sorry. I wasn't looking where I was going."

The roses lowered, and she found herself face-to-face with Spencer. "I was looking for you, Jess."

Oh, God, exactly the one person on earth she didn't want to see. "You have thirty seconds," she said, ignoring the sweet perfume filling the air between them.

He pushed the flowers toward her. "These are for you."

She glared at the roses and then at him. "I don't like roses."

He looked vaguely deflated, and she was glad. "Tell me what you do like, and I'll trade them in."

"I'm not the flowers type."

"I think you are."

"Don't," she whispered, feeling her control slip another notch. "I'm not in the mood."

"I'm not going to ask you to marry me again," he said.

"Good," she snapped, "because I've already told you my answer."

"We got it all wrong," he said, ignoring her words. "We have to go back to square one and start over."

"We're not starting anything," she said as her heartbeat accelerated. "We were a mistake. We shouldn't have happened in the first place."

"Can't undo it," he said. "We happened."

"I'm busy," she said, pushing past him. "Why don't you go home and count your trust funds?"

"What time do you get off tonight?" he asked, falling into step with her as she headed for the cafeteria.

"Midnight."

"I'll be waiting for you in the lobby."

"No!" She stopped in her tracks and spun around to face him. "Get out of my life, Spencer. I don't need or want you in it." Seeing him hurt too much. She'd rather cut him from her life entirely. Her game-playing had come with a terrible price tag attached to it.

"I'm not going anywhere."

Her eyes filled again with tears. "Don't do this to me, Spencer. Not today."

"Why not today?" He didn't sound like himself. That edge of sophistication that always unnerved her was gone. "I didn't want to make you cry, Jess. That's not why I'm here."

"Don't flatter yourself, Spencer. I'm not crying over you." *Ah'm not cryin'* . . . The more upset she got, the more Southern she sounded. Any second now he'd be calling for an interpreter. "Why are you here?" She batted the flowers away with her hand. "Why are you doing this?" Nobody ever brought her flowers. Didn't he know that?

"Why do you think?" he countered. He sounded even less like himself—ruffled and exasperated. "We started all wrong, Jess. I'm trying to get us back on track."

"Back on track? We were never on track to fall off, Spencer. We weren't anything at all." She'd thrown herself at him because she'd actually believed she could be happy with nothing more than the memory of one night in his arms.

"You're right," he said. "We were a one-night stand and we got caught, but that doesn't mean that's all we *can* be."

Her resistance was beginning to ebb. You could live just so long without hope. Sometimes she felt as if she'd lived her whole life without it. "Why are you doing this?" she said softly. "Is it for the baby or for me?"

He didn't answer right away. He was looking at her as if he'd never seen her before, and the intensity of his gaze made her wish she'd never asked the question in the first place.

"I don't know," he said after a moment. "Maybe I'm doing it for us."

"Good answer," she whispered. "Very good answer."

She buried her face in the cream and crimson blooms and began to cry.

Molly got home from Spencer's office around three-thirty and changed into a pair of loose black pants and a white T-shirt. She took an emerald green sweater from her closet and pulled it on over her head. Two weeks ago it still had that oversized look she was striving for. Not anymore. Her breasts and belly stretched the nubby fabric almost to the limit of decency. She didn't care. This wasn't a fashion statement. She needed bright colors to lift her dark mood.

Jessy was still at the hospital. Molly couldn't remember what time Rafe had said he'd pick her up. Four o'clock? Eight-thirty? She also couldn't remember why she'd ever agreed to such a ridiculous idea. She wasn't an invalid. She was pregnant. She didn't need someone to drive her around. She had all of her faculties. She could drive herself anywhere she wanted to go.

The thing was, she didn't want to go anywhere.

Not even the Caribbean for a quickie divorce?

Now, there was a swell idea. Where did Robert get the nerve to suggest such a thing?

Same place he got the nerve to walk out on you and take every stick of furniture in the house.

Good point. It made her wonder how well she'd known her husband in the first place. They'd shared a home and a bed and a life, and the truth was she didn't know the first thing about him. She knew he liked his eggs sunny side up, his shirts starched, his bath towels warm from the dryer, but she didn't know what made him happy or why he'd never loved her the way she'd wanted to be loved.

Did you love him, Molly? Be honest now. Did you love him the way he wanted to be loved?

She hated questions like that. She hated being honest with herself.

She'd loved him the only way she knew how—as a partner, as the man who would father her children. Robert had represented the security she'd never known as a child, and when he proposed to her, she said yes immediately. "We're a good team," he'd said. She'd support him during law school, then the moment he was settled in with a good law firm, she'd quit and start a family. That was their dream, wasn't it? That was what the hard work was all about.

He'd said he was happy. He said his parents would be crazy about her. He said all the right things but he never once said *I love you.*

The saddest part of all was that it took ten years for her to realize it.

She wondered how different her life would have been if she'd demanded more of Robert and the relationship, if she'd understood that being a good team meant more than a career and a house in Princeton Manor. Of course, if she'd understood that she would have seen that their marriage was doomed from the start.

She hated Robert for taking the coward's way out, but she couldn't hate him for wanting more from a marriage than they'd found together. She hated him for walking out on his unborn child, but she couldn't hate him for falling in love. Not now that she knew what they had both been missing.

The baby shifted position, a flurry of soft kicks and punches that usually preceded a nap. *It's your loss, Robert,* she thought as she gently massaged her belly. *You turned your back on a miracle.*

He made his decision the day he walked out the door on them. Now he'd have to find a way to live with it.

TWENTY

~~~~⁂~~~~

Something was wrong.

Molly hadn't said a word since she got in the car. Every time Rafe tried to engage her in conversation, he found himself slamming face first into a wall of mono-syllables.

Feel like stopping for supper? *No.*

If you're cold, I'll turn up the heater. *Okay.*

Get a lot of work done today? *Enough.*

Feel like telling me about it?

That last one didn't even rate a monosyllable.

Her lovely face was set in unapproachable lines. He tried to think of what he might have done or said to cause this breach, but his mind was blank. That morning everything had been fine between them. Whatever caused this shift of mood had happened in the hours between then and now, and she was keeping it to herself.

It was dark when he let them into the carriage house. She moved quietly about, switching on lamps, adjusting the front blinds, then drifted back to the kitchen. He heard the refrigerator open then click shut. He heard the sound of water running. She was at the sink with her back to him when he approached her.

"Need some help?" he asked.

She shook her head. Her fiery ponytail danced between her shoulder blades. "I can handle it."

A two-syllable word. He took that as a sign of encouragement. "Why should you do all the work?" he asked, moving closer to her.

"I don't mind."

He placed his hands on her shoulders, but she neatly stepped away from him. Not a good sign.

"Talk to me, Molly," he said. "If I don't know what's wrong, I can't make it right."

"There's nothing wrong." Her voice was so tight you could have bounced a quarter off her vocal cords. "Everything's just fine."

"Bullshit." He saw her cheeks redden. "Don't close up on me, Molly. We've come too far for that."

"Have we?" She spun around to face him. He noticed her anger before he noticed her beauty. That was a first. "How far have we come, Rafe? Maybe it looks different from your angle than it does from mine."

Her words stung. He had no doubt that she meant them to sting. "You want to know how it looks from my angle," he asked. "It looks like you're angry and hurt, and I'm in the line of fire."

"You're right," she said. He could see a slight softening of the worry lines between her brows. "I'm angry and I'm hurt, and you're lucky enough to be the closest one to me."

"I can take it, Molly. I'm not going to leave because you have problems."

She smiled her first smile of the night. "Maybe you should wait until you hear the problems."

He leaned back against the sink and crossed his arms over his chest. "I'm listening."

"Robert wants me to fly down to the Caribbean and get one of those quickie divorces."

He struggled to keep his expression impassive while inside he was turning cartwheels. "Will you do it?"

Her smile shifted again, this time into a line of pure steel. "He also wants joint custody of the baby."

Dangerous territory. "You wanted him to take an interest."

"Six months ago," she shot back, "not now. Now it's too late."

"The baby isn't even born yet. He—"

"Are you taking his side?"

"I'm not taking anybody's side. I'm pointing out a few things you might have missed."

"He's not coming anywhere near this baby. Not while I'm still breathing."

"He's the father."

"One night doesn't make a man a father, Rafe," she said quietly. "It takes a lot more than that."

"So you're going to shut him out."

"He walked out on me," she said. Her hands settled over her belly. "On the baby. He hasn't so much as asked if things are going well or not."

"Maybe he's having a change of heart."

"I wouldn't think that would be on your wish list," she said. Her mood went from fire to ice in the blink of an eye.

"Is it on yours?"

"That's not funny."

"You're right," he said, "it's not funny at all."

"I told Spencer to tell Robert he can go to hell. What do I need him for? This is my baby. I'm the one who's carrying her; I'm the one who makes the decisions."

He knew better than to argue with her. If he started down that road, he would end up telling her all about Sarah, and this improbable world they'd created would crash down around him. He was selfish enough to want to keep that from happening, but that didn't take away the guilt.

He had to remind himself that he had no rights in this situation. She hadn't asked for his opinion and she probably wouldn't take it if it were offered. He wasn't her husband. The baby she carried wasn't his. They were uneasy lovers with the odds stacked against them. She could tell him to go to hell, and there wasn't a damn thing he could do about it except tell her that without her he was already halfway there.

Molly couldn't shake her bad mood. She knew none of this was Rafe's fault, that he had absolutely nothing to do with her problems with Robert, but that didn't stop the sense that her whole world was somehow off-kilter.

They worked together in the kitchen in silence. She made the toast and hashed browns. He made the scrambled eggs, coffee for him, and decaf tea for her. They sat down at the picnic table near the back door and ate their evening breakfast in continued silence. She hadn't a clue what he was thinking. The truth was, she hadn't a clue to anything about him. This man who had become the central figure in her life was as big a mystery to her now as he'd been the day she met him. She didn't know him any better than she'd known Robert.

Which meant she barely knew him at all.

She wondered if this was her pattern, to skim the surface of life, to accept the obvious and not look for trouble; so when trouble showed up, it hit her right between the eyes.

She put down her fork and leaned back in her chair. Suddenly the day weighed so heavily on her shoulders that she found it impossible to eat or think or stay awake. She struggled to keep her eyes open, but it was a losing battle.

Rafe was at her side instantly. She felt herself being lifted up into his arms, heard his heart beating beneath her ear, the creak of the stairs as he carried her to the bedroom they'd shared.

"Don't be kind to me," she whispered as he settled her down on the bed. "I don't want to need you." Men didn't stay with her. Her father hadn't. Neither had her husband. He brushed her hair back from her forehead then kissed her on both eyelids. She could feel herself sinking deeper into an almost dreamlike state that was part exhaustion, part surrender. He lay down next to her on the bed and gathered her close to him in a full body hug that was as close to heaven as she had ever experienced.

"I don't know anything about you," she murmured, "not the first thing . . ." All she knew was his smell and his touch and the way he made her feel. You couldn't trust those things any more than you could trust a whisper in the night.

"You know I'll never leave you," he said.

You will, she thought as she drifted off to sleep. *One day you'll leave.*

•   •   •

She slept deeply, with her face pressed hard against his left bicep. The room filled with the sound of her breathing, the sweet smell of her skin. In a perfect world, this would be enough. This second. This moment. There had been a time when he wouldn't have asked for more, when he could have been content with a glimpse of happiness and never known the difference.

Now he wanted it all. He wanted more than a glimpse of happiness, he wanted it around the clock, every day, all week, all year. He wanted a lifetime of happiness and he wanted it with Molly and her baby. The carriage house came to life when she was there. Shadows were banished by sunshine. Birds sang from the rafters. The smell of perfume wafted through the rooms like a blessing from God.

She took it all with her each morning when she left.

One day you'll leave.

He heard her say it before she fell asleep, in that one unguarded moment not even Molly could prevent. He knew she couldn't turn to her family for help. She'd told him about the multiple marriages and half-siblings scattered about the country. Her husband had been her real family, their house her only home. She carried herself with strength and dignity, but he knew what that cost her. He could still see her the way he'd first found her, bent over at the waist with her arms wrapped across her belly, moaning low like the wolf he'd found in a trap all those years ago. She never talked about her pain, but he knew it was there. There was so much he didn't know about her, so much yet to be discovered.

She was right, of course, when she said that she didn't know one damn thing about him. Most women peppered a man with questions. Where are you from? Who are your people? Tell me who you've loved. How did you come to live in this carriage house so far from Montana?

Molly asked nothing. She didn't ask about Miriam or about his ex-wife. She didn't ask if he had children or dreams or skeletons in his closet. He wasn't sure if she didn't care or just didn't want to know. It unnerved him, this lack of interest. He had no experience in dealing with a woman who lived solely in the here and now. Karen had spent half of their brief marriage worrying about where they would be in five years' time, where they'd been five years earlier. There had been no present with his ex-wife—only where she was going and how fast she could run away from where she'd been. She told everyone within earshot that what she had wasn't enough, that she was destined for better things.

He'd thought it was just talk, the kind of dream-spinning his Ojibwa *mamaw*—grandmother—used to do by the light of the fireplace, playing *what if* in a world that never seemed to know she was there. He'd thought once the baby came Karen would settle down and be happy with him. He'd thought dead wrong.

He hadn't been listening. She'd told him exactly what she wanted. She'd told him exactly what she was going to do, and somehow he hadn't heard her. He probably couldn't have stopped her even if he had realized what was going on, but he might have held onto his daughter.

Lately he'd been thinking a lot about Sarah. Being with Molly, lying there at night with his palm flat on her belly, his thoughts trailed back to that little house on the far edge of the ranch. To that little cradle he'd made with so much love and so many dreams. He had to remind himself that round-cheeked baby girl with the big blue eyes existed only in his heart and in the handful of snapshots stuffed in his drawer. She was almost a teenager now. She had her own thoughts and opinions and hopes and fears. For all he knew Karen had presented her second husband as Sarah's father. His daughter might not even know he existed.

He'd come close to telling Molly tonight. He'd almost told her the whole story, how he'd let his family walk out the door and he hadn't done anything to stop them even though he loved them more than life itself. She'd never understand.

It was his mistake. His broken heart.

His secret.

Molly woke up as Rafe bent down to pin a note to his pillow.

"I have to give a bid on some work over in Lambertville," he said, kissing her gently. "I'll be back in an hour or so."

She sat up, still half-asleep, and tried to focus on the clock. "Wh-what time is it?"

"Early," he said. "Not even seven. Go back to sleep."

"I'm wide awake," she protested, stifling a yawn. "I'll have a cup of tea and start working on the manuscript I brought with me."

"I wish you'd get some more sleep."

"And I wish you'd quit worrying so much. Go give your estimate. I'll have coffee ready for you when you come back."

"You're feeling okay?"

"A good night's sleep can work wonders," she said then kissed him. "I'm fine."

He didn't look convinced. The furrow between his brows was deep as a crevasse.

"You're sure?" he asked.

"Positive." She gave him a gentle push. "I'm going to shower and get down to work."

She showered after he left but found she wasn't in the mood to jump right into work. She and Jinx had reached an accommodation of sorts, and the cat now allowed Molly to pet her and feed her. She'd never had a pet before. Her parents moved too often, and Robert said he was allergic to everything with fins, fur, or feathers. She liked it when Jinx curled up on her lap and cast annoyed looks in the direction of Molly's belly each time the baby kicked.

This was the first time she'd been alone in the carriage house. It was ablaze with sun, more beautiful even than usual. Rafe was slowly remodeling the place, and the first thing he'd done was open it up to light. Huge windows and skylights seemed to pull the sun right into the room with her, dancing across the polished oak floor and skimming across the kitchen tiles. He'd bought those red tiles in Mexico, he said, and lugged them all the way back in his truck. She wondered why he'd gone to so much trouble for floor tiles, but she'd never asked him.

That was one of many things she'd wondered about but never asked him to tell her. When you grew up shuttling between warring parents, you learned quickly not to ask questions, not to volunteer information. There were secrets upon secrets, layer after layer of *don't ask* and *it's better you don't know* and *what happens here is none of his/her business*. Questions rocked the boat, and that was the one thing the young Molly didn't want to do. She'd been desperate for a home, so hungry for family life that she would have done anything to keep her parents happy and together. That was a lot to ask of a high-spirited little girl, and it changed her.

Another woman might have seen the changes in Robert as they happened. Another woman might have questioned him before he walked out the door. He might have walked out the door anyway, but at least she would have had a few answers.

She made herself a pot of decaf English Breakfast tea and was about to settle down at the picnic table with the manuscript when she heard a knock at the door.

"I'm sorry," she said when she opened the door and saw Ginny, the housekeeper. "Rafe's out giving an estimate."

"I'm not here for him," Ginny said. "The old lady wants to see you pronto."

Molly took a step back. "You're kidding."

"Nope. She watched him drive away, waited to make sure he was really gone, then sent me over here to get you."

"What does she want?"

"To check you out, I'd figure."

"Good," said Molly. "That's exactly what I want from her." She grabbed her sweater from the back of the rocking chair and followed the housekeeper across the yard to the back door of the main house.

"Go upstairs," Ginny said when they stepped inside the surprisingly modern kitchen. "Third door on your left. You can't miss it."

Molly was appalled to realize her hands were shaking. She wanted Miriam to like her. Probably more than she cared to admit. Rafe had made it clear that the woman was important to him, even if Molly didn't exactly know why.

Maybe she'd remedy that this morning.

"Don't stand out there breathing," Miriam said when Molly approached her open door a minute later. "Come in, come in. That's why I invited you, isn't it?"

"You tell me," Molly said as she stepped into the room. "That wasn't much of a hello."

"I don't have time for hellos," Miriam said, looking her up and down. "I'm dying."

Molly must have gasped, because the old woman's eyes narrowed.

"He didn't tell you?" Miriam asked.

"Not a word," Molly said. "I'm sorry."

"I'm not. I'm ninety years old. I've lived a long full life, and it's my time to go. Nothing to be sorry at all about in that." Her voice was strong, her words perfectly enunciated.

"When you put it that way, it sounds natural," Molly said. Despite herself, she was impressed. She'd never heard anyone face death with such calm acceptance. She rubbed her back and smiled. "Do you mind if I sit down?"

"My manners aren't what they used to be," Miriam said. "Please do."

"I've been wondering about you," Molly said. "I was hoping we'd get to meet."

"He was keeping us apart," Miriam said. Her gaze settled on Molly's hands. "No wedding ring."

"I took it off the day my husband left me for a judge's daughter."

"I hope you made him eat it."

Molly choked on a laugh. "That's not the reaction I expected from you."

"I know." She had a radiant smile, the same kind of smile Molly remembered on her grandmother near the end. It was totally without fear or self-pity. It was also the smile of a woman who was going to say what was on her mind, whether or not you wanted to hear it. "So did you make your ex eat the ring?"

"No, I didn't," Molly said, "but sometimes I wish I had." She hesitated for a second then pushed forward. "He isn't my ex yet."

"And that isn't Rafe's baby."

"That's right," she said, meeting the woman's eyes. "This isn't Rafe's baby."

The silence between them was long. Molly resisted the urge to look away from Miriam's intense gaze.

After what seemed an eternity, Miriam spoke again. "He loves you, you know."

Molly felt her cheeks flood with color. "I don't think you—"

"Don't be coy with me, young woman. You must know that."

"No," Molly said, "I don't." She'd prayed, hoped, dreamed that he loved her, but she didn't know. "We haven't talked about it."

"Are you stupid then or being difficult?"

"Neither one," Molly said, growing annoyed. "As I said, we haven't discussed it, and, quite frankly, I don't think it's any of your business."

"Oh, it's my business," Miriam said. "I know everything there is to know about that boy."

"There might be a few things you don't know," Molly said, her tone sharper than she'd intended.

"I know that I'll move heaven and earth before I die to make sure you don't hurt him."

"Hurt him?" Molly stared at the woman in utter disbelief. "How could you think I'd ever hurt him?"

"Because it's clear to me you don't understand the kind of man you've found, and I'm not about to let you step in and break his heart."

What an odd thing to say. Molly didn't know whether to be amused or annoyed. "And what kind of man have I found?"

"You're a smart one," Miriam said. "You asked the one question I love to answer."

Miriam told Molly about how she met Rafe during a Nor'easter a few years ago. He was living in his pickup truck. Everything he owned fit in the backseat. He'd spent the five years before that moving from place to place, moving before he found himself caring too much about anything or anyone. He wanted to be anonymous, invisible. He'd done things he wasn't proud of, Miriam said, things that had changed him forever, made him tougher in some ways, more vulnerable in others. "It's not for me to tell you about them," Miriam said simply. "It's up to you to learn."

Miriam was still driving back then. She was on her way home from a reception at McCarter Theater in Princeton when the Nor'easter blew in. Wind whipped the rain horizontally against the car windows, making it impossible for her to see the tree that was down across her side of the road. She slid into it, spun across the road, and came to rest in a ditch at the side. She was shaken but unhurt. She was also quite obviously stuck. Nobody stopped for her. The few cars that went by ignored her. She was shaking from the cold, a little disoriented, growing more frightened by the minute. A battered red pickup truck angled in beside her. Her heart hammered against the fragile bones of her rib cage as a dangerous-looking dark-haired young man climbed out and made his way toward her. If he'd wanted to beat or rob her, she couldn't have defended herself. How many stories about such things had she seen on *Eyewitness News* over the years—thousands, maybe? She whispered a prayer as he tapped on her window.

Two hours later, she whispered a prayer of thanks that the man who found her in distress was Rafe Garrick.

The two struck up an unlikely alliance. She offered him a place to stay. He refused. She said it would be a business arrangement, not charity, that she needed someone to do repairs at the carriage house. They both knew that there was more to it than that. Somehow they had formed a deep and lasting friendship. Rafe moved into the neglected carriage house and brought it back to life. When Miriam offered to sell it to him, he accepted. To his surprise he'd put down roots right there, along the banks of the Delaware River.

"That's enough, Miriam."

Both women turned to see Rafe looming in the doorway like a thundercloud. Miriam didn't so much as blink when she met Rafe's angry look.

"That's not half enough," she said. "I want to make sure that—"

"I can handle my own life," he said, cutting her off.

He and Miriam continued to stare each other down while Molly watched in fascination. In a way she was glad Rafe showed up when he did. She wasn't entirely sure she wanted to hear whatever else it was Miriam had to say.

"I'm glad you're both here," Miriam said finally in a neat change of conversation. "I want to invite you to Thanksgiving dinner with me on Thursday."

Rafe and Molly locked eyes.

"I can't believe I forgot that Thursday is Thanksgiving," Molly said.

"I can't believe it's November," Rafe said.

Miriam laughed. "Then it's settled. Ginny is cooking. I invited Dr. Van Lieuw and his sister Agnes." She turned to Molly. "If you'd like to invite that little doctor who lives with you, feel free. I'm sure they'd have a lot in common."

Molly glanced over at Rafe. He was obviously quite the talker around Miriam. She felt almost jealous. "I'll do that," she said. "Thank you."

She no sooner got the words out than Miriam's eyes closed and her head fell to her left shoulder. Thank God she was still breathing. The sense of otherworldliness about the woman was almost palpable, and suddenly Molly knew the end was coming sooner than Rafe was ready to accept.

TWENTY-ONE

Jinx was waiting for them at the door to the carriage house. Rafe reached down and scratched her behind her right ear.

"I used to be able to bend down like that," Molly said ruefully. "Back when I had a waist."

"I like you this way," Rafe said, pressing a kiss to her belly. "Fertile."

"Fat."

"Voluptuous."

"Bovine."

He grinned. "Bovine?"

"I look like a candidate for *Baywatch*."

"I've never watched it."

"Don't," she said. "Not if you're lactose intolerant."

They set about fixing tea and coffee and toast. Rafe put down some scrambled eggs for Jinx, who vacuumed them up in an instant.

"Thanksgiving with Miriam," Molly said as they settled down at the picnic table. "Should be interesting."

He grunted something.

"She didn't divulge any of your secrets," Molly said, "if that's what you're wondering." She waited for him to make the expected comeback: *I don't have any secrets.* He didn't. He drank his coffee and spread blackberry jam on his toast and didn't say a word, which made her wonder all the more about what secrets he did have.

"Actually I'm lying," Molly went on. "She told me that you're a CIA operative on hiatus in western New Jersey while they build you a new identity."

"Close," he said, tossing Jinx a corner of toast. "I'm not on hiatus, though."

"So what are you?" She hadn't meant to ask that, but now that the question was out there she was glad.

"What am I?" He looked puzzled, a bit uneasy.

"Yes," she said, warming to the topic. "What are you?" She gestured widely to encompass the entire carriage house. "I've seen the work you do." The cradle that was almost finished, every piece of furniture in the bedroom. "I can't believe you're satisfied building fences and remodeling bathrooms."

"What if I *am* satisfied building fences and remodeling bathrooms? Would it make a difference to you?"

She didn't even have to think about it. "No," she said, "absolutely not."

He pushed away his coffee mug and met her eyes. "It made a difference to my wife."

She pushed away her teacup. "It made a difference to my husband, too," she said. "I'm not a doctor or lawyer or CPA. All I ever wanted was to raise a family. He didn't find that very exciting."

"You can't aim higher than that."

"Robert thought I could."

"He was a fool."

"That's how I feel about your ex-wife."

He gave Jinx another corner of toast. "I wasn't out giving an estimate today, Molly."

"No?" Her stomach knotted. *Please,* she thought. *Please don't do this to me . . .* They'd moved too far, too fast, too everything, and he wanted to put some space between them. She read the women's magazines. She watched the talk shows. She knew what was coming.

"I had an appointment with the owner of a furniture shop in Buck's County."

She sat up straighter. "And?" *Good news. Please, God, let it be good news.*

"They commissioned six pieces—three chairs like the one in the bedroom and three side tables."

She leaped from her seat as quickly as a very pregnant woman could leap and threw her arms around him. He looked shy and proud and embarrassed all at once, and the emotions inside her heart were so sweet she almost cried. Her excitement seemed to unlock something in Rafe, and he began talking about his craft, about the smell of wood and the feel of it beneath his fingers, about the shapes and visions he saw in oak and pine and walnut and mahogany.

He hired himself out on building crews, did odd jobs, repaired fences and remodeled kitchens as a way to pay bills and buy materials for the work that really mattered, and now it was beginning to pay off.

She poured him a fresh cup of coffee and refilled her teacup from the stoneware pot on the counter. The words spilled from Rafe like water tumbling over rocks. She wanted to drink them up and make them part of her.

They were so much alike. They held the most important things deep inside. She knew what it meant for him to share these things with her. It was as close to a declaration of love as they had ever come.

He loves you, Miriam had said. Maybe she was right. Maybe she'd finally come home.

The pains started after lunch. At first Jessy thought they were payback for that mayo-heavy tuna salad on rye, but she quickly realized it was something more serious.

She called Spencer at his office. "Something's wrong," she said, bypassing the amenities. "Please meet me at the emergency room."

He arrived as they were wheeling her in for a sonogram.

"I'm bleeding," she told him as he reached for her hand.

"Jesus," he murmured. "The baby—?"

"Still with us," she said. "Heartbeat is still within normal range. We'll know more after they take the pictures."

"They're ready, Dr. Wyatt," the orderly interrupted. "We really shouldn't delay this any longer than necessary."

"I'm coming with you," Spencer said.

Jessy was so surprised she couldn't speak. He'd shown a marked reluctance when it came to the more physical aspects of pregnancy. She was even more surprised when he held her hand through the procedure. The pains were growing more intense, and she bled through two pads before they wheeled her upstairs to a room on the sixth floor.

"I can't believe this is happening." She couldn't hold

back her tears any longer. "I don't want to lose this baby."

"You won't," he said. He brushed back her hair from her forehead in a gesture so tender she almost believed he loved her. Which he didn't. She knew that. She couldn't let herself forget it. He was just being kind, that was all.

"Your life would be easier," she said. "You could walk away from me and never look back." The rich boy from Greenwich and the poor doctor from Mississippi—it sounded like a 1950s B movie, the kind that always had an unhappy ending.

"Do you see me walking away?"

"You're here for the baby," she said. "I understand that. I don't mind."

"Damn it, Jess, I'm here for you."

It was the right thing to say. She appreciated the effort even if she didn't for one minute believe the words. But as the hours wore on and the doctors waited to see if they could get the bleeding under control, she began to wonder if just maybe there might be more to his words than she'd first thought. He held her hand. He dealt with the doctors and nurses. He made it clear that she was the first priority, that her health and well-being came even before the baby's. She disagreed, but his concern moved her deeply.

"It's touch and go," Jack Rosenberg told her after he'd evaluated the test results. "If we can stop the contractions and get you through the next twenty-four hours, I think you're home free."

He explained the situation with a string of medical jargon that she explained to Spencer when Jack left. Spencer turned white.

"Sit down," she said. "You don't look very good."

"I'm fine," he said. "I'm worried about you."

"Don't," she whispered. "Don't be so kind to me. I know you don't love me. You don't have to pretend."

"I'm not pretending anything, Jess. I care what happens to you."

"I don't want you to care what happens to me," she said. "I want you to love me."

"I do," he said quietly.

Hospital noises, the harsh glare of the bedside lamp—they all vanished. There was only Spencer.

"Would you say that if I lost the baby?" Her voice was scarcely a whisper. The question frightened her even more than the answer.

"I'd say we'll have other chances."

"You're lying."

"Not about this, Jess. You're the last thing I think about at night and you're the first thing I think about when I wake up in the morning. When you look at me with those big eyes of yours, I think I can conquer the world. I don't know if that's love. I only know that I've never felt this way before and I don't want it to end."

"Yes," she said.

His eyes met hers. "Yes?"

She nodded. "Yes."

"You won't be sorry, Jess. We can make this work."

And because she wanted to very much, she almost believed him.

Jessy was released from the hospital on Wednesday morning with a clean bill of health.

"And you're sure she's okay?" Molly asked Spencer, who had called her at Rafe's to give her the good news.

"She and the baby are both fine." He sounded exhausted but elated. "I have some more news."

"Personal or professional?"

"Both," he said. "Which do you want first?"

"Professional," she said without delay. "Let's get it out of the way."

"Robert wants a meeting with you this afternoon."

"You know my feelings about that."

"I think you should consider it, Molly. He's willing to make some concessions."

"Forget it," she said. "I'm not interested."

"You don't know what you're letting yourself in for," Spencer said. "If he decides to play hardball, the first thing his attorney will zero in on is Rafe. I don't think you want that to happen."

"I'm not doing anything wrong," she said. "I'm not the one who walked out and straight into the arms of another woman."

"That's all true," he said, "but it won't sound that way after the other side gets through with it."

"It's the day before Thanksgiving," she said. "What kind of idiot would suggest a meeting today?"

"I'm not going to touch that one," Spencer said, "but I do recommend that you let me schedule something with him for next week."

"We'll talk about it tomorrow. You and Jessy will be able to have dinner with us at Miriam's, won't you?"

"That's the second thing I wanted to talk with you about," he said. "Jess and I are getting married tomorrow, and we want you there."

The next twenty-four hours were like outtakes from an old Marx Brothers movie. Molly called Miriam to tender

Jessy's regrets, and the second the old woman heard the reason she popped up with an offer that amazed everyone involved.

"They can get married in my house," Miriam said in a tone that brooked no disagreement.

"But you don't even know them," Molly protested. "That's asking much too much of you."

"I'll decide what's too much, missy. If you can't offer hospitality to strangers on Thanksgiving, when can you?"

Molly could find no argument for that. She set about making phone calls to florists and bakeries, trying to find somebody who could deliver on the shortest notice possible. A bakery in Flemington said they could help out and volunteered to send someone over with a cake meant for a canceled day-after-Thanksgiving wedding.

She called Jessy and was surprised to hear how nervous the woman sounded. This was eveything she'd ever wanted, and she sounded as if she was scheduled to appear before a firing squad. Spencer was the one who sounded relaxed and happy. None of it made the slightest bit of sense, but she didn't have time to worry about it. There were too many other things she needed to get done.

Like finding out whether or not the fridge in the main house was big enough to hold a chocolate mousse cake.

She grabbed her sweater and dashed out the door. She was halfway across the gravel drive when she heard the sound of a car crunching its way toward her. It was either the bakery or Rafe. She turned around and almost fainted dead away when she realized she was looking at Robert behind the wheel of a slate gray Saab with New York plates.

He looked at her and didn't smile, which was fine with her. She wasn't in the mood to smile at him. She hadn't laid eyes on him since the day he walked out. She waited, expecting to feel a rush of anger or warmth or something, but instead she felt as if she were looking at a stranger.

That was her husband climbing out of that fancy car. She'd lost her virginity to him. She was carrying his baby. You'd think she would feel something, wouldn't you, some small burst of emotion. Any emotion.

"You're looking well, Molly," he said as he approached. "Pregnancy agrees with you."

"Oh," she said sweetly, "you noticed. You missed a trimester or two, Robert. I guess even you can't ignore the changes." She met his eyes. "So how did you find me?"

"People talk. I listen. It wasn't hard." He held out his hands, palms forward. "Believe it or not, I didn't come here to fight."

"So why are you here?" As if she didn't know. "I already told you I don't have time for a meeting."

"Diandra and I are leaving tonight for the Caribbean."

"How wonderful," she said. "Thanksgiving on the sand."

He reached into the breast pocket of his jacket and withdrew an airlines folder. "I bought you a ticket," he said. "Two tickets really. I reserved a suite overlooking the water. You can even bring your boyfriend. This whole thing could be over by Sunday."

"Forget it," she said. "Not interested."

"There's no chance for us," he said. "I thought you knew that."

"You just don't get it, do you?" she asked. "We're not playing by your rules any longer, Robert. I have a say in things now, too, and I say I'm not going to the Caribbean."

"The divorce is inevitable, Molly. It's going to happen. Why not let it happen sooner rather than later?"

"The baby," she said simply. "You gave up all rights to the baby the day you walked out the door."

"You can't cut me out of the child's life."

"Really? Just watch me."

"You've seen the settlement. I'm being more than fair. I'm willing to own up to my mistakes."

"Doing that well, are you?" She couldn't keep the edge from her voice. She didn't even try. "You must be a happy man, Robert. That's what you always wanted."

"I told you I regret my mistake. What if I made the custody issue negotiable? Would you fly down to the Caribbean this weekend and get the divorce?"

"Our marriage might be negotiable, but my baby isn't. I'll make a deal with you: You keep the house and the car and the money. I'll keep the baby."

She didn't wait for his answer. This time she was the one who turned and walked away.

The wedding of Jessica Wyatt and Spencer Mackenzie took place at twelve noon on Thanksgiving Day in the library of Miriam Cantwell's house. Dr. Van Lieuw gave Jessy away while his sister played Lohengrin on the piano. Ginny the housekeeper and her husband Harry were in attendance as were a few of the neighbors who were home for the holidays. Welcome candles glowed at every window, both in the main house and the carriage house. Miriam presided over the festivities from a motorized wheelchair that was festooned with flowers. She wore an elegant pale blue dress with a brocade collar and she appeared to be having the time of her life.

Which was more than anyone could say about the bride.

"Jessy's hands are shaking," Rafe whispered to Molly. "She looks as if she's going to faint."

"Look at Spencer." Molly shook her head in amazement. "He looks calm and collected." And happy. She couldn't help but notice the look of happiness in his eyes as he and Jessy exchanged rings. None of it made the slightest bit of sense. Nobody in his or her right mind would ever have predicted this wedding, and they certainly wouldn't have predicted Jessy to be the one who looked like she wanted to bolt and run.

Molly had been the picture of contentment at her own splashy wedding. She'd sailed through the proceedings on a cloud of happiness, secure in the knowledge that this marriage would be forever and a day, that nothing— not time or circumstance—could possibly come between her and Robert. She hadn't figured that life itself would do exactly that. Seeing him yesterday had left her with nothing but relief and a mild touch of residual sadness that she could have settled for so little the first time around.

But there was the baby, the one wonderful thing she had to show for her years with Robert. She wouldn't have missed this baby for the world.

She wondered about Rafe's wedding. His marriage. Had he believed it was forever, too, or had he somehow known it came with an expiration date like milk and cents-off coupons? Did he ever think about his ex-wife and wonder how he would feel if she walked through the door? Suddenly Molly wanted to know everything there was to know about him. She couldn't get the image of him, alone and living in his pickup truck, from her mind. She couldn't bridge the gap between his married life in Montana and that. Miriam's words had cut deep into her heart. At first she'd been so afraid of what she might hear that she'd blocked out the sheer wonder of the story. He'd been as low as a man could get, but nothing had been able to crush the basic kindness in his beautiful soul.

How had he ended up living in his truck? What had happened between him and his wife that sent him across the country into a downward spiral of loneliness?

Tonight was the night she'd ask those questions. It was time she found out more about the man she loved.

The bride and groom left not long after dinner. Rafe shook Spencer's hand then hugged Jessy. She felt like a hummingbird in his arms, all fluttering heart and fragile bones.

"It's going to be okay," he said to her. "You're going to be happy."

"I must be crazy," she whispered. "We don't stand a chance."

"Nobody does. It's up to you to beat the odds."

She looked up at him as if he'd said something profound, and when Spencer pulled out of the driveway, Jessy turned and blew a kiss to Rafe.

"What was that all about?" Molly asked. "Flirting with new brides isn't kosher."

He grinned and draped an arm around her shoulders. "Jealous?"

She shot him a saucy look. "Should I be?"

"No," he said, no longer kidding around. "You shouldn't be."

He tilted her face up toward his and kissed her deeply. She tasted like ice cream and pie. Tonight, he thought. Tonight he'd tell her how he felt, the wonderful things he saw in their future, the father he wanted to be to her child.

"Miriam's exhausted," Molly said as they walked slowly up the drive to the main house, the candles glowing warmly in each window. At that moment he had everything he'd ever wanted in life, and it could only get better.

Dr. Van Lieuw met them at the door. "The happy couple left on their honeymoon?"

"Two nights in a B and B, then it's back to work for both of them," Molly said. "I guess they'll schedule a honeymoon later on."

Van Lieuw nodded, but Rafe sensed he wasn't paying attention.

"What's wrong?" he asked the doctor.

Van Lieuw glanced over at Molly then back again at Rafe, and there was something about that look that told Rafe everything.

"It's Miriam, isn't it?" he asked.

"Yes," Van Lieuw said quietly. "She's gone."

TWENTY-TWO

Three days later Miriam was buried in the family plot north of Stockton. She had specified in her will that she wanted a brief, private funeral, and her wishes had been met. A few people took the lectern to say a few words of praise, but it wasn't until Rafe started to speak that Molly began to cry. She didn't really know Miriam, of course. Her loss was one of association, not history the way it was for Rafe. He spoke briefly and eloquently about what Miriam had meant to him, and when he sat down again, there wasn't a dry eye in the house.

He reached for Molly's hand, and she held it tightly, wishing she could ease the sorrow he felt over the loss of his friend. Of course Miriam was much more than a friend to him. She was family. His sorrow ran deep and wide. He hadn't slept last night. Neither had Molly. She'd lain awake upstairs, listening to the sound of chisel against wood as he worked on the cradle.

She hadn't told him yet about Robert's unexpected visit. With the preparations for the wedding, there had been so much going on that she simply hadn't had the chance. Or at least that's what she told herself. Then Miriam's sudden death had relegated Robert's visit to an even lower level of importance. Besides, she'd handled it. She'd stood up for herself against his offers of money and her freedom and proved she was no longer the needy pushover of a wife he'd known. When she'd turned her back and walked away, she'd regained a part of herself she'd believed lost forever.

The mourners went back to Miriam's house for a buffet meal put together by Ginny and her husband. Miriam's relatives surrounded Rafe, peppering him with hugs and questions and memories. Molly mingled the best she could, but she felt terribly out of place. Rafe must have sensed it because a second later she felt the familiar, loving weight of his arm around her shoulders.

"You look beat," he said. "I know you didn't sleep last night. Why don't you go back to the carriage house and take a nap?"

"I would," she said, "but I can't sleep in the afternoon."

"Go rest," he said. "There are some books on the nightstand that'll put you to sleep."

She didn't want to leave but she knew that she needed to get off her feet for a little while. "Just for an hour," she said. "I want to be with you when they read Miriam's will."

"There won't be any surprises," he said. "I'll continue paying off the carriage house to the bank, same as before."

She hoped he was right. Death had a way of changing everything. Agreements that worked smoothly suddenly fell apart in the face of family pressure and legal wrangling.

Jinx was waiting on the top step. "Poor baby." She bent down and tried to scratch Jinx's head but couldn't quite reach. "You can sleep on the bed with me," she said as she opened the door. "I promise."

She fed Jinx while her tea was brewing, then carried the mug upstairs. Rafe was right. She was beyond exhausted. The thought of undressing for just an hour was terribly unappealing, so she lay down carefully on top of the feather bed and closed her eyes. She heard Jinx's nails tapping their way across the floor then felt the slight dip of the mattress as the cat landed next to her. Jinx fell asleep within two seconds.

"You snore," Molly muttered. "What a dirty trick."

Rafe had said he had some sleep-inducing books on the nightstand, but she didn't see anything more than a woodworking catalog. That would do it, she thought, but she'd been hoping for something a little more intriguing. Maybe he meant to say in the nightstand, not on it. She slid open the drawer of the one closest, on Rafe's side.

Perfect. A dog-eared copy of *On the Road* was buried under a pile of old letters, bank statements, and photographs. Her father had worshipped at the altar of Kerouac and Kesey, which was probably one of the reasons she'd never read either man's work. Now was as good a time as any to see what the attraction was all about. Her dad no longer had a hold over her life. She was in charge now, and it felt wonderful.

She sat up against the headboard and opened the book. She hadn't finished the first paragraph when she noticed a photograph on the comforter next to her. He must have been using it as a bookmark. *Sarah*, it read on the back. His wife? She turned it over and was surprised to see a photo of a newborn baby, one of those *I'm two hours old* shots of a wrinkled little red face swaddled in blankets.

A niece, she told herself. A friend's daughter. Maybe one of Miriam's grandnieces. She put the photo aside.

She couldn't get comfortable. Jinx's snoring was too loud to ignore and, to add insult to injury, the baby woke up and decided it was time for calisthenics. She sipped some tea, flipped through the book. She found the story unsettling. This wasn't the time to read about a group of men who kick off the confines of real life and hit the road like a group of overaged Peter Pans. No, it wasn't the right time at all.

She must have fallen off to sleep at last because suddenly she realized ninety minutes had slipped by and she was late for the reading of Miriam's will. She quickly brushed her hair and her teeth, put her shoes back on, then headed across the lawn once again toward the main house. These things never started on time. They were probably all still eating Ginny's tuna casserole and reminiscing.

The kitchen was quiet except for the whir of the dishwasher. She moved into the hallway. No sign of anyone. She heard a faint rumble of voices coming from the living room—no, wait. The library. She hurried down the hall and ended up face-to-face with a closed door.

"'. . . my sister Agnes, my portfolio of stocks and bonds with the proviso that she . . .'"

Oh, great. They were already deep into the bequests. She couldn't barge into the room now. She barely knew Miriam. Joining them now would be a sign of disrespect, and that's the last thing she wanted. She could hear everything from out here. Maybe she'd just stay and listen so she'd be there for Rafe when it was over.

Rafe was paying minimal attention to the proceedings. The funeral had been bad enough. Listening to Miriam speak from the grave was too damn sad. She'd thought of everyone from Ginny to Dr. Van Lieuw to her family. He didn't want anything from her. She'd already given him more than any parent ever could have given a natural-born child. She'd given him friendship and guidance and a kick in the butt when he needed it. She'd given him a home and the sense of family.

He could move on now with only his memories and not feel cheated. He had Molly and the baby, and that was enough for any man.

The lawyer turned his attention toward Rafe. " 'And now we come to Rafael Garrick, who is the son God granted me late in my life. Rafe has been my son, my friend, my defender. Knowing him, watching him grow roots, I want those roots to continue to grow, and so . . .' "

Rafe's brain shut down. He couldn't hear over the roar inside his head. Miriam had left him the carriage house free and clear.

"Mr. Garrick," the lawyer broke in. "Did you hear what I said?"

Rafe shook his head. He was beyond speech. All he could think of was telling Molly the news.

"There's more to this bequest."

Miriam had left him more than the carriage house: She'd left him the main house and grounds and prepaid taxes.

He glanced around the room, expecting to see anger

and resentment. He saw nothing but happiness.

"All I ask of Rafael is that he approach my family if the time comes when he chooses to sell any or all of the above-named properties."

He nodded again. He would do that. It was the right thing. Anyone could see that. "You have my word."

"There's one final item," the lawyer said. He withdrew a long white envelope from his briefcase. Rafe could see his name neatly typed in the center. "Let me go back to Miriam's words." He cleared his throat and continued. " 'I know that you have tried more than once to find Sarah with no success. I've found your daughter, Rafael. Now it's up to you to learn how to be a father.' "

Thirty minutes later, the reading of Miriam's will was completed. Rafe felt as if he'd run head first into a brick wall. A gold-plated brick wall, but a brick wall no matter how you looked at it. His daughter. His baby Sarah. The envelope in his hand contained her new name and address and a photo. She was beautiful like her mother, with shiny brown curls and a big white-toothed smile. He saw himself in her straight nose and high cheekbones and maybe in the expression in her big blue eyes. Maybe. It was hard to say. This lovely young girl had little in common with the baby he'd held years ago. This lovely young girl was a stranger.

"A lot of changes for you today, Rafael." Miriam's lawyer extended his hand in farewell. "I wish you the best."

Rafe edged toward the door, fielding good-byes and fond wishes. All he wanted was to find Molly. Somebody must have been watching over them. This would have been too much of a shock for her—finding out about Sarah in a roomful of strangers. If he felt shell-shocked, he could only imagine what the news would have done to her. He was glad she was in the carriage house, asleep. That would give him time to find the right words to make her understand something he didn't understand himself.

He'd waited too long to tell her. He knew that now. Sarah had always been his darkest secret. As the years went by, he found it more and more difficult to understand why he'd ever let her out of his life, why he'd believed he had no rights in the matter. Why he'd believed a father didn't matter.

How did you tell that to the woman you loved? He felt as if she'd been in his life since the beginning of time, but that wasn't the case. They'd bridged the gap from acquaintances to lovers in one random heartbeat, and he still hadn't found the moment or the words to tell her about Sarah.

Leave it to Miriam to force his hand.

She'd given him a home and now she was giving him back his daughter.

It was up to him to hold onto Molly and her baby.

The door to the carriage house was open. That wasn't like Molly. She checked and double-checked doors and windows. He felt a cold knot form deep in his gut. He took the stairs two at a time and ran down the hall to the bedroom. Jinx was sprawled, sleeping, in the middle of the mattress. There was no sign of Molly. He saw his old copy of *On the Road* facedown near her pillow and he saw his snapshot of newborn Sarah.

No reason to be concerned. It could be his niece or his godchild. She wouldn't take off because a snapshot of a baby girl fell out of an old book. Not unless she knew who the baby girl was.

He threw himself back down the stairs and outside. His truck was gone. Why hadn't he noticed that before? She must have grabbed the keys from his jacket pocket and hit the road herself.

Okay. No reason to get upset. Maybe she needed something from the store, decaf teabags or honey or those sesame seed bagels she loved. Maybe she got tired of waiting for him and went out for a ride. There was always the possibility that she'd slept longer than she'd planned and felt funny about joining them in the middle of the proceedings.

But it wasn't any of those things.

She'd heard about Sarah and she was gone.

Molly drove for hours. She followed the river north, then when darkness fell she turned around and followed it back down south. She stopped for gas not far from Stockton. Three dollars' worth. That was all she could find stuck in the empty ashtray. She'd left her purse back at the carriage house along with her money, not to mention her license. If she made a left and followed that curving road she'd be back where she'd started from, at the carriage house with Rafe. If only she could turn back the clock as easily.

She couldn't drive forever. It was late, and exhaustion was beginning to slow her reflexes. She knew that even if she could drive forever, she still wouldn't be able to outrace her thoughts.

Rafe had a daughter.

She tried to comprehend the words and came up short each time. He had a child. A baby girl. He'd pressed his lips to a woman's pregnant belly, felt the baby kick beneath his hand, said and done all the things he'd said and done with her. Things she'd believed he was doing for the first time. She could have lived with all of that. They'd both been married before. They both had histories. If he'd told her, she could have lived with it, made his child part of her life.

But his child wasn't part of *his* life.

Rafe had walked away from his daughter the same way Robert had walked away from their unborn child. He'd turned and walked out the door, and he needed a dead woman's persistence to remind him he was a father.

It didn't make any sense. None of this characterized the man she knew. The man she knew understood what love meant. He understood about commitment and loyalty. His relationship with Miriam was proof of that.

He'd found Molly at the darkest moment of her life, when she thought she'd lost everything that mattered. He was the one who caught her when she fell. She hadn't been looking for him. She'd tried her best to maintain her distance, but he'd showered her with passion and warmth and kindness until she forgot why she'd ever held back. She'd learned more about love and generosity in her few months with him than she had in all of her years with Robert.

Funny thing, though, either way she ended up alone.

Her three dollars' worth of gas didn't get her very far. The needle flirted with Empty, and she knew she'd run out of options. She had no choice but to go home. How she was going to get in the house was another story. Her keys were back at the carriage house. She could break a window or try to pick the lock. If worse came to worst, she could sleep in the truck then call a locksmith in the morning. All she wanted was to make it all the way up Lilac Hill Road without running out of gas.

The guard waved her through without even looking at her. So much for security. She wasn't about to complain though. She didn't have a single scrap of identification with her.

All of the houses lay dark and quiet. The windows stared blankly at the street. She loved early evening when lamplight illuminated the rooms, throwing lives into sharp relief. She used to walk the length and breadth of the subdivision, pausing in front of different houses as she pretended to tie the laces on her running shoes so she could look inside the windows and see how families worked. Because she really didn't know. She'd grown up in chaos that she'd accepted as normal family life. Family life with Robert had been more like partnership in a small, moderately successful law firm. She'd been on the outside looking in at her whole life. She didn't want that for her baby. She wanted warmth and laughter and so much love that her child wouldn't have to stand in front of other people's windows at dusk and pretend she was part of a family.

She made the turn onto Lilac Hill Road. She hated the thought of that big empty house. No Rafe. No Jessy. No Jinx. Nothing but four thousand square feet of broken dreams. Not like the carriage house.

Forget about the carriage house. That part of your life is over. It's time to move on.

He hadn't even bothered to come after the truck. She'd kept an eye on the rearview mirror all night, expecting an irate Rafe to come swooping down on her for stealing his pickup; but she supposed he had other things on his mind now. Like the daughter he'd left behind.

The first thing she noticed was the strange car in her driveway. A late-model Caddy with New Jersey plates. She didn't know anyone who drove a car like that. She parked next to it then climbed down from the truck. Had Robert decided to retaliate by sending somebody around to scare some sense into her? She felt more angry than scared. She'd lost as much as she was willing to lose without a fight. She had started up the walkway when she realized what she was seeing. A small candle flickered at the living room window. The curtains were pulled wide, and she could make out the shapes of the sofa and chairs behind the candle.

Fear and anger and elation all filled her heart. Only one person would place a welcoming candle in the window. Only one man knew what it meant.

The door was unlocked. That didn't surprise her. He always thought of everything. Well, almost everything. He had forgotten to tell her about his daughter.

She stepped into the foyer. He was standing to the left of the staircase, in the same spot she'd first seen him months ago.

"Here," she said, as she tossed him the car keys. "Thanks for the lift."

"I brought you your purse and house keys," he said. His voice was level, his tone neutral. "They're on the kitchen table."

"Thank you," she said.

She started toward the kitchen. He stepped in front of her.

"Don't," she said, her voice low. "It's too late."

"I'd been trying to find a way to tell you," he said. "I didn't expect Miriam would do it for me."

" 'Molly, I have a daughter. Molly, I walked out on her.' " She met his eyes. "See? That wasn't so hard. Eleven words, and you've told me everything I need to know."

"That's not how it was."

"I heard the whole thing, Rafe," she snapped. "You didn't even know where your daughter was until this afternoon."

"There's a reason for that."

"I'll bet there is," she said with a harsh laugh. "Indifference. Disinterest. Fatherhood. Pick one."

"I made a mistake."

"Of course you did," she said, pushing past him. "That's a good way to describe it. A mistake. Robert tried that one with me. It didn't work for him either."

"I want to tell you the story."

"I don't want to hear it."

"Don't shut me out, Molly. Don't do this."

"Shut up," she said, storming into the kitchen. "I don't give a damn about your story. Your story doesn't mean anything to me."

"I'm admitting I made a mistake. If you'd stop and listen to—"

She grabbed her keys and purse from the table. "I put a new tape in the answering machine," she said, gesturing toward the telephone. "Leave a message, and maybe I'll get back to you."

He reached for her, but she darted past him and hurried toward the front door. If he touched her, she didn't know what she would do. Hit him. Cling to him. Either choice was wrong. If she touched him, she'd be doomed. She wanted to put as much distance between them as she possibly could and she wanted to do that now, before she could think or wonder or long for all the things that were impossible right from the start. Nothing was forever, not love or hope or happiness.

She swung open the front door.

"It's easy to leave, isn't it, Molly?"

She tried to leave, but his words stopped her cold. She heard him walking toward her and yet she stood with her hand on the doorknob and she didn't move.

"Nothing hard about walking out the door." He was so close she could feel his breath against her cheek. "Nothing so tough about leaving."

"Shut up," she whispered. "I don't care what you have to say."

"Staying is what's hard, Molly."

The baby kicked hard against her left ribs, and the surprise pushed her into action again. She stepped out onto the front porch.

"Karen was pregnant when we got married."

Why wouldn't he let her go? Why was he still talking and talking when she'd told him she didn't care?

"I loved her and was glad to find a reason to get her to finally accept my proposal. We were both too young—I can see that now—but I thought I was in love enough for both of us."

She gripped the porch railing. "I know that feeling," she whispered, despite herself. She'd believed that she loved Robert enough to make up for the fact that he didn't love her the way she'd dreamed about being loved.

Rafe had been overjoyed by his wife's pregnancy. He'd shared doctor's visits and Lamaze classes, he'd been there in the labor and delivery rooms, coaching and breathing and exulting when his baby daughter came into the world and he cut the cord then held her slippery body in his trembling hands.

She could see the blood and the triumph. She could feel his love and his joy. He was describing her own dreams with one important difference: she never would have left them behind.

"You still walked away from her," Molly said as he joined her on the porch. "For all of that, you still walked out the door. How much does that bond mean if you were able to leave your wife and daughter? You're no different than my father or Robert. You say all the right things but sooner or later, you all walk out that door."

"You've got it all wrong, Molly." He took her hands in his.

"The hell I do." She tried to pull away from him but he held her fast. "I heard what the lawyer said, Rafe. Your daughter must be what, ten years old by now? You didn't even know where she was. Miriam had to hire a private investigator to find her. She had to force you publicly to reconnect with your own child."

"Karen walked out on me, Molly. She took the baby and she walked. I wanted my child. I wanted to hang onto my daughter, but Karen told me I was being unfair. Sarah wasn't even a year old yet, she said. Karen had another guy waiting in the wings. She wanted to build a life with him, and I'd only complicate matters for Sarah."

She doesn't even know you, his wife had told him. *She'll never miss you. She doesn't need you.*

"You should've known better," Molly said, as her eyes filled with tears. "How could you believe such a thing?"

But that was all he knew of family life. His mother

had killed herself when he was a little boy, and his father's position in the family was one of resentment and anger. It was hard to believe you mattered when all you'd heard your entire life was how worthless you were, how unimportant, how goddamn good for nothing.

"I couldn't give Sarah any of the things this other guy could give her. I lived on a broken-down ranch. I had no prospects. My life was going to be the same as my old man's and his old man's before him. Karen wanted better than that for herself and Sarah. Hell, I wanted better for them. How could I blame her for that?"

He'd seen enough kids pulled between parents after a messy divorce. They ended up straddling two homes, two sets of expectations, and failing both.

Molly saw herself in his words. He was describing her adolescence, her teen years, when she'd needed a stable family life and had to marry in order to achieve it.

"I thought I was doing the right thing for Sarah," he said. "I thought she'd have all the things she deserved, the kind of life a little girl dreams about. That's why I did it. I thought I was doing the best thing for her."

A year later Karen had moved on to husband number three and had headed west toward California with Sarah in tow.

"She used to send me one photo a month. That stopped once she got to California. I never heard directly from her again." A tiny muscle in his jaw twitched as he obviously struggled for control.

"You could have hired a private investigator," Molly said. She knew she sounded harsh, but there was so much hanging on his answer. Three lives hung in the balance.

"I did," he said, "but investigators cost money. I tried twice, and both times the guy got nowhere. I've been putting money aside to try again early next year."

Something inside her heart shifted, and she turned slowly to meet his eyes. "You won't have to do that now," she said. "You've found her."

"I've found her," he said, and she could hear the wonder in his voice, see the happiness in his eyes. Karen was married to her fourth husband and living outside Seattle with Sarah and her two other children.

He wasn't going to rush into anything. The one thing he didn't want to do was drop a bomb in the middle of his daughter's life. He had to find out if she even knew he existed then proceed from there.

It was enough for the moment to know she was alive and well.

"This picture was taken six months ago." He pulled a snapshot from the pocket of his leather jacket. There was no mistaking his pride.

"She looks just like you," she said. Her voice broke on the last word, and she turned away. *He didn't leave . . . he didn't leave.* She felt as though someone had handed her the keys to heaven.

It was coming back, that miraculous sense of connection that she'd experienced the first moment she saw him. He was right. Leaving was easy. Dangerously easy. Staying together required understanding and patience and so much love.

We can work past this, she thought. They were working past it. He'd made the wrong decision with the best of intentions. He'd done what he thought was best for his child, and look at what it had cost him.

"You're doing the same thing, Molly," he said. "You're making the same mistakes."

She spun back around. "What did you say?"

"Your husband's a son of a bitch. I'm not going to argue that with you. But he wants a chance to be a father. Don't—"

"Robert walked out on us," she snapped. "It was his choice. I'll be damned if I reward him for it."

"You're right," Rafe said. "The bastard doesn't deserve either one of you."

"Then why should I do it?" she asked. "Why should I let him be part of my life?"

"For the baby," he said simply. "Because the baby deserves all the love she can get."

"Damn." She quickly wiped her eyes with the back of her hand. "I wish you wouldn't say things like that." She looked up at him. "Why do you care? What difference does any of this make to you?"

He looked awkward and vulnerable, and in that instant it all came clear for her: the secret to life. Sometimes, if you were very lucky, you found it in a man's dark blue eyes.

"You haven't figured it out yet?" he asked.

"No," she said. "I want you to tell me." *Tell me the secret. Tell me that you know it, too.*

"I love you," he said. "I've loved you from the first moment I saw you standing right where you're standing now. I wanted to kiss away your pain. I wanted to carry you off to the carriage house and keep you safe. I love the baby you're carrying as much as I loved Sarah, as much as I'll love any babies we have together." He stopped, her quiet man, and cradled her face between his hands. "I love you," he said again, "and I'll never leave."

She'd never been good at making speeches, sweeping declarations of love and longing like the ones she read in books, but this time it was easy. All she had to do was let her heart speak for her.

"I love you," she said to him. "I never knew just what that meant until I met you." It went beyond sex and beyond friendship and beyond anything she'd ever imagined possible between a man and a woman. "You're my family, Rafe. You and the baby. The two of you are all I've ever wanted."

"You're going to marry me," he said. "Now."

"I'm still a married woman," she said, laughing softly.

"Then we'll have to do something about that as soon as possible."

"I think that can be arranged." Not on Robert's time schedule, but on theirs.

"And then we'll get married," Rafe said, "and this time we're going to do it right."

"As in forever?" she asked.

"As in for always."

Love.

The secret of life.

Love made all things possible, even happiness. She looked at the welcome candle twinkling in the living room window, at her belly bursting with life, and Rafe's beloved face, and she finally surrendered herself to joy.

EPILOGUE

"What do you think?" Jessy Wyatt Mackenzie performed an awkward pirouette in front of Molly. "It's terrible, isn't it? I look like a whale."

Molly crossed her arms over her belly and peered closely at the very pregnant doctor. "You're nine months pregnant, Jess. You're supposed to look like a whale."

Jessy eyed her grimly. "You're not exactly a sylph yourself."

"I know," Molly said. "Isn't it wonderful?"

Jessy groaned as she studied her reflection in the fitting room mirror. "Three babies, and you're still glowing about the process. You should have been the obstetrician, Molly, not me."

"Oh, quit griping," Molly said. "You know you love everything about being pregnant, Jess. Why don't you just admit it? I won't tell Spencer."

Jessy's serious expression dissolved into the brilliant smile that had become her trademark over the last five years. "You're right," she said. "I love every single thing about it, even the fact that my ankles look like drainpipes, my stretch marks have stretch marks, and that I no sooner get one out of training pants than I'll have another in diapers."

Molly threw back her head and laughed. "No sympathy here, old friend." Her hands cradled her belly, a gesture that was second nature to her now. "Three in five years."

Jessy pretended to shudder. "Look at you," she said with affection. "You're a glutton for punishment."

Jessy and Spencer had celebrated their fifth anniversary last month with a trip to Paris. Molly wouldn't have given them a one-in-a-million chance, but they'd defied the odds and found happiness together. Spencer had become a devoted family man, while motherhood had opened Jessy's heart to both her family and her career. As much as you could tell anything about the state of someone else's marriage, Molly guessed the Mackenzie union was in fine shape.

"Mommy!" Four-year-old Lizzie burst into the fitting room. Her tumble of red curls was gathered up in a big bright blue ribbon the color of her eyes. "Daddy says to hurry. He wants pizza."

Robert was Lizzie's father, but Rafe was her daddy in every way that mattered.

Molly opened her arms wide, and the little girl hurled herself into her embrace. "Did Daddy tell you to say that?"

Lizzie nodded vigorously then looked up at Jessy, who was trying to wriggle back into her own clothes. "Charlie wants pizza, too." Charlie was Jessy and Spencer's four-year-old son. He and Lizzie were best pals and sworn enemies. It depended on what time of day you asked them.

"How about you, Tizzy Lizzie?" Jessy asked. "Do you want pizza, too?"

Lizzie buried her face against Molly's chest and giggled. Lizzie was prone to bouts of shyness, even with the people she loved most.

"I think that's a yes," Molly said. "No daughter of mine ever missed a chance for pizza and ice cream."

A few minutes later they joined their men outside. Rafe leaned against the side of the new red truck they'd bought with the proceeds of his first showing of hand-made furniture. Two-year-old Josh sat on his daddy's shoulders. Father and son both wore jeans and cranberry-colored sweaters. Molly's heart almost burst with pride. Their son was the mirror image of Rafe, right down to the dark blue eyes and stubborn chin. Sometimes late at night she'd get up while the house slept. She'd go from room to room, marveling at Lizzie, exulting in Josh, and glorying in the new life growing once again inside her body. That cradle Rafe made had served them well, and would for many years to come.

She thanked God every day for bringing Rafe Garrick into her life. From that chance encounter on the worst day of her life a brand-new family had been created. Miracles were everywhere if you opened your eyes and your heart to the possibilities.

"Daddy!" Lizzie tugged on Rafe's sleeve. "Mommy bought a new dress."

Rafe met Molly's eyes over their daughter's head. "I hope Mommy bought a pretty new dress," he said with a wicked grin.

"Mommy bought a very pretty new dress," she said,

"and she'll be happy to model it for you when we get home."

He put his arm around her shoulders and brushed her ear with his lips. "Better be careful," he murmured low. "That's how you ended up this way." He gloried in each of her pregnancies and seemed to genuinely find her just as sexy with child as without.

Jessy and Spencer each took one of little Charlie's hands. "Come on," Spencer said in his best lawyerly tone of voice. "There's a double pepperoni at Tony's, and it's got the Mackenzie name on it."

"Me, too," Lizzie said, lifting her hands toward her own parents. "I want pizza."

"I guess I want pizza, too," Molly said, taking her daughter's right hand.

"Won't catch me arguing with a double pepperoni," Rafe said, taking his daughter's left hand.

"Pizza!" crowed Josh, and they all laughed.

"Happy?" Rafe asked her as they waited for the light to change at the corner.

"Very," she said. "And you?"

He looked at their children then met her eyes. "I think you know the answer to that."

"Hey!" a familiar voice called out. "Wait for me!" Sarah, Rafe's teenage daughter, popped out of the record store and joined them. She was tall and slender, with her mother's light brown hair and Rafe's beautiful blue eyes.

"I thought you were meeting us at Tony's," Molly said, smiling at the girl.

"I got sidetracked," Sarah said with a grin. "Acid Bath released a new CD, and I had to check it out."

Rafe launched into a critique of modern music that

had Sarah rolling her eyes, Lizzie giggling, and little Josh pulling on his hair.

"I give up," Rafe said finally. "I know when I'm outnumbered."

"Come on, you guys." Sarah put Josh on her shoulders and took Lizzie's hand. "I think the parental units feel like singing some Barry Manilow."

"Barry Manilow!" Rafe bellowed. "The day you catch me—"

"She's only kidding, sweetie." Molly winked at Sarah. "She knows you don't listen to Barry Manilow."

"She thinks I'm an old man," Rafe muttered as Sarah and the kids moved away from them.

"She's supposed to think you're an old man," Molly said. "You're her father."

"Next thing you'll tell me the rest of our kids will feel the same way."

"If we're lucky," Molly said. "That's the way these things usually go."

"Mothers get a free ride?"

"No such luck. Sarah reminded me that Engelbert was playing down in Atlantic City this weekend. She thought I might like to know."

"Looks like we're in this together," he said as they walked hand in hand toward the pizzeria. "Us against them."

She squeezed his hand. "I like those odds."

"Would you do it again?" he asked as they stopped to wait for the light to change. "I might never be able to give you Paris."

She thought about how it felt to fall asleep in his arms each night, how it felt to wake up to the sweet sound of her children's voices. She thought about the laughter that filled the house and the warmth and the love.

"I don't need Paris," she said as he drew her into his arms. "I already have everything I'll ever need right here."

A home. A family. A man who loved her the way she'd dreamed of being loved. Paris couldn't compare to what she'd found right there in New Jersey.

"Guys!" Sarah's voice floated toward them from across the street. "Come on! The pizza's waiting on us."

He cupped her face between his hands, the way he had the first time he ever kissed her.

"You heard what she said." Molly touched a finger to her husband's lips. "The pizza's waiting on us."

"Let it wait."

He kissed her long and slow and sweetly, right there at the corner of Main and Church streets with the late-afternoon sun warm against their backs and the delighted laughter of their children filling their hearts.

"Daddy, stop kissing Mommy!" Lizzie's high-pitched little voice rang out from the other side of the street. "We're hungry!"

Their kiss ended in gentle laughter.

"I think she means business," Rafe said, brushing a lock of Molly's hair back from her face.

"She always means business when there's pizza on the horizon." Molly rubbed away a smudge of lipstick from the corner of his mouth.

He took her hand in his, and together they crossed the street to catch up with their future.